DEAD AGGIES DON'T DRIVE TRAINS

Other Books by Don Bemis

Heavens to Louie

Count Otto's Dragon

Mary in Transit

DEAD AGGIES DON'T DRIVE TRAINS

DON BEMIS

DEAD AGGIES DON'T DRIVE TRAINS

Cover Photos by Don Bemis:

Front: Turkey vulture over Southeast New Mexico, somewhat altered. Vultures are graceful, but beautiful only to other vultures. September, 2010

Back: Coyote in Jasper, Alberta. So Jasper isn't desert. The photo otherwise seemed to fit. May, 2010.

ISBN: 978-0-9848070-5-5

CLAIMER:

My name is Don, and I am an Aggie.

DISCLAIMER:

My degree was in geography, so it hurts me to rearrange New Mexico as much as I have done. However, it is a big state, and there is plenty of room to put things. I can live with the pain.

This is a fiction book. If you think you see yourself or somebody you know here, you don't. I made these people up. There probably are lots of folks like you and your acquaintances. I didn't write about them either.

The same goes for places, except for those on a real map. As to businesses, they are fictional, too.

There really is a New Mexico State University, but its resemblance to anything in this story is pretty vague. I got a good education there, and it's where I met my wife.

D.B.

The sun beat down upon Yootibibit. That was normal. In fact, it was the source of the name. "Used To Be Blue Truck". U.T.B.B.T. Yootibibit.

Janet had come up with the name. "It sounds sort of Navajo, doesn't it?" she asked.

"I suppose so, if you don't speak Navajo," replied Rex. "But it'll do."

Things eventually got names in outstate New Mexico, any place far enough from Albuquerque and Santa Fe that movie stars didn't move there and politicians only showed up often enough to be reelected. There were not too many people to talk to, so eventually one got around to addressing whatever was available. Even a faded pickup truck.

Rex Albert had been talking a lot more to Yootibibit of late. The same sun that bleaches paint had done in Janet. She was one of the many on campus who, a lifetime ago, had exposed as much flesh to it as possible. Her light brown hair faded nearly to white, her white skin darkened to brown, and she was beautiful. They married while in college.

Hither and Thither had resulted. "Heather" and "Arthur" may have been written on their birth certificates, but the twins had been Ithers ever since the ultrasound showed two of them. The names proved appropriate when the children took up toddling. Their tired mother remarked more than once that it might have been better to call them "Sit" and "Stay".

One night while fourth grade Ithers slept, Rex heard the shower turn off. He cracked open the bathroom door. Through the steam he studied Janet, who studied herself in the mirror.

She reached for a towel without turning around. "Go away."

"Why?"

"I'm turning into a raisin. You might notice."

"I like raisins."

"You'd better."

"Shall I show you?"

Years later, after the children were grown, Rex had a growth removed from the bridge of his nose. "It shouldn't be a problem, but we'll send it to the lab. anyway," the doctor explained while applying a bandage.

"Actinic keratosis," he called it a few days later. "The sun does it. It'll heal fine." And it had.

The doctor had not said the same thing when Janet showed him a scaly patch on her shoulder. Neither did a bandage heal it.

A few months later, Hither and Thither returned to help their father bury their mother on a sunny July day. The cemetery sprinklers had automatically turned off shortly after sunrise. By afternoon, dry grass crackled beneath shuffling feet. Watery eyes watched the casket descend permanently into shade, and sunburned mourners returned to air-conditioned cars.

The three of them were silent as the limousine started away. Hither gazed through the heavily tinted side window. "Why aren't there any trees?" she sniffled.

"There will be," decided Thither.

"What do you mean?"

"I'm going to plant one in the spring."

"They won't let you," warned Rex.

"I won't ask."

Janet's health insurance had not succeeded at ensuring health, but it paid most of the medical bills until the time came for similarly misnamed life insurance to take over. That policy paid for the funeral, the sunbaked cemetery plot, and a gravestone with room for two names ("We can put one casket over another," the salesman had explained).

Rex's job outlasted his wife by two weeks. Mines don't need mining engineers after the ore is gone. That's the trouble with ore seams and oil patches. Cities like Mailpie, full of hope and good paychecks, spring up in places like the badlands of the Malpais where no sane person would settle otherwise. Residents avoid thinking of the day when they successfully extract that last bit of whatever is buried below the lava beds, or alkali flats, or miles of nothing surrounding their Mailpie.

His ten-mile drive to work had been the last ordinary occurrence of that day, if one didn't count biological necessities. The first clue that the morning would be different was a sheriff's vehicle parked just in front of the plant on the shoulder. The officer might have been waiting for some night shifter to race toward home, but for the second clue.

The parking lot and railroad gates, always open at the twenty-four hour operation, were padlocked. A new sign announced that the mine was permanently closed. Former employees were invited to a meeting that evening at the high school auditorium, where their rights and benefits would be explained. Thank you for your valued support.

The squad car window was open, with an official looking elbow sticking out. Rex pulled alongside. "Hey, Stan, what happened to the graveyard shift?"

The deputy turned his head. "They were escorted out half an hour ago. Early enough to collect 'em all, and late enough they couldn't rile up the day shift before you all got here. Right after a team of specialists came in to mothball the mine. They've got it down to a science."

"You mean people don't even get two weeks' notice?"

Stan sighed. "Rex, y'all know better'n that! Them New York types think different from us. Don't want nothin' vandalized before they can sell it. Now can you move? Cars are pilin' up behind you. The last thing we want's for somebody to think there's gonna be a riot."

"Are you kidding?"

"Nope. State Police were notified just in case."

"Yeah, well, thanks. You gonna be at the school tonight, too?"

" 'Fraid so. Now git a move on!" The elbow retracted into its window, and the glass slid shut. The discussion was over. Rex released the brake just as a white helicopter with a glistening gold shield decal chop-chopped over the office building. Its name, according to the bottom, was "ECILOP".

The evening meeting went as expected. Spokesmen with neckties and Yankee accents explained that closure of the mine should be viewed as an opportunity. Some people qualified for retirement. Pensions were fully vested. No, nobody had raided the pension plan. All displaced workers were eligible for unemployment. An outplacement firm would teach job search skills, and a retraining program would be set up with the schools. Yes, former employees would be considered for other company jobs if they had the right qualifications. Where? The closest facility was in Nebraska. What was it? A bank. Was it hiring? Not at the moment. What about other mines? The company was getting out of the mining business. Sorry. Good luck.

Rex learned over the next few months that, "We'll get back to you," usually is a lie. Whenever it isn't, "How are you doing?" means, "Employed, we hope." He considered writing a how-not-to book on resume writing. About the time his unemployment ran out, he began to call his situation "retired early".

Come springtime, Thither, Thitherette, and the Grand Dithers came to town long enough to plant a tree as promised. Cemetery groundskeepers pulled it up. The manager sent a stern letter warning that Rex would be billed for landscape repairs if he persisted in damaging the property with unauthorized plantings. Rex returned the letter, wadded up and taped to a five-dollar bill, in a shipping envelope stuffed with silver leaf maple seeds.

The phone rang two days later. Rex checked the number before answering. It was local, vaguely familiar, but not quite so. Not another out-of-town lawyer or grief salesman, anyway.

"Hello?"

"Mister Albert?"

"Speaking."

"I'm Richard Walters, at the cemetery. I'm the manager. We got your package."

It *was* a grief salesman, after all. "Okay."

"The secretary opened it in front of the air conditioner. We have an office full of maple whirligigs."

"Good."

There was a pause. "I'm – um – I think I understand. Mrs. Albert was my wife's favorite teacher, but we just can't have folks planting things all over the place. We can't keep them all alive."

"That seems sort of fitting."

Mr. Walters coughed. "Can you hear me out? Please?"

"If you'll listen to me afterward."

"Deal. How would you feel about a pecan tree? I'll put your five bucks toward one and plant it where it'll shade Mrs. Albert's plot in a few years."

There was silence.

"Mister Albert?"

"Thank you!" Rex hung up and sobbed.

《 》

A new July finally arrived, just as hot as the previous one. Yootibibit was one year less blue. Rex's hair had surrendered the last vestige of dark. Repainting was not considered in either case. He still had both; that was enough.

It would be more difficult to say if his chameleon eyes had changed. They were always changing: blue to match the sky, green when excited, or grey when bored. Dust storm red didn't count. The eyes were Yootibibit color at the moment.

"Well, Truck," confided Rex, "I guess it's just you and me for a while longer. Can't afford to trade you in." Man and machine bounced along a rutted path paralleling the train track. The railroad had announced plans a month earlier to pull up the rails as soon as they rounded up everything they had left along the line. Lawyers and legislators were scrambling to prevent it, but they might be too late.

A mostly empty cup of gas station coffee rode in the front middle holder. Janet's cup had always ridden just behind it. Her no-question-about-it blue eyes would have had something to say about the candy wrappers that had since taken up residence.

A full half-gallon canteen, once a necessity when he had spent shifts underground, rode on the floorboard. An oil-soaked lunch bag stained the passenger seat where nobody sat anymore. Taquitos, fried clams, and chicken gizzards had been the choices that morning at the food counter. Sorry, no eggrolls today. Taquitos won. Six of them, plus coleslaw. Clams or gizzards might go bad after a few hours in a truck. Rex would have gone bad soon afterward.

He wasn't really going anyplace, geographically or otherwise. Prospective employers weren't eager to hire people in their fifties who cost more to insure, expected pay for experience, and didn't fully buy into modern management philosophies. Age discrimination was illegal, of course, but it didn't much matter. There were always reasons if one looked hard enough. In another sense, Rex had no particular destination on that particular day. Along the railroad line they bounced, just him and Yootibibit and the taquitos thirty miles south of home. Vultures soared overhead, maybe wishing he had chosen the clams.

Desiccated plains extended leftward to the flat eastern horizon. Steel rails pointed ahead, straight as a string, toward their distant junction with the east-west trunk line at El Paso. The view to the right was more interesting, growing ever lumpier and higher. A black cloud in an otherwise blue sky was squeezing its way through a low spot in the Continental Divide.

If a man stood atop the Divide and looked toward Mexico, he could spit to the right and befoul the Pacific Ocean. Spit to the left, and the Gulf of Mexico got it. Then it might eddy into the Gulf Stream and wash onto a British beach. That was only theory in New Mexico. Spit would evaporate shortly after landing. Prevailing winds virtually guaranteed that spit vapor would favor the Gulf.

Cell phone reception was nonexistent. Phone companies only erected towers where customers would pay for service, and coyotes were too cheap to buy phones. Snakes had no friends to call. Horned toads were poor conversationalists. Jackrabbits lacked pockets to put phones in. Possums had pockets but didn't live in New Mexico, and cattle couldn't work those little buttons with their hooves. Who was left?

Radio was nearly as bad. No FM stations were in range. The only audible AM station finished a song that Rex didn't enjoy, crackled a bottom-of-the-hour story about a drill rig disappearing somewhere in Texas, and crackled further into unintelligibility. Crackling usually meant heat lightning but seldom meant rain. Rex switched off the noise. "The oil company probably gave 'em two weeks' notice," he muttered to Yootibibit.

The truck, not replying, lumped down the side of an arroyo by the half shade of a trestle. Trains were lazier. A beat-up silver-nosed locomotive chugged straight across, backwards, pushing a traveling junkyard: a crane with a claw hook, a dented gondola, a splintered wooden boxcar, an ancient business car that had been recycled into a rolling field office, and a pair of flatcars, one with a pickup truck and wheeled tractors chained to the deck.

The last train to Mailpie was on its way to the mine. From there it would slowly work south. A few more engines would run up and down the line before then to empty the yard of unemployed freight cars and any remaining equipment, but the last train, like a fugitive in an old Western, would sweep up their tracks behind them.

The unbroken foreground finally broke nine miles later, but barely, when a tiny circle showed dark against the brilliant sky. It slowly grew into a red steel disc welded to the top of a metal post like a petrified lollipop, announcing a railroad switch. A weedy side track swept toward Rex and curved west. He had not even known there was a side track. Where did it go?

That question was soon answered by a faded white sign:

COMUNICADO JCT.

One M. It was either misspelled or Spanish.

New Mexico was full of historical parentheses: events that had seemed important once but in hindsight made no difference. This was the path to a parenthesis…

《 》

(Late in the 1870's, speculators decided to punch a two-mile tunnel for rail communication through a narrow part of the ridge that was the Continental Divide. They laid out a town at the eastern portal. The effort was abandoned just before completion when a competing railroad, working around the clock, laid a track to the south where the mountains petered out. The southern route was flat enough that nobody could really locate the Divide to know which direction to spit. Legend had it that most derailments on the successful line occurred on stretches laid at night.

Comunicado eventually was sold. Emboldened by New Mexico's transition from territory to statehood in 1912, a fresh batch of dreamers blasted a smaller passage through the last few hundred feet of untouched rock. They also constructed a dam in the canyon on the Pacific side of the ridge, just downstream from the hole through the mountain. Period photos of the Comunicado side showed the blocked-up outline of a tunnel high enough for smokestacks and wide enough for one set of tracks. Water formerly bound for the Pacific shot through a powerhouse next to the tunnel and irrigated crops on its way to the Atlantic instead.

All such photos could be dated within a three year time span. That was how long it had taken the equally new state of Arizona to win a lawsuit for theft of water rights. The lake was drained. Comunicado's new peach trees withered before producing their first crop. Water flowed again toward Arizona when it flowed at all, but it seldom arrived. Nobody could help it if the climate was getting drier. Texas and Arizona took to suing New Mexico every few years for water it didn't have, and New Mexico wouldn't send it to them. New Mexico periodically would sue Colorado, and Old Mexico to the south would sue the Gringos, with similar results.

Nothing was left of Comunicado but a dusty hamlet at the end of a gravel state road, with a Class B high school that played six-man football and fielded a tiny marching band. Class B high schools had zero to seventy students. Comunicado was closer to the zero end. The gym had sentenced itself to death by electrical fire, and it had not been replaced in thirty years. Inspired by the gymnasium's example, the county building inspector condemned the stadium bleachers.

Comunicado Coyotes only played away games after that.)

《 》

Rex parked by the switch, instinctively staying far enough from the rails that a nonexistent train on the defunct spur would not hit him. He rustled inside the lunch bag and captured a taquito, so-called Mexican food only a Gringo would eat. Mooshed-up animal parts, textured soy protein (whatever that was), and quasi-Mexican seasoning were rolled up in a tortilla and cooked crisp. All luncheon entrees at the gas and food store were deep-fried, as usual. This one had a crunchy shell with a pasty interior, peppery nose, and oily finish. He wondered as he chewed if deep-fried cockroaches might be described the same way, but with less salt. The thought did not improve his meal.

His eyes wandered down the spur line. He had never been to Comunicado. He wasn't due to be anywhere. No road paralleled those rails, though, because trucks had been nonexistent in its day. Would it be wise to drive along the track? Trains didn't use it.

A flicker of lightning over the mountain decided the issue. Arroyos down here originated up there. If it *did* rain for a change, one could flood without warning. He pointed the truck back toward Mailpie. It was time to go home.

No, it was past time.

A trickle of water shimmered below the first trestle. Rex stopped at the lip of the arroyo. He rolled down the window and killed the engine. As long as he was going to be trapped, he might as well enjoy the show.

A rumbling introduction heralded the main act: wild brown surf, sparkling in the sunlight, roaring down the channel. Uprooted yuccas swirled toward the Gulf, with only fifteen hundred miles to go. A dead steer wedged itself between the trestle embankment and a piling. Rex might have joined it if he had tried to beat the flash flood.

The water would recede in an hour or so, but the impromptu riverbed would be a quagmire for a couple of days. The five remaining taquitos would not last that long, not even with coleslaw. Only the vultures would be happy if he waited. He backed away from the edge and turned around again. The road bumped across the spur line and continued south. Hopefully it would intersect something passable.

It took a couple more miles, but finally a grayish line humped inchworm-like over the rails. Three silhouettes marked the crossing: a railroad crossbuck (this road did not rate one on each side), a stationary automobile with the hood open, and a moving human. The car was parked crookedly on the opposite side of the crossing, pointed more or less toward the tracks. The human slammed the hood shut and shook a fist at the car.

Unnoticed or ignored, Yootibibit pulled from the rutted two-track onto the marginally better road, and stopped.

Rex could not tell whether he was looking at the back of a man or a woman. The hair was fairly long, but that didn't mean anything anymore. No-nonsense jeans, a loose long-sleeved shirt, and a well-used cowboy hat kept the sun at bay. They were the same type of clothes that he had favored since his nose's visit with the doctor. Janet had not had time to change her wardrobe tastes.

The car's MacPherson strut had degraded into a MacPherson stumble, leaving the near front wheel cocked at an odd angle. The human yelled. Female, but not too feminine. She proceeded to insult the offending vehicle, describing its provenance in colorful and highly personal but unlikely terms. The warmish off-white paint job seemed to blush on the sides where it had not faded quite as badly as the top.

The tirade ended when Rex exited his truck. The woman did not turn around, not yet. She squared her shoulders and gathered breath for one last round.

"Useta, you can't DO this to me!" she screamed before pivoting to face the newcomer.

Many, but not all, long-time ranch women can be lumped into two classes. One variety is strung together with barbed wire: sinews and spikes. The other is more solidly constructed, looking like they could beat a bull into submission. There are plenty of other ranch women, of course, built for appearance, but this specimen fell into the second major classification.

Height, five six or so, plus hat. Width, best not to ask. Tonnage, closer to battleship than light cruiser. Two-tone hair strung onto her shoulders. Steel grey for the first four or five inches, it shifted to a darkish color born in a bottle. Apparently she had given up trying to look younger some months back.

"Can I help, ma'am?" he asked.

She bit off a retort. "Yeah. Shoot Useta."

He jolted. "Sorry, ma'am, but I don't have my rifle."

The woman stared incredulously. "What sorta- ? Never mind! Hang on a minute!" She stalked back to her car and yanked open the driver's door. The upper half of her torso disappeared into the opening. She extracted herself and an oversized purse a few seconds later, after which she pulled a large pistol from the bag and positioned herself in front of the radiator.

"I might as well do it myself!" She released the safety, took dead aim at a grasshopper stuck to the grille, and pulled the trigger. The pistol roared and jumped. There was no more grasshopper. Useta bled rusty radiator fluid into the ruts.

"There! I feel better now." The shooter returned her weapon to its purse.

"*I hope so!*" thought Rex to himself. "Need a ride?" he asked.

"Looks like. Either that or I'll have to steal your truck."

"Druther you'd let me drive."

"If you insist. Just let me get my stuff." The passenger emptied the contents of her car into Yootibibit's bed. Groceries and junk. She didn't bother to close Useta's doors.

Rex retrieved his greasy lunch bag from the freshly oiled passenger seat but didn't comment. There was nothing he could do about it. She climbed in.

"Where to, ma'am?"

"Comunicado. The only place this road goes."

"Except ranches, I guess."

"Nope."

They turned toward the hills. The railroad crossing looked no rougher than the rest of the road, which had not been graded for some time. Every so often, Yootibibit's tires would launch a rock past the shoulder. Dust boiled up behind them. The mountain storm had dried out before reaching the plains, as usual.

"Want some lunch?" Rex asked.

"I might. Whatcha got?"

Without taking his eyes off the road, he pulled a tepid taquito from the bag.

She recoiled. "I'd rather eat cat food!"

"You're outa luck then. The cat died at Christmastime."

"I'm sorry to hear that. It musta found one of these in its stocking."

"Times were tough. I couldn't afford a mouse."

She snorted.

He shifted subjects. "Why do you call your car Useta?"

"It useta be pink."

"Pink's pretty rare."

"Yeah, like steak."

Rex glanced curiously at his passenger, and she decided additional explanation was in order. "Never mind. That's not why. I useta sell cosmetics."

"Did they work?" He immediately wished he could reel the words back in. "I mean. ..."

She scowled. "You just chewed your foot off, Mister!"

"Sorry. But I ..."

"Don't start on the other one!" There was no sound except for Yootibibit and flying gravel. "Yeah," she finally muttered. "No."

"Hmm?"

"I useta be married. Till my husband ran off with my best customer. So yeah, they worked. But I couldn't smear enough on myself to keep him, so no. After he took off, I lined up the rest of the bottles and used 'em for target practice. Bright red lipsticks were the best. They were her favorites. His too, I guess. Then I quit the business, but I still had the car. Till now."

"You probably coulda got it fixed if you hadn't shot it."

"Nah, it was the right thing to do. You know what I thought of when I pulled the trigger? My ex. The only thing better woulda been if Useta'd died on the tracks. Now *that* would be something to watch!"

"It's too late now."

"Yup. Useta's dead."

"No, I mean because you're fresh out of trains. A wrecking train ran up to Mailpie a couple hours ago to start yanking tracks."

She gasped. "Oh, no! They can't! It's in court!"

Rex shook his head. "They must figure it's easier to ask forgiveness than permission. Did you ever hear of Meigs Field?"

"No."

"It was a little Chicago airport on an island. The Mayor wanted to turn it into a park, but the Feds said no. So one night bulldozers dug up the runway. Airplanes were stuck. Folks complained, and it cost the city more than a million bucks, but Meigs Field is gone."

Both of them lapsed into silence. The empty spur line that had run roughly parallel to the road began to sweep left and right, finding the shallowest grade into the hills. The county road took a more direct route, climbing over ridges and across arroyos. Finally it rounded a bend in the hillside to reveal kind of a town.

COMUNICADO
ELEV. 4,722

The ground sloped upward toward a jagged granite mountain devoid of trees. Dilapidated houses and trailers straggled across crumbled stone at its base. A defunct gas station greeted visitors on the left side, the better to catch people leaving town with less than a full tank. A tall, ancient hand-jacked fuel pump with a ten gallon glass top stood at attention by its stoop-shouldered electric replacement. The old-timer was ready to fill cars when the power went out, assuming there was gas, which there wasn't, and a customer, which there wouldn't be. The pop machine by the front door had not held a cold cola for years. Coyote Lounge across the street once had sold stronger beverages to nighttime revelers, but revels were passé in Comunicado.

"Just past the filling station on the left." She pointed toward a cinder block house with a corrugated roof and a failed flowerbed by the door. A greasy spot in the side yard showed where Useta had lived.

She had the passenger door open before Rex came to a full stop. "How're you going to get around?" he asked as she escaped.

"I have friends." Her newly greased jeans walked to the back of the truck, where she began swinging freight from the bed onto the side of the road.

"Need help with your stuff?" he called through the window.

"No, I'll get it when I get around to it. Nobody'll bother it. Thanks!" She hurried into the house. It had not been locked.

He shrugged and shifted into drive. As long as he was in Comunicado, he might as well see Comunicado. It did not take long. A peeling white church on the left side of the road stood counterpoint to a derelict, half-finished adobe train station across the street. A rusty chain link fence with bullet-riddled "No Trespassing" signs in front of the station spoiled what could have been a decent photograph. The fence continued along the weedy track toward the mountain that defined the back edge of town.

The street diverged slightly to the left and dead-ended at a rutted turnaround in front of a two-story brick school building that had been out of date for seventy years at least. It still appeared to be in use, but barely. A faded wooden sign boasted:

HOME OF THE OMUNICADO OYOTES

Two once bright red C's had turned a sickly yellow. A smaller sign pointed to Comunicado Elementary, a permanent cluster of temporary buildings just south of the turnaround.

A stone field house to the right of the high school hugged the base of the cliff, at the far end of a tumbleweed-studded once-upon-a-time football field. Undoubtedly splintery bleachers slouched between the railroad right-of-way and the field. A playground snuggled against the near side of a sagging security fence around the unused stadium. The playground seemed to be in better shape than either school.

Partly hidden behind the bleachers and the field house, the town's origin and downfall could be seen where the top of a high stone arch bit into the face of the mountain. Row upon row of tan stone blocks, laid perfectly straight, sealed it shut.

The sun disappeared behind the jagged range. The mountain's shadow began its daily march down a field where no band had marched for decades. It would be a few more hours before the eastern plains went dark.

"Well, Yootibibit, we've seen Comunicado. Now our lives are complete." They started down the long road to Mailpie.

« 2 »

Rex stood in line at the grocery the next day, waiting for the lady in front to finish emptying her cart onto the belt. Loads like hers explained why shopping cart wheels wore out so quickly. He would be stuck for a while, unwilling witness to a long conversation. Hopefully it would not be about female surgery or scummy husbands.

"What's Choo-Choo goin' to do when they pull up the tracks?" the customer asked, glancing toward the door.

"I dunno," replied the worried clerk. "I reckon it'll just about kill him."

"Does he know?"

"Not yet, I don't think. We ain't tellin' 'im. But here he comes." They changed the subject to hemorrhoid treatments when a perpetually smiling young man pushed a string of carts into the store. He spotted Rex immediately as he always did, thanks to Janet. Miz Albert had been one of his favorite teachers even though she had never actually been his teacher. She didn't teach Special Ed, but she was pretty and she would talk to him.

"Howdy, Mister Albert!" he called excitedly. "Didja see the wreckin' train?"

The medical discussion screeched to a halt.

"Hi, Charlie!" Rex replied. "What train?"

"The one that's gonna pull up the tracks now that the mine's closed. A three thousand horsepower EMD SDP40F left over from some passenger run, two forty-foot flatcars, a forty-foot gondola, a tool car, a 1957 Budd business car, an' a claw crane. I only seen 'em in pictures, an' now I'll git to watch one work!"

"Congratulations! How do you know they're forty-foot cars?"

"They all was once. Cars was forty feet an' rails was thirty-nine so they'd fit on cars. Now they use unit rail an' it don't matter, but that old yard rail's all thirty-nine feet. They can peel it up an' haul it away easy!"

Choo-Choo Charlie was good at two things: train lore and bagging groceries. He could read and do math at a sixth grade level because he had worked at it. That put him ahead of some "regular" schoolmates who hadn't, but reading and math were not necessary for his career or his field of interest.

A year earlier, grocery customers had quietly chipped in to buy round-trip Amtrak sleeper tickets between El Paso and Los Angeles for him and his grandmother, as a twenty-fifth birthday present. There could have been no better gift. His little house by the freight yard was decorated with railroad flotsam and jetsam. He had painstakingly constructed a walk from the street to the front door with discarded steel tie plates held in place by reused spikes pounded into the hard caliche soil. The rusty path was deadly hot in the summertime, but hardly anybody except Charlie ever navigated it. Inside the house, an extensive collection of train videos substituted for television. He made scrapbooks of railroad articles and pictures.

The view from his back door until recently had been freight trains being made and unmade around the clock. That had changed to a few stationary cars and shimmering sky-blue mirages punctuated by mesquite. At the moment, there also was a wrecking train parked on a siding by a concrete loading platform. A skeleton crew had taken the train to Mailpie, jockeyed the pickup from the flatcar to the dock, and driven back to their base of operations in El Paso. Charlie could study the rig at his leisure.

"What'll you do after they pull up the tracks?" the hemorrhoid lady asked. The clerk glared at her.

Charlie thought a bit. "I dunno. Move, I guess. Find a store that needs a bagger in some town with trains."

"You can't do that! We'd miss you," protested the clerk.

"Y'all can move too."

Several minutes later, Charlie left with Hemorrhoid Lady, pushing her groceries and chattering about trains. The clerk watched him with pity and turned to Rex. "Can you believe that? Choo-Choo thinks he can just run out and find another job anywhere he wants. It's sad."

"Maybe he's happier'n us for not knowing any different."

The clerk could scan, slide packages, and talk simultaneously. "I guess you're right. They're talkin' about layoffs here too, now that there's less people in town to buy groceries. Mailpie's gittin' quieter'n quieter. I ain't feelin' too good about it."

Mailpie was not quiet that night. The police received a tip of a major dope deal about to occur at the Turquoise Motor Inn on the east side of town. After a flurry of phone calls between the County Sheriff, the State Police, and the Feds, a drug team raided a motel room. Nobody was there. However, a kilo of white powder and an open bathroom window in the back indicated the tip had been accurate. A broken bag of powder and dusty footprints led to the Hoist House ("Hoist One Here," flashed the neon sign), a nearby bar long suspected of selling more than alcohol. Police questioned everyone they could round up, but without any results beyond a drunken magistrate and some high school football players. That was about the time that the Sheriff's Office received a complaint about somebody flinging trash from a car as it sped north on the highway. The "trash" was more one-kilo bags.

Sirens and police radios kept East Side residents awake. Across town, the nighttime start of track demolition was largely ignored in a community where round-the-clock crashing and banging of train cars had been background noise for fifty years. Those who did notice generally grumbled, "The railroad must be in an awful hurry to get the tracks out before the lawyers stop 'em," and went back to sleep.

The rail yard was not quiet the next day, either, after reporters converged on the scene. Lucky members of the wrecking train's crew costarred on television news until railroad lawyers got wind of the situation and ordered them to shut up. The workers had driven a hundred miles to Mailpie that morning to begin their job, but somebody else had started it for them. The wrecking train was stranded on its siding. It would be there for a while. Rails and roadbed ended in a water-filled ditch five feet from the locomotive. Even the ties and ballast had disappeared.

Four lengths of track were missing. If Choo-Choo Charlie had been present, he would have told everybody that was "a hunnert an' fifty six feet," but he wasn't, and he didn't. Charlie was missing, too.

《　》

The *Mailpie Courier Herald* finally had something more interesting than births to report. Grand larceny, vandalism, and drugs sold papers. Scandal never hurt, either. It was a good week to be in the newspaper business.

The railroad offered a substantial reward for information regarding an unmarked white semi-tractor-trailer rig that had been parked by the freight yard the previous evening, but which had since vanished down one highway or up the other.

Unnamed minors had been arrested for possession of alcohol in the Hoist House raid. Two local football heroes were suspended for a rules violation. The school administration declined further comment, citing confidentiality laws. Not mentioned in the article was the fact that everybody in town knew who the boys were, where they had been, and what they had done. Their beverages of choice were not much of a secret, either. The next School Board meeting promised to be interesting.

The magistrate apologized for appearing to be drunk. He had been feeling ill, and that was why he spent thirty minutes in the men's room while the police were rampaging through the bar. Rampaging, mind you! No decent officer would violate the privacy of a stall to see if somebody was crouched fully clothed on top of the seat. The fact that the judge had toppled off was no excuse, even if he had made a lot of noise doing it. The automatic flusher had startled him.

《　》

Two weeks elapsed with no more word on Charlie's whereabouts. The hunt for drug dealers was equally fruitless, except for several kilos of heroin rounded up during the chase.

Opinion at the grocery store was divided, whether Choo-Choo had suffered foul play at the hands of the phantom wreckers ("You *know* he woulda watched 'em!") or had made good on his plan to find another town with a train ("I'd like to be there when he walks into their grocery store lookin' for a job!"). Foul play had the most votes. He did not drive. Nothing, not even his video collection, was taken. A pumpkin-colored plastic lawn chair sat outside his back door, facing the place where the tracks had been.

Hours later and blocks away, a cool night breeze wafted through Rex's bedroom window. Crickets and dogs furnished background noise, but not enough. It had been too quiet ever since the railroad went still. Maybe that was why he was dreaming about trains, sort of.

He slept fitfully, somewhere in that twilight zone where thoughts and dreams shift seamlessly into each other. He and Yootibibit were driving alongside the railroad, away from the flash flood and toward the Comunicado switch indicator silhouetted dark and round against the azure sky.

Suddenly he awoke.

Was that what he had seen?

No question about it.

But that was wrong! The circle would be visible from his angle only if the switch had been turned to the side track. A train had come down the main line less than half an hour earlier. Either the switch had moved in those thirty minutes, or the indicator lied.

He cracked an eye at the clock. Four seventeen. A couple of years earlier, he would have rolled over to catch that last hour and forty three minutes before the alarm went off, but the alarm didn't go off any more. There was no reason to set the thing. No matter, though; sleeping was hopeless. Or was it? He could try.

Was it working? He peeped at the clock again. Four eighteen. *Get up!* it seemed to say. *If you don't, I'm going to say four nineteen, then four twenty. You'll lie there and watch, trying to guess the instant that I change, until I drive you crazy. If you close your eyes, you'll wonder what time it is until you <u>have</u> to know. Make you look! I'm gonna make you look!*

Four nineteen. He threw back the sheet and rolled out of bed. Groping along the wall, he found the power cord and pulled. "Take that!" he grunted. He didn't need to know the time anymore. The clock beeped in protest.

Four twenty. He had forgotten about the battery backup. Once it had been important, but now it was just an instrument of torture. It was not the only one, though. His bladder also demanded attention. *Flash flood! Remember that dream? That was my doing! Ignore me at your peril!*

Four twenty four. The coffeemaker said so when Rex passed by the kitchen on his way from the bathroom. Coffee would start to brew automatically as soon as it said seven. The gurgle and aroma usually helped pull him out of bed, but not this morning. He could not wait that long and pushed the "Start" button.

As long as you're up, you might as well feed me! growled his stomach. He glanced down at it, lapping over the waistband of his boxers. A predawn snack did not look necessary, but still it felt like a good idea. He padded to the refrigerator and inspected the hoard. What was easy? A translucent bag of two-week-old taquitos lurked to the left of the milk. No coleslaw, though; it had gone limp on the way back from Comunicado.

Microwave one, or eat it cold? Decisions, decisions. Cold was faster. Then again, those taquitos were pretty old. Heating might be safer, and hardened lard didn't sound too appetizing anyway. Score one for the microwave.

Four thirty one. Rex sat, still in his boxers, at the kitchen table. A cup of coffee was in front of him, one swallow shy. The coffeemaker sputtered angrily beneath the pot, complaining about his clumsy attempt to pour a cup before it was ready. Three taquitos lay on a plate in a puddle of orange grease. He bit into the first one. The outside tried to fry his tongue. The inside was cold. The end, just inches from his eyeballs, was a fuzzy blue. Cat food might have been better.

He stopped in mid-chew.

Cat food.

Useta.

Meigs Field.

The taquito returned to the plate. All of it. The coffee cup rose to his lips. This would be at least a two-cup problem. It might even take a real breakfast to figure out. He imagined a phone call to his deputy friend.

"Hello, Stan, this is Rex. ... Fine, yeah. Say, I might have something on that train business. ... Like it's partly my fault. ... No, no, not me really! ... Some lady. ... Who? ... Now that you mention it, I don't know who she is. But her car's named Useta. ... What's she like? Ranch lady. Built like a bull. Well, not quite like a bull, but you know the type. ... Hair, grey and bottle brown. ... Eyes? I can't recall. I was watching the gun. ... Yeah, gun; she shoots cars. ... No, really,

Stan, honest, I'm sober as a judge! ... Well, not that judge. ... In Comunicado. ... No, not incommunicado. In - Comunicado. ... You gotta be kidding! Whaddya mean, material witness? ... Hello? Hello?"

Some research would be in order before calling the cops.

Cup in hand, he headed for the computer. Then he imagined what somebody might think if they happened to see him sitting in his skivvies staring at the Internet at not quite five in the morning. He should put on some clothes.

Four fifty two. Rex was passably dressed but not showered. Maybe he'd get around to that later. E-mail came first: a Grandither picture, the usual collection of exotic investment opportunities, medical aids that would do him no good in his current social environment, and forwarded inspirational messages that *had* to be forwarded again if he was a decent human. He had quit being a decent human long before, though, and deleted all but the baby picture.

Then he opened a satellite mapping site. There was Mailpie, and there was the railroad. Zooming in, he could identify blurry rails. It was amazing how pictures could be so detailed from thousands of miles in space. Rex had enough trouble taking sharp snapshots at ten feet. He scrolled south and located Comunicado Junction. The roadbed of the branch line was easily identifiable as it wound toward the mountains. Oddly, though, he could not see rails. He had crossed rails. Maybe the shadow angle was wrong.

The line dead-ended at the mountain. Comunicado looked fuzzier than Mailpie, but Rex had noticed before that the sharpest resolution was generally reserved for places that interested the most people. Nonetheless, he could easily pick out the gasless gas station and underpopulated school with its football field-cum-tumbleweed patch. Useta's former home was a square blob.

He scrolled across the mountain. The Continental Divide was the easternmost, but not necessarily the highest, of a series of more or less parallel north-south ridges. Canyons west of the Divide fed the Gila River when they felt like it. The crooked canyon separating Comunicado Ridge from its western neighbor looked the same as every other canyon in the area, except for a fuzzy line across it just south of where the tunnel would have been. That would be the abandoned dam.

The tunnel's western approach was not visible. Rex wondered about the lack of fill where the portal ought to be. Blasted rock had to go someplace. Then he realized it would have been used for dam material after the change in plans.

He scrolled north. The image became blurrier. That was not uncommon for New Mexico, where two thirds of the land was government owned. The

Defense Department in particular was touchy about what people should know about their property.

Six oh two. How time flies when you're having quandaries. Rex's stomach grumbled, either from lack of taquitos or essence of taquito that the coffee had washed down. The Headframe Café should be opening for breakfast around six unless the Health Department had come by again.

Health Department inspections were posted in the newspaper, but that meant you had to read it. Things had been easier in the old days when a decal would be posted in the window. It was disconcerting when a bright green "A" sticker was replaced by an equally bright red "C", especially when the "C" was backward because you noticed it on your way out. "D" was a padlock.

Time to kill the computer and get a move on. Click Start. Then not the Off-On icon; that only put it into hibernation. One of these days he would learn how to fix that. Or not. Right Arrow would do until then. Shut Down. "Do you want to save your settings?" No. "You have unread messages." Later. "Try our mail order movie service." No. "A dialog box is open." Just die. Rex pulled the second plug of the morning.

Returning to the kitchen, he emptied the coffeepot into a travel container. Lukewarm, it would still be better than a hot jug of Headframe swill. Not as much better as usual, though, since he had decanted a high octane cup before it finished brewing. He sloshed out the canteen and refilled it with water. He tugged boots onto his feet, put a hat on the other end, and started ferrying supplies to Yootibibit. Sunglasses, a .22 rifle, and a box of ammunition completed the kit.

Yootibibit was hungry too. Rex filled the tank at the gas station. He also checked the tires, the oil, and the radiator. Once upon a time, people with limited academic skills and caps worn backward would have checked those things for him, but now all stations were self-service. He wondered what those people did anymore. Walked around in packs with their caps on sideways, he supposed. Lately it had become more fashionable in some circles to shed the caps and don hooded sweatshirts instead. That seemed counterproductive in hundred-degree weather.

The Headframe's last health report had said something about low and moderate risk violations. In the days of decals, a bright yellow "B" probably would have greeted diners. Rex was the only diner so far. "Hey, Smitty," he called, "what's a low risk violation mean? Puny germs?"

The proprietor was not amused. "Structural issues. Not, I repeat *not*, germs!"

"OK, sorry. What sorta structural issues?"

"Nothin' much. The kitchen plaster's crackin' up. A chunk fell in the rinse sink."

"Just the rinse sink, huh?"

"Yep, so there *ain't* no germ problem!" He muttered to himself, "Lucky it didn't knock out the sanitizer sink!"

Rex overheard. "How many sinks do they make you have?"

"Three, now. Used to be two. At this rate it'll all be sinks one of these days an' there won't be no room in the kitchen to cook nothin' but dishwater! So git y'all's order in early. What'll it be?"

"A couple eggs, over hard. Bacon. Crisp."

"Still don't trust me, huh?"

"Never mind. A big grapefruit juice too." Frozen or canned, it should be safe enough.

"Coffee?"

"Might as well." It was boiled.

"Comin' up!"

"And a Lunch Bucket Special." That was a large take-out meal designed not to spoil if left unrefrigerated.

Smitty paused. "Not much call for those since the mine shut down, but I'll see what I can scratch up."

Not long afterward, Rex traded cash for a toothpick and exited onto the sidewalk. The bank sign across the street recited all the news it cared about. Six Colon Fifty Eight. Seventy Six Space F. Twenty Four Space C. Two Point Nine Percent. New. Cars. Six Colon Fifty Nine. Yootibibit popped a yooey from the curb and headed south. Seventy Seven Space F. It would be a hot day.

Driving was a lot faster on the two-lane highway, where the speed limit was seventy, than along the rutted path paralleling the railroad. Seventy there would have killed at least Yootibibit and maybe both of them.

The Mailpie bank sign, long out of view, was flashing Seven Colon Thirty Nothing and Eighty Three Space F when Rex turned toward Comunicado. Fifty or maybe sixty would be the limit on the gravel road.

The railroad crossing was doubly marked, first by the traditional bullet-riddled crossbuck, but also by Useta on the shoulder with her (she had to be female) useta-be-pink doors still hanging open. They had become perforated over the past few days. Sparkling cubes of glass lay below every window opening. It was a western fact of life that flat surfaces attracted bullets. That differed from other parts of the country, where bullets usually flew in town and hit softer things, like people. Rex had never seen much sport in targeting anything as large and motionless as a car door, but maybe some folks really needed the practice.

He bumped across the crossing and turned north onto the rutted service road. The red circle of Comunicado Junction came into view a few minutes later, meaning the spur line should be open. He parked Yootibibit and hiked to the switch. It was shunted to the left, so the indicator did not lie. The mechanism seemed to be in good repair. The spur track was old bolted rail, but functional. The tops were shiny.

Maybe they used it as a siding. It would make sense. The ninety five mile line from El Paso to Mailpie was single track. Choo-Choo had told him train speed was fifty miles an hour. Unless there were sidings, a train could not start one direction until an opposite train cleared the line.

Probably the work crew had turned the switch to lock out the track segment they were to dismantle. That made sense. Rex was glad he had not called the police.

How long was the spur? Mailpie trains could be a mile long. The day was getting a bit warm for hiking up and down a mile of track. Yootibibit wouldn't mind, though, and was air conditioned. Rex turned onto the spur. As he expected, the tires straddled the rails. He could run to the end of the line, and if there were no place to jump the tracks and turn around, he could back up all the way to the switch. It would only be for a mile or so. He zeroed the trip odometer.

Years of giving paternal advice left him a bit uneasy. He had solemnly warned both Ithers about driving on railroads. "What if there's a train?" he would ask. But what train? This line was out of business. He was grateful anyway that no Ither was around to see what he was doing, or worse, give him a hard time about it.

A sign stood between the rails 1.2 miles later. Four feet square, it bore diagonal stripes and three words:

**TRACK
MAINTENANCE
ENDS**

A tire might pop off the rim if Rex tried to jump the rails, and it was a long walk to town. It would be wiser to back to the switch. Shifting into reverse, he laid his right arm across the back of Janet's seat, gripped the steering wheel in his left hand, and turned his head to look behind.

And saw, against the shimmering sky, the shadowy blue nose of a locomotive inching up the siding.

That was bad enough, but a deer rifle trained on him from the cab side window made it somewhat more serious.

The rumbling engine, leading a short string of mixed freight, did not stop. Yootibibit lurched forward when the coupler contacted the bumper. Rex instinctively pressed the brake pedal as hard as he could, but he could not stop a train. The whistle blew, long and loud.

The stranger with the rifle shook his head repeatedly and waved the truck forward. Rex jerked his head around and saw to his amazement that the sign, apparently motorized, was flattening itself between the rails. He also felt to his amazement that his jeans were wet. There was no time to worry about that, though. He shifted into Drive and crept ahead.

The train tooted. It bumped Yootibibit again. Rex pressed uncertainly on the throttle. Another toot, and he pressed a bit harder. The rifleman in the rear-view mirror nodded to him.

They eventually settled on thirty miles an hour. Then a trestle came into view, looking very narrow from Yootibibit's cab. The train did not slow down. Planks laid alongside the tracks allowed the truck to traverse the ties. The rails would nudge the wheels back into line whenever they drifted off course. An acrid smell of hot rubber permeated the cab. "This can't be doing my tires any good!" Rex shakily said to himself.

The engine never left more than a hundred yards between itself and the truck. Onward and upward they wound, through narrow cuts, over fills, and across trestles. Comunicado came into view after a tight bend. The train slowed down as it passed the unfinished station. It did not stop, though, but urged Yootibibit toward the blocked tunnel.

The tunnel unblocked.

Mortar seams between rows of blocks were strictly theoretical. Stone veneer was secured to the panels of a high roll-up door that slowly wound open, exposing all but the top of the arch.

The locomotive chugged toward the dark opening. Rex had no choice but to proceed. The engine switched on its headlight, which shone above Yootibibit's cab and illuminated everything except the space immediately ahead of the truck. Rex pulled on his headlights. The tunnel throbbed with racket.

A red light glowed ahead. Shortly afterward, the profile of a streetcar appeared against the blackness. Sparks flashed above where a pantograph fed it electricity from a catenary line. The streetcar was proceeding in the same direction as the truck and train, but only at about ten miles an hour.

Yootibibit was sandwiched between the streetcar and the engine. After what felt like an hour but the radio clock claimed was only six minutes, the streetcar stopped. So did the train.

"Out of the truck!" blared a bullhorn.

Rex shut off the ignition, killed the headlights, and obeyed. As loud as the noise had been inside the cab, it was immeasurably worse the moment he opened the door. The roaring Diesel shook the air. There also was the whine of a large fan.

No sooner had he closed the door than the engine's headlight went out. The streetcar's lights also were extinguished. Rex was engulfed in total blackness, but not total silence. The whistle blasted. There was a stinging pain in his shoulder, and he dropped in a heap.

《　》

3

Rex awoke, cold and thirsty. His ears rang. At least he wasn't dead. If he were in Heaven, he wouldn't be thirsty. If he were in Hell, he wouldn't be cold. So where was he?

One eye cracked open. He was on a bed with white sheets and a blue flowered pillow. Not a casket. That was good. He wasn't dressed in a suit, either. That also was good, because he only expected to wear one of those when he was in a casket. Instead, he was draped in a green hospital gown with nothing beneath it but him. That explained the cold part.

The door was closed. Locked, too, probably. Whoever these people were, they didn't play around.

He turned his head. No tubes stuck out of him, and no wires were attached. A drinking glass sat on a little white table. Could he reach it? The arm worked. Yes, he could. The drink wasn't quite water, but it was wet and welcome. Like that lizardaid stuff, he decided, that only tasted good when one was thirsty.

A window high in the wall admitted white sunlight from a blue sky, filtered through a green tree, with jagged brown mountains in the lower background. A hummingbird feeder hung from the eave outside. Below the window, a French horn rested on a chair.

"Mister Pierce?" A doctorish voice with just a hint of Italian inflection came from the next room.

"Yeah, doc?" A gruff, quick accent, not New Mexican at all. Maybe Chicago or Pittsburgh. All Easterners sounded alike to Rex. East was anything to the right of Dallas on a map.

"No, no!" corrected the inflection. "You must remember never to go by that name again! Your life depends on it!"

"So gimme a new one and I'll forget, okay? I've been in this dump a week already!"

There was a deep sigh. "That's normal. It-"

"Not for me it isn't!" the accent complained.

"It takes time to study you and decide what new persona will suit you best. You must become somebody your enemies would never suspect. Plastic surgery isn't the whole answer, you know. It only completes the conversion. We learn who you are, and then we change you into somebody completely different. First comes the surgery, and then we start work on your persona. As soon as you're ready, we move you to your new home, all expenses paid. But I have some good news!"

"Yeah?" The brusque voice sounded almost hopeful.

"We have found your persona!"

"Yeah? What is it?"

"There are two questions first. How do you feel about moving to Tahiti?"

"Sign me up!"

"And how do you feel about unmarried women?"

"You know me, Doc! The more, the better!"

"Excellent! Then we'll start surgery in the morning."

"It's about time! So what's my new name?"

"Sister Clarisse."

There was silence, broken by the doctor. "You will be working with the Sisters of Mercy at a Hansen's Disease hospital. They need burly sisters to help with some of the larger patients. You will do fine."

"Hansen's-?"

"At one time it would have been called a leprosarium, but you must never use that term. It'll be easier because you will speak either French or Tahitian, whichever you prefer."

"Uh, Doc, this surgery...?"

"Only what is necessary so you won't be suspected as an imposter. We have taken the communal sanitary facilities into account in planning the conversion."

"But-"

The doctor interrupted. "I understand. 'But plastic surgery will not be enough,' you say. That is true. You must not just act the part, but *be* a caring, devoted nun. Watch your vocabulary. No cigars, of course, but there will be wine. Over time, other urges will trouble you less and less. But now you must rest. We have given you a sedative. You will wake up in time for Nurse Lew to prep you at ten tonight for tomorrow morning's operation. Lew may look big, but he's gentle as long as you don't cross him. Now have a pleasant nap. See you in the morning!"

A door opened and closed. Somebody, presumably the doctor, walked whistling down the hall. Somebody else, not the doctor, transitioned from swearing to mumbling to snoring.

Rex was not comforted. He sat up. So far, so good. He walked to the door steadily enough. His back was a bit drafty, though. He pushed the lever. Locked, as expected. There was a peephole, but it didn't work. Turning around, he inspected the window. It would not open, and the glass was reinforced.

The French horn taunted him from the chair. He crossed the room and picked it up. It made little breathy popping noises when he pressed the keys in succession. The mouthpiece went to his lips, and his right hand into the bell.

"Play *Aggies, O Aggies*." The doctor called from the hall.

Rex nearly dropped the horn. The peephole must be backward, not broken. "Are you kidding? I haven't blown one of these in thirty years!"

"Don't worry about that! Remember how you make a trumpet sound like a French horn?"

"Yeah. Stick your hand in the bell and miss half the notes."

"So blow it."

It was not a good rendition of *Aggies, O Aggies*, but it was recognizable to anyone who had heard the song for four years. The lock rattled. A grinning, balding physician in a lab coat entered the room. His name badge said, DR. COGNITO.

"Teerex?"

"Berno!" Rex yelled. They embraced laughing and self-consciously separated. "What're you doing here?"

The doctor sat on the chair. "I run the place. Bio major, remember? Then medical school. A small town doctor does pretty much everything, but plastic surgery's my specialty. Cognito Clinic. The place to go if you want to be incognito. It's a natural. I run a good business with the federal witness protection program."

"Like my neighbor?" Rex gestured at the wall.

Berno frowned. "Yeah. A rotten piece of work, he is. He ran an international business of professional women. Most weren't volunteers. But he turned state's evidence against a mobster, so now he gets to run free."

"Not the way I heard it through the wall."

The doctor regretfully shook his head. "I can't really do that. 'First, do no harm.' Hippocratic Oath. I wish I could, but it wouldn't be fair to the convent." He smiled a grim smile. "No, he'll take care of himself."

"How's that?"

"I told him the nurse would be in at ten. He'll wake up about nine, scoot out his door as fast as he can go, and hightail it out the nearest exit, which happens to be across from his room. Straight up the hill, won't look back. Rattlesnakes are bad this time of year. If they miss him, it'll be sunstroke tomorrow. He's a city kid."

"Then what?"

"Buzzards gotta eat."

A vulture glided through the bit of sky outside the window. Maybe it was waiting for Sister.

"What about the Hippocratic Oath?" Rex asked.

"'*First*, do no harm.' This is second. And he's doing it to himself."
Berno was a world-class rationalizer.

"Do you still get paid?"

"Of course not! That'd be crooked. This is a *pro bono* case."

Rex glanced uneasily at the door. "What about me?"

Berno grinned again. "You're okay. We confirmed your ID."

"My wallet, I suppose."

"That's where we started, but you verified it for us. Horn players are pretty rare, especially Aggie horn players. *Especially* Aggie horn players who answer to Teerex."

"It's been a long time since I answered to that, until now. But speaking of wallets, where's my stuff?"

"Your clothes are being cleaned. They needed it, especially the pants. The truck, too. I'm afraid the guys were a little hard on you. They meant well. The more frightened you were, the faster the tranquilizer would get to your brain. They could use a smaller dose. They didn't think about shock. You taught them about that, though. I've never seen the trolley shoot out of the tunnel so fast!"

Rex stared, bewildered. "Berno, where am I?"

There was a pause. "Comunicado."

The light began to dawn. "But – but, Comunicado is …"

"No place, I know. Think of this as West Comunicado if you prefer, even more no place. We're in Comunicado."

"Who is 'We'?"

"Us."

"You're mighty helpful. I'm stuck here, right?"

The doctor shrugged. "It's up to you. We could use a horn player. But the Director says you can leave."

"The Director?"

Berno glanced toward the door before he continued in a lower voice. "Dictator would be closer to the truth, but I didn't say that."

"Nice guy not to know, I take it."

"You could say that." The doctor paused. "The Director wanted you dead, Rex."

Rex jumped. Berno had never called him anything but Teerex. "What-what changed his mind?" He could barely speak.

"I don't know, except that I wouldn't do it." He spoke through gritted teeth. "So I kept you conked out for almost two days. If I pushed it too far, I'd be dead, too. Finally the Director said okay, you could stay in town, or you could leave on two conditions."

"Which are?"

"First, we're a secret."

"And?"

"To make sure we stay a secret, you have to leave your .22 here as collateral."

Rex shrugged. "That old gun isn't worth much."

"Not to you, maybe. The Director says you'll understand."

"Wrong."

The Grandithers decided the matter. Rex did not wish to be permanently separated from them. "Then I'll go."

Berno sighed. "I expected as much. A nurse will bring your clothes. The trolley comes by in –"he checked his watch – "forty five minutes. Your truck will be waiting for you. Just remember: not a word after you get out. That's no joke." He started for the door. "I'll meet you when it's time. Be ready."

The door clicked shut. Yes, it was locked.

Five minutes later, a hulking male nurse, probably Lew, ducked his head and entered. After delivering the clothing, he left, locking the door. The jeans were ironed, and even the hat had been cleaned. Rex gladly swapped the drafty hospital wardrobe for more familiar garb.

Half an hour later, Berno escorted Rex down the hall past snoring would-be Sister Clarisse's room on the right and an exit to a steep trail on the left. At the end of the hall, he pressed a button, and a door opened into the lobby. One more button and one more door, and they were on a station platform.

A pink trolley rolled in from the right. *"Tammy the Tram"*, declared the side. "Ding!" declared the bell. It rang again after the doctor preceded his guest into the conveyance. Steel wheels rumbled beneath them.

Rex gaped at the invisible town, unseen on any map. It was in a steep valley that terminated suddenly at a tall dam. A blue pond lay at the base, surrounded by a green park. Houses and shops lined roads on opposite sides of a stream. Trolley wires stretched above both roads. Pedestrians and bicycles shared the streets with streetcars and a few horses, but not cars. Modified golf carts hauled deliveries up, and garbage down, sloping side paths.

A small rail yard lay to the north, but the trolley did not go that direction. It swung rightward onto a trestle that stapled the sides of the valley bottom together.

"How do you keep this a secret?" Rex asked over the rumble.

Berno glanced toward the eastern ridge. "The Continental Divide's up there. No crossing except the tunnel. Behind us, the Gila Wilderness. No people, but plenty of snakes. Mexican wolves, too, recently planted and doing fine. Wizmer's a few miles north."

"Wizmer?"

"White Sands Missile Range. Not the big one, of course. It's kind of a branch, with a hush-hush launch site. They're used to secrets, so if they hear there's a Black Budget facility next door, it's no skin off their nose. They patrol their side of the fence and don't see us."

Tammy the Tram would not be asked to climb the Divide. She turned to the right as soon as the bridge was behind. "And south of here?" asked the passenger.

"Canyons and lava beds. We borrowed some Wizmer 'Keep Out' signs, too."

"But none of this shows up on satellite photos!"

Berno nodded. "So you looked. The same fine folks who airbrush out military bases make us disappear."

"Because you're black budget."

"Not really. We aren't even government-owned, but we don't need government accountants nosing around to find out." He paused. "Or others."

"I hear you." The artificial southern horizon drew closer and higher. "Nobody notices your dam?"

"Nobody sees it. Sky blue paint on the other side. And the canyon's crooked."

That's not all that's crooked! Rex kept that suspicion to himself. "What about airplanes?"

His guide grinned. "A friend in the FAA. Wizmer's no-fly zone's a bit oversized. Not even the Air Force is allowed. Wizmer's a Navy base. No ocean, but plenty of beach. Sometimes smugglers fly low up the canyon to hide from radar, but they only get one chance. If they come around the bend and hit something like a surprise dam, we wait a couple of days for the coyotes to clean up. Then we repaint the dam and scrap out the plane."

Rex eyed the doctor. "More *pro bono*?"

"Kinda."

"What about the contraband?"

Berno glanced away. "We don't want it."

That subject wasn't up for discussion.

The tunnel's high mouth swallowed them up. Daylight dwindled to a point and was not replaced, as the trolley ran without lights. Blackness was sporadically broken by arcs from the overhead wire. The stone passage reverberated with rumbling wheels and crescendo whine from a large ventilation fan. A breeze blew through the car and diminished with the whine.

Just as it seemed the Stygian journey might go on forever, the car decelerated. Lights switched on to reveal a spotless, blue tiled subway station labeled COMUNICADO EAST. The three trolley riders were the only occupants. The track disappeared below a high, closed roll-up door just past the platform. A low side tunnel, tiled and lighted, extended to the right past a turnstile. A red EXIT sign glowed above it.

Berno stood up, rocking as the car came to a halt. "End of the line. Your truck is outside. New tires, courtesy of the Director. The old ones smelled pretty hot." He lowered his voice. "The French horn spot'll be open for a while. Think about it."

"Fat chance! I have grandkids to spoil."

Berno's face reddened. "You don't quite catch on sometimes."

Rex curiously watched his friend. "Maybe not," he conceded. "So if I *did* change my mind, how would I sign up, anyway?"

"The gate combo is 1888. Play *Aggies*. Until then, be careful!"

No sooner had Rex clicked through the turnstile than Tammy the Tram dinged the bell and began her return trip. The station lights went out, except for the exit passage. It turned to the left and ended at a windowless steel door with a crash bar.

The door snapped closed behind him, leaving him in a dusty field house. He walked past locker rooms with faded signs: HOME to the left and VISITORS to the right. The hall ended at rusty double doors with cracked chicken wire sandwich glass.

The outside doors looked old, but they swung quietly and locked solidly. How many six-man football teams had run this way into the end zone, to the cheers of tiny crowds? Now they only went through other teams' doors onto other schools' fields.

No crowd, tiny or great, greeted Rex. Only a washed and waxed Yootibibit with shiny new tires awaited him in the morning sun. How long had he been away? A couple of days? It didn't matter. Even if it had been fall, and even if it had been a Friday night, his truck would not interfere with local sports.

It would have been a spectacular setting for football. Little bands would sound twice as big with the echo off the mountain. The delay would interfere with musical crispness, but small town bands were not renowned for musicality.

He drove down the weedy running track to an open gate and started through downtown Comunicado. East Comunicado. The only Comunicado as far as most people knew.

Children scampered and dug holes in Useta's yard. Others refueled their tricycles at the gas station. "Must be grandkids," he decided. "There sure are a lot of them." A second look suggested otherwise. Unless some were friends, the family had developed multiculturalism into an art form. Virtually every skin tone but green was present. Roswell was underrepresented.

Comunicado disappeared behind the first bend. There was no traffic, not even dust stirred up by distant vehicles. Yootibibit's wash job quickly disappeared beneath a layer of dirt. Powdery brown avalanches slid down the windows. The only interruptions in the cloudless sky were soaring vultures and a brown dust devil whirling across the plain, maybe wishing it was a big tornado, black as a buzzard. There was nothing for the would-be twister to destroy, though; just a few tumbleweeds to relocate.

The railroad crossing was visible miles before it materialized. The crossbuck stood as still as ever, but there was movement around Useta. Vultures overhead were not aimlessly prowling for carrion. They spiraled down, looking more like a twister than the dust devil had.

Rex's heart accelerated. Black, baldheaded birds slouched in and out of the car. One landed on the hood and ducked through the shattered windshield. A coyote slunk out the right rear door as Yootibibit clattered across the tracks and stopped by the hulk.

Dreading to do it, Rex lowered his window for a clearer view. Vulture breath rolled into the cab. Two bodies, clothed, tied, and chewed, slumped in Useta's back seat. One had very red lipstick.

He yelled. He honked his horn. Birds boiled from the car, taking to the air and waiting patiently in a holding pattern. Maybe if they were lucky, he also would die. He turned for his rifle to scare them away, but there was no rifle. Instead, he closed the window and fumbled for his cell phone. No service. Mailpie would be in sight before he could call.

There really was no need to hurry. The people were long beyond help, and the killer was equally long gone. That made no difference. Rex raced away as instinctively as he had hit the brakes when pushed by a locomotive. Behind him, the circling vultures spiraled back down to Useta.

He reached the paved highway in record time and made a sliding left turn. A minute later, flashing red lights approached from the north. He automatically checked his speedometer (ninety) and stopped on the shoulder just as he had taught the Ithers to do. This would be an interesting conversation. *("Going to a fire, Mister?" "No, Officer, from a murder." "Oh, really?")*

A state police car raced past, siren blaring. In the rear view mirror, Rex could see it fishtail onto Comunicado Road. He would not have to report a murder after all. Not right away. He could go home first and decide what to say.

Nerves and close attention to the speedometer made the road to Mailpie seem longer than usual. More flashing lights approached, but not as quickly. An ambulance eventually passed.

Yootibibit seemed more shaken than Rex. The pell-mell race down the last few miles of Comunicado Road had knocked the freshly shod wheels seriously out of balance. That would have to be fixed soon.

Finally Rex reached his street. Reaching over the sun visor, he pushed a button. The garage door opened. He pulled into the shade, killed the engine, and pushed the button again. The clattering disappearance of the outside world was too tunnel-like for comfort.

He beelined through the stifling garage to the utility room. The "click" of the spring-loaded door to the garage reminded him again of Comunicado, as if he wanted reminding.

The house was not as hot as the garage, but it was muggier. The swamp cooler had seen to that. The refrigerator was colder yet, sheltering milk and beer but not much else. Beer was tempting, but milk won. It would cool his brain without fogging it, while he decided what to do next.

Two days of normal life had run off. He thought of Ithers and Grandithers, who had unknowingly beckoned him home. Maybe there would be an Ithergram in the e-mail.

Nostrums and opportunities flooded his inbox, but no Ithergrams. Something else did catch his attention, though. There, between "$5 Million Cashier's Check Needs Your Attention" and "Make Her Happy", was a message entitled, "COMUNICADO Collateral". Heart pounding, he clicked.

"Read attachment, then delete!"

He opened the attachment.

"Each victim died from a .22 shot to the head."

Rex stared at the screen for over a minute, willing the message to change. It did not. He clicked the "Delete" icon. It didn't delete. He closed the mail. It didn't close. Start. Arrow. Shut Down. Click, whirr. "Shutting Down... " "Shutting Down..." ...

He pulled the plug.

At least he knew what to report to the police. Nothing.

《　》

Frame. The word had two dozen definitions. *"'I was Framed,' Claims Magistrate"* shared the front page with *"Solons Frame Bill to Save Rail Line."* The want ads were no better. Below "Chester Drawers" and just above "Purebread Beagle Mix Puppies", somebody wanted to sell "Picture Frames".

Rex threw the paper toward the wastebasket and leaned against the doorframe. Then, remembering what it was, he jerked away as if burned. It would be a long afternoon.

As long as he was going to hide from the world, maybe he should study Comunicado. He turned on the computer. Nothing happened. Oh, yes. He crawled below the desk and plugged in the cord. On. Click, whirr, blinkety-blink. That was better.

"Trojan Horse Detected! Click here for details…"

That was not better. Click. It was a nasty one, tracking keystrokes and resistant to elimination. He unplugged a blue wire from the back of the machine. Whoever was on the other end could wait as long as they wanted for that next keystroke.

The phone jangled. Rex jumped.

"Hello?"

"Dad?"

He relaxed. "Hi, Hither."

"Are you all right?"

Relaxation time was over already. "What do you mean?"

"You didn't call on Libby's birthday. Then I phoned yesterday and you didn't answer. And today you sound a little different."

"Her- Oh, no! I'm sorry! I forgot all about it. I was- uh, things have been kinda crazy around here."

"What do you mean?"

"My computer's been hacked."

"Oh, Dad, that's awful!" She switched to mother mode. "You didn't open some attachment, did you?"

"Nothing but grandkid pictures."

Then he remembered: "COMUNICADO Collateral".

"Dad?"

"Yeah?"

"Are you sure you're all right? You scared me when you quit talking."

"I'm fine, Baby," he lied. "Is Libby there? I can apologize."

"She's napping, and I doubt a three-year-old notices. I'm the one who noticed."

"Thanks for worrying. And calling. Someday I may need that checkup call."

"Don't say that!" protested the phone.

"Why not? It's true."

Hither changed the subject. "What are you going to do about the computer?"

"Well, I can't trust it, but it's full of things I don't want to lose. Maybe I'll just use it offline and get a little one for the Internet."

She hesitated. "Dad, do you mind if I ask a question?"

"Ask away."

"Can you afford it? I mean, you've been sorta retired for a while now."

He had wondered the same thing. "There's not much choice."

"What if we make it a Christmas present?"

"It's August!"

"So? One less thing to buy in December."

Rex laughed. "That makes sense!"

"Let me know what it costs."

"Can *you* afford it?"

"At the moment."

"Funny. It used to work the other way."

He hung up, wondering how much the Comunicado Gang knew already. They had investigated his wallet while he boarded at Berno's. There was no telling what information the computer had passed on before he pulled the plug. Would they use his credit cards? Could they track his purchases?

He *did* have one card they wouldn't know about. It was a freebie that came with a senior citizens' bank account, which he had meant to cut up. He would activate it instead.

The Data Mine was going out of business, done in by the other mine and the big box store on the edge of town. Rex drove to their shop, a block past the Headframe Café. His new credit card made its first purchase, not a "Mainframe Special", but a tiny computer loaded with the world's finest hacker protection. It said so.

He drove straight home afterward, not stopping for the "Framing Lumber" sale at the lumberyard. As soon as he locked himself into his house, he started the old computer.

"Internet Cable Disconnected!" That was too bad. A snitch could not expect to be trusted. Temptations would be removed from its presence.

E-mail worth saving went onto a red memory stick, pictures onto a green one, and important but boring files onto yellow. Then he washed the

Snitch's brain. Not everything; just what hackers shouldn't have. Try to cure the virus? Nope. There was deception to be done.

He reattached the blue wire. "Internet Connected!" boasted the Snitch.

Rex opened the map application and zoomed in on Comunicado. First, he printed a picture of the invisible town. Scrolling east across the Divide, he printed that side too.

The cursor chugged down the undead railroad to Comunicado Junction, and up to Useta's crossing, where it jumped the tracks and drove the road straight through Mailpie. Scrolling on and on to the north, Rex would occasionally zero in on nothing in particular. Finally he clicked a motel link in Albuquerque, made a reservation not for that night, but the next, with his old credit card, and shut down the Snitch.

He swapped the blue cable to the new machine. It fired up without even a Trojan pony. Rex installed the map program and resumed exploration, but a different direction: south from Mailpie to Texas.

It was a lonely track. Miles and miles of nothing but miles and miles, then Comunicado Junction, more miles and miles, under I-10, and miles and miles again to the next switch. Just outside El Paso, a branch led into a factory yard teeming with train cars. Another switch reconnected the south end of the yard to the Mailpie route, which continued down a weedy right-of-way between a truck route and an irrigation ditch. It ended at a monstrous rail yard on the east-west main line.

He blew up the factory image. Shadowed, brooding steel cranes tended ragged heaps resembling oversized nests. An advertising link beckoned visitors to a lounge across the street, "just drinking distance from Environmill." Rex had heard that name. He would see what the computer could tell him about it.

Environmill was a steel mill. It burned no coal and needed no mine. The furnace was electric. The ore was junk: steel scrap, dead automobiles, and condemned railroad cars. They were cut into chunks and dumped into the pot. Old, rusty debris turned into bright, shiny ingots ready to be pounded, cast, and rolled into new shapes so they could rust all over again.

The company kept a low profile. Privately held, it did not release financial reports. Owners' identities were not published.

Public opinion was mixed. Some folks were pleased that Americans were being paid to recycle our own junk instead of shipping it across the Pacific on a Japanese ship to a Chinese steel mill so we could buy a nice new Korean car.

Others were less tolerant. An environmental blog complained, "They think if they paint the entire plant sky blue, nobody will see it. What sort of idiots do those idiots think we are???"

A sky blue steel mill.

A sky blue dam.

A blue locomotive.

One thing was not sky blue. The sky outside Rex's window had turned purple going on black during the study session. He still had two things left to do before turning in. Cancel the motel reservation, and cancel the credit card he had used to make it.

Then to bed, and if lucky, to sleep.

《　》

The *Mailpie Courier Herald* had another good week. Deaths, especially violent ones, attracted even more readers than scandals and drugs.

Rancher Billy Flaherty and his wife Bambee were found dead in an abandoned automobile on Comunicado Road. They apparently had been abducted, transported to that location, and shot. Police suspected foul play. The registered owner of the vehicle, Wanda Flaherty, was being sought as a person of interest. No other details were available.

The railroad learned that there are many white semi-tractor-trailer rigs in this world, at least when rewards are involved.

Letters to the editor reflected a strong division of public opinion on the football suspension matter. Some said it was still summer, so there was plenty of time for the players to be rehabilitated before the opening game. No, wrote others, they should be expelled.

Three persons announced their candidacies for the magistrate's position.

Police were following several leads in the drug case. They could not comment further.

Charlie "Choo-Choo" Phillips, age 26, was still missing.

« »

Rex awoke at ten. Life had gotten simpler since he unplugged the clock. Usually, anyway. A glance at the morning paper nearly ruined his coffee. It was time to get a move on.

If anybody had seen him peering at and fondling every inch of Yootibibit inside his closed garage a few minutes later, they would know he had gone over the edge. He was not completely surprised to feel a lump under the bumper molding. The black plastic thingamajig he worried out might be a tracking device.

He backed into the street. A few more "For Sale" signs had popped up in the last couple of days. It might be too hot for dandelions, but the sign crop was doing well. Harvesters were few. Would a sign eventually sprout in his yard? He hoped not. He needed a respite from the craziness.

The truck stop café had a nice seat with a lovely view of the gas pumps. Late breakfast with toast and coffee sounded good. A tiny plastic tublet of strawberry jam went onto the bread. A tublet of peanut butter went into his pocket. Nursing the coffee, he admired the view.

A commercial van labeled "Duke City Tools" pulled in from the south. The driver headed straight for the men's room, in a hurry. Rex dropped a twenty on the table and left. It was an awfully big tip, especially for mediocre service, but there was no time to wait for change.

As soon as he was behind the tool truck, he looked around. Nobody was watching. He reached into his pocket.

Not long afterward, a black plastic parasite started for Albuquerque on the roof of a commercial van, stuck in place by a glob of peanut butter. It was anybody's guess how long the makeshift adhesive would hold in the August sun.

Yootibibit went only as far as the auto shop. The mechanic shook his head. "I can't work on 'er today. Too busy. If y'all'd called earlier, maybe. How 'bout tomorrow mornin'?"

It was just as he had hoped. "I won't be able to bring it in then. Can I leave it here now?"

"Sure, but it won't git done any quicker."

"That's okay. It's not too hot out yet. I'll just walk home."

The mechanic stared as if his customer had just sprouted two extra heads. Nobody in Mailpie walked any further than the nearest refrigerator. Some of the younger ones bicycled, but all ages rolled. "Aw, c'mon, one of my boys will drive you there!" He stuck two greasy fingers into his mouth and whistled.

A salesman drove Rex home. "We have a special on frame alignments this week," he suggested.

"No, thanks."

I was wrong, Rex decided as he unlocked his front door. *It's too hot already.* He felt out of place. Only strangers, usually unwelcome ones, tended to call at that entrance. Normal people used the side door by the driveway.

He turned the deadbolt. Going from room to room, he closed the curtains. Nobody needed to know anybody was home. The phone could ring its head off if it cared to. Locked away in his hermitage, Rex would read a book, but not a whodunit. Then whomp up some supper to end a pleasant wasted afternoon, and back to work.

The Snitch was the computer of choice that evening, but not for cybergossip. Instead of its favorite blue cable, it got a microphone cord.

Hither and her husband had given Dad a new recliner for his birthday, maybe because old folks needed their naps. Grunting, he jockeyed it from the living room into the study, across from the desk. Next to it went a TV tray topped with sandwiches, beverages, microphone, and loaded pistol.

Thither and Thitherette had given Pop a painfully bright halogen gooseneck floor lamp the previous Christmas. Whether they thought his eyes were going bad, or they intended to make them so, he could not tell. The Grandithers had given Grandpop a remote control contraption for the lamp, maybe thinking anybody so old would be too feeble to walk over and turn it on to blind himself. Quietly blessing the monsters, Rex plugged the contraption into the wall and plugged the lamp into the contraption. He set the lamp three feet inside the study door, and pointed the goose's face toward the hallway.

He settled into the recliner and kicked off his shoes. He hated to admit it, but the shiny new chair really was more comfortable than the ratty old one.

Paranoia was funny. Probably nothing would happen. Most likely, he'd just get a good night's sleep in his chair. He wouldn't roll over in bed and reach for the Janet he had lost. He fell asleep thinking of her.

A rattle woke him about midnight. Somebody was unlocking the front door.

Paranoia had its uses, after all. Heart beating wildly, Rex straightened his seat to an upright landing position, palmed the remote switch in his left hand, and took the pistol in his right. He released the safety just as the front door creaked open. The entry was out of sight from the study, but yellow light from a flashlight glowed dimly on the hall floor.

Quiet footsteps padded away toward the kitchen. The door to the garage shuffed open. Probably they were making sure he was gone. The door shut more loudly. Whoever the person was, they seemed more certain of themselves.

Show time was about to begin. Rex slid the microphone switch to "On". At least, he hoped it was on. He got it right about half the time.

The yellow light started up the hall, preceding footsteps that grew louder by the second. *Good!* he thought to himself. *Maybe they won't hear my heart beating. This'd be a great time for a coronary!* He mentally recited the drill: *Left hand first, then right!*

The stranger stepped into the study. Rex pressed the remote with his left hand. The halogen light flashed on, not two feet in front of unsuspecting eyeballs.

Built like a bull. Well, not quite.

"Tell me about Comunicado, Wanda."

《　》

The intruder whirled toward the voice.

"I'm armed," warned the speaker on the desk. "You can't see. I can. Drop everything you're holding."

A flashlight and a pistol clattered to the floor.

"Hands up, walk to the desk, and sit down. Don't turn around."

Hands in the air, Wanda obediently walked toward the voice. Rex rose from the recliner. Keeping his attention and pistol aimed at her back, he retrieved her weapon. The safety was off. It was good that she had not seen him, or he might have resembled Useta. And its cargo. He engaged the safety and slid her gun between the recliner arm and seat cushion. He settled back into the chair. After raising the footrest, he propped his pistol on his stomach, its butt on his gut and the barrel pointed her direction.

"Now turn around and tell me about Comunicado, or I'll make you eat taquitos."

She cautiously rotated the desk chair. Her face was as close to chalk white as a desert tan would allow. Wide hazel eyes would have been striking if her hair was a real color.

"You- you- you're more trouble than you're worth, Teerex!" she chattered.

"Not really," he retorted, "just in more trouble than I ought to be. Those were your ex and your best customer you killed with my gun, weren't they!"

"NO!" She glanced at the curtained window. Facing Rex again, she hoarsely whispered. "Yes, they were, but no, I didn't!"

"Right."

She shot him as sharp a look as she dared. "You think you're the only one being framed?" Her voice shook.

"It makes sense to me!"

Wanda took a deep breath and puffed it back out. "I guess it would. Maybe I'd better tell you about Comunicado."

"Maybe you should. Which one?"

"All of 'em."

He nodded. "Good! But first, how did you get here?"

"I was dropped off."

"How do you get back?"

"They pick me up at two."

"Here?"

"Where else? Nobody's home."

Rex sighed. "You're lucky the mine shut down."

"What do you mean?"

"I mean, if people still worked shifts around here, somebody'd be awake to see a woman let herself into my house at midnight and leave at two. It'd be all over town by lunchtime."

Wanda blushed. Apparently that was still possible. "But they might not know I'm a woman," she suggested.

He groaned. "That *really* helps! Never mind; we're wasting time. Tell me a story. A true one."

"Once upon a time…"

He raised his left hand. "Wait. If you're going to tell a bedtime story, we need to change the lighting. Turn on that desk lamp." As soon as she did so, he pressed the remote button, and the halogen light went out. "Now start over."

She sat stiffly. "Once upon a time …"

4

Once upon a time, there was a university band. It had two hundred members, if you counted twirlers and flag carriers. They marched; they played music; they twirled batons and waggled flags. Some fell in love, and a few even married each other. And behold, it was fun most of the time, if one didn't count practicing in hundred-degree weather in a field full of prickly weeds, or four-mile parades, or marching where circus elephants had recently trodden but cleanup crews had not, or twenty-eight degree football games that their team usually lost.

There were special times, like when the fire baton ignited the football field, and when the drum major's shako was mysteriously replaced by a Seuss hat at the last minute. There was the Saturday night when a horn player and flautist marched in tuxedo and white gown respectively and were wedded in the halftime show, followed by a five-yard delay of game penalty because the ceremony ran long. A shorter kiss might have been in order.

There were plenty of twirlers, but one particularly stood out, a paragon of pulchritude named Wanda Beebe-

« »

"Wait a minute!" Rex exclaimed. "You're Wanda Bee?"

She looked down at her acreage. "Got over it, didn't I? I was Wanda Bee until I married a Flaherty. Now I'm Useta Bee."

"I still remember that halftime show when you and Sidney Boyle did a Jitterbug in honeybee costumes!"

She gazed off, remembering. "I'd have to wear a bumblebee outfit now."

« »

Good things come to an end. A school band is evanescent by nature. The organization might continue for decades, but members are like midges. The band only lasts about four years for any particular student, during which a few hundred musicians are stirred into a bigger, less musical, and progressively older world. Instruments might never be picked up again except at moving time, or when they are about to be sold.

Wanda Beebe wedded tackle Billy Flaherty shortly after graduation. They had much in common. She looked good. He liked that. He had an athletic physique. It appealed to her. She had a taste for beer, and so did he. Both enjoyed poker. She owned a horse, and he managed his ailing father's ranch. Eventually he stood to inherit the spread.

Things did not continue in this idyllic manner. First, the horse died. Wanda and Billy observed over time that the beer was amplifying each other's profiles. She acquired something like a linebacker's build, and he looked more and more like a washed-up color commentator but without the flashy suit. He wore his hat outdoors to protect a premature bald spot from sunburn, and he wore it indoors to hide the bald spot. Wanda's garb also changed. Her neckline moved upward as her attributes moved down.

A medical miracle for Mister Flaherty, Senior, pushed Junior's potential inheritance far into the future. Sale of the ranch to pay for the miracle finished off all but five acres surrounding the house. A five-acre ranch could feed about half a cow. Billy and Wanda moved in after Big Bill and the Little Woman bought a retirement condo in Truth or Consequences.

Billy took a job with the railroad. Wanda began selling cosmetics. They had hoped children would eventually pull them closer together, but they never had the opportunity to find out.

They still liked poker, though. She liked it even better than he did, because she was better at it. When Billy lost, he drank. When he drank, he lost. Drinking made poker seem worthwhile to him. They had friends who shared his philosophy. Not least among them were Mel and Bambee, proprietors of the Coyote Lounge.

Comunicado's social establishment did not get much business, but overhead was low. Saloons have low light bills. A lack of air conditioning increased the demand for cold beer. The free sign bore the logo of a beverage sold on the premises. The barroom was in the front of the building, the house behind. It got lonely standing behind the bar in hopes a customer would come, so Mel installed a bell on the door. He and Bambee could watch television, or do whatever else, in the privacy of their domicile until the bell jingled. They were not often interrupted.

Mel and Bambee encouraged personal friends like the Flaherty's to socialize in the house end of the building rather than the bar. The chairs were better and not as sticky. There were business reasons, too. Mel did not want his friends to feel they had the run of the inventory. He had learned as a young man that guests' tastes are more expensive when refreshments are free. If confined to the house, they could clean out no more than the refrigerator. Hard stuff "for company" in the home liquor cabinet had a higher than advertised water content for the same reason.

Eight people came one Saturday for poker night. Four left early, either due to lack of luck or lack of skill. Mel was ahead, as usual. Nobody begrudged him that, since the bets and drinks generally came out about even. Billy was doing as badly as the escapees, but Wanda held a good share of the dollars the others had left behind. She also was in slightly better driving condition.

Billy laid his remaining dollars on the table. Wanda matched. Mel and Bambee folded. Billy displayed his hand face up. "Three aces!" he chuckled.

"Twos and threes," Wanda replied, reaching for his cash.

He clamped her hand beneath his own. "Hang on, Lady!" he slurred. "Three of a kind beats two pairs."

"Look again, Mister! Full house. Now unhand me."

Billy stared at the cards. "Huh! Oh, well, I guess the money's still in the family. This calls for a beer." He hoisted himself to his feet and lurched to the kitchen. "Good thing I'm the designated drunk tonight!"

"I'll make sure he don't drink the Worcestershire sauce by mistake!" Bambee flashed a bright red smile at Wanda and followed her other guest.

Mel watched them leave the room. After they were out of sight, he sighed. "I love that woman!" Then he turned to Wanda. "That stuff you sell works, you know. Bambee ain't much to look at first thing in the morning, but she shines up right nice."

There was laughter in the kitchen. Mel rounded up the cards. "Who's your lawyer?" he asked.

"Ernie the Attorney. You know, the guy on TV. Why?"

"Just wondered. Wanna play a hand for a buck?"

"Why not?"

"Okay, hang on a minute." Mel went into his office and returned shortly afterward with a manila envelope. He laid it on the table, shuffled, and dealt. "You're first."

Her cards weren't that good. She looked up. "A buck, huh?"

"I'll match. Call this a buck." He slid the envelope forward.

"Whaddya mean?"

"Never mind. Call it a buck."

"If you say so. I'll take two cards." She laid a couple down, and he dealt her two new ones.

Mel replaced one of his own cards.

"I'll stay," Wanda said.

"Same. Let's see what you got."

"A pair of sixes."

"Two fours. You win." He slid the envelope across the table.

She frowned. "Are you sure? Wanna try again?"

"Nope. It's yours." He glanced sideways at the kitchen door. "It's takin' him a long time to git that beer, don'tcha think?"

"Prob'ly gettin' a couple."

"I reckon they're both gittin' a lot more than beer."

Wanda colored and started to push herself up from the table. Mel shook his head and laid his hand firmly on hers. "Forget it, Wanda. Siddown an' open that envelope. There's plenty of time."

Unwillingly, she did. A stack of old stock certificates and other official looking papers slid out. *COMUNICADO LAND COMPANY.* She looked up at Mel.

He looked straight back. "You are now the sole stockholder. It's all of the stock, the deed to the tunnel and the land at both ends, et cetera. Bambee don't know about it, an' I don't want her to git it. Now Billy's got Bambee, and you've got the shaft." He chuckled sadly. "The tunnel, anyway. Don't let on you've got it."

Wanda stared. "But Mel, you can't do this by yourself! New Mexico's a community property state!"

He shook his head. "We ain't married. Never have been. She wouldn't, an' now I'm glad of it! First time I ever was glad of it, I reckon. Now put those away before our lovebirds come back."

"But what about you?"

"Never mind me. I know what I'm doing."

Her eyes dropped to the papers. There were a hundred or so identical printed documents, decorated with steam locomotives belching black smoke at the top and angels blowing on trumpets in the corners. Century-old dreams that had come to nothing. It seemed appropriate. She slid them into a pile, straightened them, and slipped them into the envelope. It disappeared into her purse just as footsteps echoed in the kitchen. Billy stumbled out.

"Whooee! That was a *good* – uh, beer!"

"We're leaving!" announced Wanda in a voice colder than the beer. She gathered her bag. "Thanks, Mel," she whispered.

"Tell Bambee thanks for me!" slurred Billy.

Mel looked down at the floor.

Wanda dragged her husband to Useta and pushed him into the passenger seat. It was a voiceless ride. She didn't know what to say, and he passed out. When they arrived at home, she left him in the car and went to bed alone. She left the house unlocked, except for the bedroom. The outside door slammed an hour later. Billy made it as far as the couch.

The phone woke them in the morning. The jangling bell was only a few feet from the sofa, where Billy lay groaning. "Good!" his wife grumbled in the bedroom. "He can answer it! I hope they talk loud!" She heard mumbling, screaming from the telephone, and swearing from the living room.

"Wanda! Mel killed himself! I gotta help Bambee!" Billy bolted to his truck and roared away.

In that shocking instant, Wanda realized two things. Mel was gone. So was Billy.

"No, Mel!" she howled.

Still sobbing, she packed everything she wanted to keep into Useta and drove away from the ranch for the last time. Her red eyes were dry by the time Mailpie manifested itself in the windshield. She arranged to rent a small house that had been empty for months, if one didn't count cockroaches. One couldn't count the cockroaches.

That was Sunday. Bambee told everyone who would listen how awful it had been. Mel had dropped the bills into the mailbox by the road, and then he headed into the bedroom. He called her to come in and see something. What she saw was Mel sitting on the edge of the bed with the business end of a shotgun in his mouth and his finger on the trigger.

The busy week continued. Wanda visited Ernie the Attorney on Monday morning. Billy was served divorce papers at the railroad yard on Tuesday. Bambee moved to the ranch that evening. Mel's closed-casket funeral was Wednesday. Billy sat with Bambee, and Wanda sat alone.

On Thursday morning, Billy called Ernie to say if Wanda was going to up and leave like that, he would not contest the divorce as long as she would settle for what she had taken with her.

She did not hesitate. "Tell him yes."

Ernie looked curiously at her. "Wanda, we can do better than that. You're entitled to half."

"So's he. I want done with him. If he'll settle for what he's got, so much the better!" She fished in her purse and pulled out a manila envelope. "Can I trust you?"

"I hope so! That's my job."

"Good! Tell me what you think of this."

He studied the papers. "Old stock certificates generally aren't worth much."

"How about if there were a hundred shares, and there's a hundred certificates? I think that means I own the whole shebang."

"If there's any shebang left. Where'd you get these?"

A tear started down her coarse face. "Mel. He gave them to me Saturday night. He told me about Bambee and-and Billy and gave me these. He musta planned it all!"

Ernie was silent. At length, he said quietly, "Wanda, you realize they'll accuse you of – pardon me if I'm blunt – killing Mel for these."

Her eyes flashed. "I doubt it. Bambee's been blabbing all over the county about what she saw."

"Well, there is that. But his wife still gets his property, no matter what type of person she is."

Wanda shook her head. "She never was his wife. Mel told me she wouldn't marry him."

The attorney frowned. "She might wish she had now. There's palimony, you know."

"Only if she knows her pal had something worth suing for, and I'm not telling."

"I suppose not. But Billy's entitled to half anyway, and I *know* you two are married. Otherwise you wouldn't be trying to get unmarried."

"You heard his offer. I got these after he alienated my affection or whatever it is. Mel gave 'em to me the day before he died, and I took 'em with me when I moved out. Billy says I can have what I took. If he wanted 'em, he shoulda said so! So there!" She took a breath. "What're they worth?"

Ernie shrugged. "I don't know. We'll have to see. I'll make a few copies, and then you can put these in your safety deposit box."

"I don't have one."

"Get one."

"If you say so. Oh, and Ernie, I think the Coyote liquor license says something like "DBA Comunicado Land Company". I'd wondered who they were."

"Hmm! Sounds like Comunicado Land's still in business. They might be you now. Of course, the state'll have to run a police check on you if you're going to own a bar."

"No problem. I'm clean. Can I sell the license after that?"

"If it's yours."

"Good! I can use the cash! You're about to clean me out."

He shook his head. "Now, Wanda-"

"Never mind. It's worth it."

Wanda spent the rest of the day moving her meager belongings around her Spartan house so it wouldn't look quite so Spartan. The roaches didn't offer to help.

Ernie called her to his office on Friday morning. "I have something for you."

"What is it?"

"A letter. Also some information."

"A letter? From who?"

"You'd better come see. How about eleven?"

She nervously drove to the office. Had Billy had second thoughts? Had he learned about the stocks some way? Was she going to be sued? Anyway, who would write her at Ernie's office?

Ernie was waiting in the reception room with an envelope in his hand. He led her into his office, shut the door, and handed over the envelope. It had been slit open. A sealed envelope was enclosed. Wanda read the outside:

Ernie the Attorney
Mailpie, NM

The return address was Coyote Lounge, Comunicado, NM.

"That's Mel's handwriting!"

The attorney nodded. "I expected that. The inner envelope is addressed to you. You don't have to open it here."

"No, I'll do it." Her hands shook. The inner envelope did not open nearly as neatly as the outer one had. She pulled out a pair of documents, stared at one of them, blinking back tears, and handed them to Ernie. "You read 'em. I can't."

He studied the larger sheet. "It's a bill of sale for the Comunicado Land Company, notarized last week, contingent upon Wanda Flaherty paying the purchase price of one dollar." He picked up the other paper. "And this is a receipt to Wanda Flaherty for one dollar, signed and dated last Saturday, in payment for the Comunicado Land Company. There's a key taped to the receipt."

"But I didn't really buy it!" protested Wanda. "I won it with two sixes!"

His eyebrows rose. "For a buck?"

"Well, yeah. But he had fours."

Ernie chuckled. "He probably cheated. If he'd won, I'll bet there would have been another round. It doesn't matter; it's yours. I've done some looking into your company, by the way."

"So did I get my money's worth?"

"You tell me. You own an abandoned railroad right-of-way, a tunnel a train won't fit through, a dam you can't fill up, most of a town that nobody much wants, a section of land you can't get to, a mountain in between that you can't run a road over, sixteen acre-feet of water per year if it ever decides to rain that much, and minerals if there are any. Plus a liquor license." He looked over his glasses. "And a football field."

She gasped. "A- a - How could I own a football field?"

"The land company let the school use the property for educational purposes. Football's educational around here. The field hasn't been used for decades, though."

"He knew," she said in a tiny unWanda-ish voice. "And he's been planning this for some time, hasn't he?"

"Looks like."

Her head snapped up. "But what if there's a will?"

Ernie smiled. "It doesn't matter. He can only bequeath what he owned when he died. He didn't own Comunicado Land Company by then."

"Couldn't somebody say he was crazy?"

"I doubt it would stick. He had to be pretty with it to figure all this out."

"What if he didn't keep the taxes up?"

The attorney laughed. "Wanda the Worrywart! They're paid. I checked."

"How?"

"Who knows? But they're paid."

"Well, they won't stay paid." She faced Ernie. "How do I sell a liquor license? There's nobody much out there but jackrabbits, and they drink less than Baptists. And – and the building's sort of a mess." *Especially the bedroom*, she thought to herself.

Ernie understood. "Well, there're people who make a living buying and selling liquor licenses."

"Can you find me one?"

He shook his head. "It's better if I don't. Potential conflict of interest. Tell you what: You get a name, and I'll check 'em out."

"What do you suppose the thing'll be worth?"

"Well, I did look up recent sale prices. The average is about a quarter million."

Wanda whistled.

"The *average*," he cautioned. "Some are lower, some higher. Minus sales commission. And capital gains tax. You bought it for a buck, so there'll be plenty of those."

"It still oughta leave enough for lawyer fees." Her eyes twinkled as he started to say something. "And a few groceries."

"Don't forget rent."

She laughed. "Who's a worrywart now? I own a whole town! I can move into whichever dump suits my fancy!"

《 》

In order to sell the liquor license, Wanda had to have the liquor license. That meant a trip to the Coyote Lounge. She dreaded the trip, but there was no choice. Morning would be best while it was a bit cooler.

Comunicado was even emptier than usual. School was out for the season. The families that could afford to go on vacation were gone. Goathead stickers straggled through the cracks in the sidewalk that led to the bar. Nobody had been inside since Bambee moved out.

Wanda tried the key in the deadbolt. It worked. Holding a handkerchief over her nose, she pulled the door open. A clothespin would have been more in order. Hot, dry air rolled out, bringing with it the smells of stale beer and worse. Nothing had been cleaned since the disaster.

The door to the house end of the building was closed, thankfully. A flickering neon beer sign and high, fly-specked windows provided the bar's only illumination. She didn't care to hunt for a light switch.

A beer cooler hummed. *Time to shut off the power! The stuff can explode for all I care!* She reconsidered. As long as it was her own place, she ought to at least pull a draught for herself. Mel would have understood. And so she did. She downed a swallow but would have the rest outside where the air was fresher. First, though, there was work to be done.

The back bar was mostly empty. Bambee and Billy had taken enough time to haul away the liquor. All that was left was the keg below the tap. They probably had run out of room in the truck. Wanda's first thought was fury. They had stolen her property! Then again, they had no way of knowing it had changed hands before they got their hands on it. It was not worth pursuing the issue. The longer they remained ignorant, the better. Had they known, they surely would have smashed every last bottle before they would let her have it.

Wanda bypassed the framed *"You must be at least 21"* placard, the likes of which had not worried her in more years than she cared to remember. *"Credit available only for persons 75 or over, when accompanied by both parents,"* would stay too. She considered sending the *"We reserve the right to refuse service to anyone"* poster to Billy but thought better of it. What she had come for was a less entertaining placard with smaller print. She stepped behind the desolate bar and removed the frame from its nail.

License in one hand and glass in the other, she left the building. She set the drink down long enough to lock the door, took another swallow, and started to read in the daylight. State of New Mexico. Liquor License. Coyote Lounge. Mel Catalan, Comunicado Land Company. Et Cetera.

Something felt odd, though. Turning the license frame over, she found an envelope taped onto the cardboard. It contained two keys and a note:

"Wanda, I'm sorry for the mess. If I'd shot Bambee instead of myself, I'd still be hurting and in jail besides.

The silver key is for the house across the street. You own it. The gold one is for the football field. You own that, too. The key fits the gate, the field house, and another door in the back. There is more for you there.

Mel

P.S.: Watch out for snakes.

P.P.S.: Take a hat."

Wanda folded the note and slipped it back into the envelope. Beverage in hand, she examined the house across the street. The galvanized roof didn't look to be rusted through. The windows were unbroken. And the key worked.

The place was cheaply furnished, but livable. There were two bedrooms, and two beds. Somebody had slept in one of them, so she would use the other. Each bedroom had an air conditioner in the window. Was there electricity to run them? Yes. Water? If it were any harder, it would be limestone, but it was still liquid enough to rinse out the beer glass. How about the other end of the water cycle? The toilet flushed. The place would do.

The Queen of Comunicado had found her castle. Now she would inspect more of her realm. She settled into Useta the Carriage and motored to the football field. The gate was locked. "DANGER. KEEP OUT!" ordered a sign. A dusty path and a gap in the fence showed that it might as well have said "COME ON IN!" to adventurous youngsters, but Wanda would not fit through the opening.

The key would fit in the padlock, though. She swung the gate open and drove in. Then she reclosed the gate but did not lock the hasp. She drove up the track to the end of the bleachers by the field house. It might be her football field, but she did not care to advertise the fact. Slipping her pistol into her pocket, she stepped out of the car.

The stone field house was far too ornate for a country school. The sun-faded steel door was out of keeping with the ornamentation, but it appeared to be solid. The lock, a good one, worked easily. Wanda stepped inside, listening for the buzz of snakes. It was quiet. A long, dried skin on the floor showed that snakes did favor the place, though. Maybe they were out shopping for kangaroo rats.

Were there lights? Yes, barely. There also was a plain steel door, just as advertised, at the far end of the hall. An electrical conduit from the nearest outlet box disappeared into the brick wall by the door. Wanda unlocked the door and tugged it open. It was tightly weather stripped. Even a snake would have trouble getting past it. Cool, stale air poured out of the dark space.

She felt for a light switch inside where the conduit ought to come through. Success! There were two switches. One turned off the field house lights, and the other illuminated a line of fluorescent tubes hanging from the ceiling of a stone tunnel about seven feet square.

The entry passage ended about thirty feet ahead at another steel door. Just before the door, the tail end of a golf cart projected from a side passage to the right. A charging cord ran from the cart to an outlet between the ceiling lights.

Wanda edged into the tunnel. She checked the door to make sure it would open easily if she decided to leave in a hurry. It worked fine, but just in case anything was wrong, she pulled out her pistol before starting forward.

The golf cart had been modified. Steel panels a couple of feet high had incongruously been welded on both sides of the driver's area, complicating ingress and egress. She was not surprised to find an envelope on the seat, or to feel a key sliding around inside the envelope. There also was a powerful flashlight.

"This would have been a silver mine if there had been any silver. They ran out of money eighty feet in, years before the railroad idea. Fifty years later, the water people connected the mine to the big tunnel and built the power house at the mine mouth. After that plan went bust, they turned the power house into a field house and bricked up the mine to keep kids out. I reopened it a few years ago.

Don't forget to unplug the charger before you drive off. Remember to plug back in when you're done."

Wanda was hooked. She unplugged, settled into the seat, and started forward. The short side passage opened into a black, much larger chamber. Upon closer inspection in the headlight, the walls were not really black, but coarse reddish granite overlaid with dust. The center of the arched roof was a good twenty feet overhead. The silt-covered floor was flat. Rusty iron rails on ancient ties disappeared to her right under a heavily tarred stone block wall. To the left, they stretched into the darkness.

She turned left, straddling the cart over one rail to ensure side clearance. Ten or fifteen miles an hour felt like a hundred as the walls flashed by. Irregular pink granite glimmered where struck by the headlight and faded elsewhere into blackness.

Three or four minutes into the tunnel, Wanda spotted a signpost to the left of the rails. SLOW DOWN. An envelope was taped to the sign. She lurched to a stop.

"When you get to the front wall, look right."

The tracks ended fifty feet ahead at a russet stone wall. Just left of center and roughly five feet above the floor, a hole about the size of the mine tunnel popped through the face. A sloping ramp connected the two levels.

That was interesting enough, but Mel had said to look right. Wanda swung the flashlight that direction. Rough steps, cut into the rock, led to a cavity high in the side wall. She stepped out of the cart and started to climb. Puffing a bit, she flashed the light into the four-foot opening. It led into a larger hole, from which white and yellow light reflected into her eyes.

There was some of the reddish granite of the railroad tunnel. Mostly, though, there was crystalline quartz.

And gold.

The chamber was not flecked with gold. It was mostly gold. A manila envelope lay in the entrance, weighted down by a three-inch nugget.

"Too bad for the silver miners that they went broke when they did! Too bad for the tunnel builders that they didn't have better aim! I bet they would have forgotten about the water project. Good for us, though. I found this while blasting for the ramp. The dust cleared, and there was gold all over the place!

Bambee doesn't know about any of this. I didn't want her to marry me for my money. I guess I got that wish.

You're on the Pacific side of the Divide. Keep driving to see your section and your dam. Watch out for snakes. Wear your hat."

How would a hat protect her from snakes? Wanda nonetheless made sure her headgear was in place. Why, she could not say. Maybe it was to honor the dead. Picking up the golden paperweight, she started back down to the cart. The rock was heavier than lead, but much prettier.

The water tunnel was dusty and claustrophobic, with walls and ceiling seeming to reach for the intruder. Tire tracks showed that the cart had been this way before. It finally emerged into a smellier repeat of the big tunnel on the eastern side. Daylight still was half a mile away. Iron rails were mostly hidden by silt, and the ties were buried completely. The western and eastern tracks had come within kissing distance of each other, if two hundred feet out of two miles counted as kissing distance, before the competitors' railroad doomed their romance.

Something ticked onto Wanda's hat. It sounded a bit like rain, or maybe a leaking roof, but nothing appeared to be wet. She shined the flashlight upward. Bats, thousands of them, hung from the ceiling. Nobody housebreaks a bat. Mel had been right about the hat.

She pressed the accelerator, and the cart hurried toward the light like a moth. It was a reasonable simile, because any moth with half a mothy brain would want out of a tunnel full of bug munchers. Wanda was eager to see what else she owned.

Bats got sparser as the light grew brighter. Finally the cart whirred through the western archway. The gaping tunnel mouth was only slightly higher than the base of the mountain. A valley several hundred yards wide separated Comunicado Ridge from its nearest western neighbor. It slowly grew narrower upstream toward the north.

Rusty tracks curved to the right and hugged the side of the mountain before venturing across the canyon on an iron truss bridge. Economical water dreamers had left the bridge and its approaches standing when they flooded the valley. The trestle didn't look bad for having spent three years underwater and decades drying out.

Five hundred feet south of the tunnel, a dam loomed upward. Made of earth and rock for most of its height, it was crowned with a cement wall that spanned the canyon. A spillway eighty or so feet above the valley floor had not spilled anything for nearly a century, if ever.

Heavy green brush at the base of the dam shaded a swale where water puddled before trickling through an open sluice gate into the discharge tunnel. That gate would not be closing any time soon. A long, threaded iron rod extended from the mud by the gate and lay askew across the valley floor. A wooden tower once had stood above the water, where an operator could turn a hand wheel to open and close the valve, but the tower had collapsed. The weight of the falling rod had torn the sluice gate from its guides. Remains of a catwalk from the dam's crest to the tower were scattered down the embankment.

"I could live here!" Wanda said to nobody in particular. "Of course, the driveway's a bit long, and there's no electricity, but the water couldn't be any worse than across the mountain." That reminded her: she had not had anything to drink since that beer, and she had not thought to bring anything.

Her stomach growled that drink was not all she had left behind. Mailpie was the nearest place with food, for humans, anyway. Bats had it made. Fly out, snaffle up some mosquitoes, and go back to bed. That was one more reason to leave. Having once visited Carlsbad Caverns at dusk, she wanted to be out of the tunnel before the bats took wing for their evening meal.

Wanda took a last look at her western realm and turned toward the cart. Suddenly a buzzing noise near her left ankle arrested her attention.

Western diamondback rattler, observed the thinking portion of her brain.

SNAKE! screamed the reflex part.

"BANG!" shouted her pistol. "BANG BANG!" And "BANG!" Fortunately, she had gotten it out of her pocket before it spoke.

The flopping snake was severely perforated. As long as Wanda stayed out of range of the head, she would be all right.

Wrong. Buzz! By the other ankle, this time.

"Click!" whispered her pistol. She threw it. Apparently a bit of the old Wanda Bee was still with her. The twirling butt of the handle caught the reptile in the head. The snake lost whatever senses a snake has, and she gingerly stepped around it. For a change, she looked first before retrieving her .38 caliber baton.

"Watch out for snakes." Mel had tried to warn her. Another one was slithering out of the tunnel.

Shaken, Wanda boarded the cart. Suddenly she understood the reason for the side panels: snake shields. Maybe living on this side of the mountain would not be so great after all. It was a long way to a hospital, or even to a phone. She motored into the dark but stopped long enough in the twilight zone to shine her flashlight across the floor. Beady eyes shone back, two by two. A warning buzz followed the beam of light. She had not met the only three snakes, not by a long shot. A moving vehicle was the place to be at the moment.

She stopped again a hundred feet in. No more snakes, no more buzz, just the chirp of bats talking in their sleep. Rattlers were lazy and preferred to stay within easy crawling distance of the entrance as long as weather permitted. They liked their food fresh. Dead bats dropping from the ceiling didn't count. Clumsy baby bats weren't very filling. The only sounds were sleepy squeaks and guano pitter-pattering onto her hat.

The bat colony ended shortly before the reduced bore of the water tunnel. That was okay with Wanda, who did not care to peel them off the roof with the crown of her hat.

She inched through her water tunnel, started past her gold mine, and noticed another envelope taped to the back of her "Slow Down" sign. It contained a note and a key:

"This fits the other door. Don't lose it!"

Finally the eastern tunnel stopper loomed before her. She maneuvered into the side passage and parked. After plugging the charger back in, she eyed the one door she had not opened. *I'm thirsty!* her throat complained. *Shut up!* commanded her curiosity. *I have to know what's in there!* Out came the key. Into the lock. *You'd better turn!* It did.

The door was heavy. The mining tunnel dead-ended about thirty feet beyond the inner door, but only the very top of the back wall was visible. The rest was full of loose gold, pried from the middle of the mountain. That was not all. In front of the pile was a box of $20 bills. Naturally there also was a note, with something paper-clipped to it. The something was a cashier's check with one more comma than Wanda had ever seen on a check.

"I closed out the Comunicado Land Company accounts the Friday before you bought the outfit. That was quicker than trying to get you signature rights. The cash will keep you going for a while until you open new accounts. It'll be easiest to open them at the same bank that issued the check. Less questions. They know me, or knew me by the time you read this.

Be careful! Folks get curious if you try to sell too much gold at once.

Wanda, you're a fine woman. Billy is an idiot to treat you so bad. If I wasn't such an idiot as to still love Bambee, I'd be after you myself.

Take care. Don't do anything stupid like me.

Mel"

She read the last part over and over until it disappeared behind a curtain of tears. Blinking, she stuffed a pack of twenties and the check into her pocket. She considered taking a bit of gold too, but decided she had better get some idea of what to do with it first. Gold, especially raw gold, would indeed make people curious. Billy and Bambee could be even more trouble than they had been already. She closed and locked the Bank of Mel.

It was time to return to the real world. Open the door. Kill the tunnel lights. Step out of the mountain. Shut the door. Check the lock. OK. Down the dim hallway toward the dirty exit windows. Push. Out. Click. Check. Locked. Onward to Useta.

The only thing in the way was a county SUV.

A big hat and a pair of sunglasses watched her through the windshield. Wanda stopped cold. Here she was, coming out of a vacant school building with a pocket full of twenties, a cashier's check that made the twenties seem like chump change, a recently fired pistol, and, three doors behind her, tons of loose gold. That should be fun to explain. Five curious children peered through the fence at the opposite end of the field, straining to hear.

Red and blue lights came to life on the truck's roof. So did a loudspeaker between them. "Hands up, Ma'am!"

Ma'am obeyed.

The driver's door opened, and a prematurely grizzled deputy stepped out. His hand hovered over an unsnapped holster. "Can y'all tell me whatcher doin' here?"

"I own it."

"Uh huh. Everybody needs their own locker room. What's yer name?"

"Wanda Flaherty."

She couldn't see his eyes for the sunglasses, but his mouth twitched. "Oh, really. Got ID?"

"Yessir." Her hands stayed up.

"Well, go ahead an' git it. Hope y'all don't mind if I point this thing atcha while ya do it."

"No, Sir." She found the proper pocket, taking care not to unearth a pistol or a wad of cash in the process, and handed her driver's license at arm's length to the deputy. Her hands went back into the air. Keeping half an eye on Wanda, the officer studied the license. His pistol returned to its holster.

"Reckon that's you. Y'all can putcher hands down," he said before returning the license. A sad smile cracked his face. "That's the name Mel said to watch out for. Told me a couple weeks ago, before he done that fool thing he done."

Wanda gaped. "You *know* about this?"

"Shoot, Ma'am, Mel an' I've been friends since we was babies. Sure, I know he owns this here football field! Owned it, I mean. His granddaddy left it to him. His dad died while he was still in diapers – Mel, that is, an' his mom wasn't worth much. Grandmom an' Granddad did most of the raisin'." The deputy shook his head. "Dunno what anybody does with a dead football field, but I reckon it's good fer braggin' rights. Not everybody has one. Now y'all can brag about it."

Mel apparently had been very good at sharing parts of a story. He had done it to her two Saturdays earlier and parceled more out to her, a note at a time, since then. It was a good bartender's skill. Tell people enough to point them the way you want them to go, and shut up about the rest. Selective truth could mislead better than lying.

The deputy's sunglasses remained fixed on Wanda. "Ma'am, can I ask you a question?"

"Ask away. You've got the gun." She instantly regretted it, but his mouth wrinkled up at the corners.

"It's pointed at my foot. Reckon I won't shoot at the moment. But this ain't business. Was your maiden name Beebe?"

"Yeah. Why?"

The grin widened into a full-blown smile. "Whaddya know! I was a freshman in the Aggie band when you were a senior!"

"You're kidding! Take off those shades!"

"Cain't see without 'em."

"Well, I can't see you with 'em on."

He removed the sunglasses. They were such a part of his being that the flesh behind them was white. She studied his face. "Cutoffs and sandals. Sideburns. Am I right so far?"

"That was half the band. Keep tryin'."

"Cymbal player. Always an extra twirl on the turns."

"You got it!"

"I'm worse with names." Then she remembered: police wear name tags. "Totten... Just a minute- Was it Douglas Totten?"

His mouth broadened. "Still is. But now I'm Deputy Doug. And Wanda Bee remembers me! Well, almost."

"After all these years! Did you major in deputying?"

"You mean police science? No, Ma'am."

"Wanda to you."

"Well, then, no, Wanda. History, but there ain't much call for history majors."

"History, huh? You don't talk like a history major."

"Neither do the folks I arrest."

"I expect not." Maybe it was time to practice Mel's skill at partial truths. She pointed past the end of the field house. "Here's a history question for you. What do you know about that?"

Deputy Doug restored his sunglasses to their usual place. "The tunnel? As much as I could find out about it. Railroad scheme went belly-up, water scheme went belly-up, and Comunicado pretty much went belly-up. Power house turned into a field house, an' Mel's granddad got stuck with it. What else?"

"Want to see some history?"

"Why not? Nothin' else is happenin'. Radio's quiet."

Wanda pulled the gold key from her pocket, taking care not to disturb anything else. "Good. How close are you to retirement?"

"Any time I want. I've got my time in. Why?"

She unlocked the door. "I may need a caretaker, or a security guard, or whatever you wanna call it."

He looked around. *"For this?* You gotta be kiddin'!"

"You'll see." *But you won't see everything*, she thought. Not yet, at least. She proceeded to the back of the hall, unlocked the next door, and pulled it open. She did not switch on the lights. The golf cart and Bank of Mel remained hidden in the darkness.

The deputy whistled. Reaching into his shirt pocket, he pulled out a pair of clear glasses and swapped specs. "When I was a kid, that was a brick wall with a bulletin board on it!"

She nodded. "Mm-hmm. With a little tunnel behind it, that connects to a big tunnel."

"Which connects to the other side of the mountain!"

"Yep."

"Can you git through it?"

"Yep."

Long-dormant history genes perked up. "So what's at the other end?"

"Bats. Snakes. A dam, empty. And a section of land."

"I'd give my left- uh, ear to see that someday!" he breathed.

Wanda smiled. "Maybe that can be arranged. I won't need your- uh, ear, but I might need some security. I haven't decided what to do with all of this yet, but there are some people that don't need to know about it."

"Like Bambee?"

"And my future ex."

Doug started. "Is *he* her new – Oh, man, I'm sorry, Wanda!"

"So am I. But it's done. They deserve each other." With that, she closed the door to the past. The two returned to the outside world, where children a hundred fifty yards away continued to watch through the fence. The five had increased to eight. Flashing lights have a way of making that happen. Wanda's focus switched from the urchins to the deputy. "Are you married?"

He eyed her suspiciously. "Twenty three years."

Do you like it?"

He put a little more distance between them. "Wouldn't have it any other way."

"Good! Kids?"

"And grandkids."

"Would your wife mind if you changed careers?"

"Depend on what it was. But she's never cared much for deputy work. Not just nuts with guns, but roads full o' drunks."

"Maybe we can ease her mind." As if in rebuttal, Wanda the Worrywart butted in. "This isn't all going into your report, is it?"

His mouth crinkled again. "Reckon it'll say something like, 'Confirmed the subject was authorized by the property owner. Investigated the premises and saw no evidence of illegal activity.'"

"You have a nice way with words."

"That's the history major. Write lotsa words nobody'll read. Take care now!" He climbed into the SUV and turned off the light bar. As Wanda walked past to Useta, he rolled down the window. "An' y'all oughta lock the gate next time, not just hook the chain. Otherwise you cain't keep kids and cops out!"

"I can't keep the kids out anyway!" she laughed.

"Then fix the fence." Dust boiled from behind the tires as he U-turned onto the track.

"Yessir, Deppity Doug!" Maybe if there was a decent playground, they'd stay outside the fence. She could afford it.

《 》

"So Doug became a cop," interrupted Rex. "If you're telling the truth."

Wanda bristled. "Do you think I could make up a story like that?"

"Probably not and keep a straight face. Not that you aren't smart enough, but you'd probably go for something more believable."

"Thanks!"

"Don't mention it. I never knew Doug that well, but I remember the twirls on the corners. Drove the director crazy. You probably knew most of the band folks better than I did. You were a people person."

"Yeah, and you were a person person, pretty much wrapped up with Janet."

Rex flinched. His almost-a-smile vanished, and his eyes bored into her. She stopped suddenly.

"How's your foot?" His voice was chilly.

"A little chewy. I'm sorry!"

He sighed. "Never mind. You're right. I was, and I am. It's not your fault. Would you like something to chew on besides your foot?" He motioned toward the sandwiches on the side table.

"You won't shoot me, will you?"

"Not yet. I want to hear the rest of the story first."

She edged toward the food. "Maybe I should talk real slow."

"I wouldn't recommend it. I might get antsy. Take a beer, while you're at it."

Her eyes brightened. "Just one, thanks. I've cut way back. Gettin' drunk got me Billy."

《 》

Queen Wanda kept a low profile. She decided to stay in the house next to the filling station where she could keep an eye on her realm. The few other people in Comunicado accepted her as one more recluse in a land of loners. Sure, she owned the football field and spent a lot of time in the field house, but what business was that of theirs? Maybe she was an artist. Everybody knew artists were crazy. So she lined up bottles on her back fence and shot them. Who didn't?

Then she did something really crazy.

A semi rolled into town and dropped off a load of boxes by the football field fence. A curious kid asked the driver who it was for.

"I dunno. Lemme check." He inspected the manifest. "Somebody named W. Flaherty. Could be Walter; could be William or even Wilbur. Who knows?"

The boy's eyes opened wide. "Wanda! The crazy lady by the gas station!"

"Might be. We'll see if she signs for the delivery."

So she did, with a gaggle of children watching. The truck rumbled out of town, leaving a cloud of dust, a cluster of dusty urchins, and a field full of crates. The same boy piped up again. "What happens now?"

Wanda studied his face, like an ox contemplating a jackrabbit. "What's your name?" she asked.

"José."

"Well, José, we're going to work a deal. You and your friends tell your parents we have a playground to build."

"YAY!" shouted the children.

"On one condition!" she shouted as they began to scatter.

"Oh." The mob stopped.

"No more sneaking through the fence into the football field. It isn't safe, and I don't want you hurt. It's too far to the doctor. Anybody caught on the other side of the fence will be banned from the playground!"

"Are you joking?"

"Nope. If you don't agree, I can call the trucker and have him haul all of this away again. Whaddya think?"

A chorus of little voices responded. "Don't do that!" "We promise!" And other such things.

She nodded, trying to look serious. "It's a deal then. One more thing: How are you all doing in school?"

There were uncomfortable glances all around. "Okay."

Wanda shook her head. " 'Okay' isn't okay. If you all can do better than 'okay' this year, maybe we can add some more equipment in the spring."

"YAY!"

The playground was completed within a week. The gap in the fence was repaired, and goathead runners began to grow undisturbed across the path that had cut through it. However, no good deed goes unpunished. A whispered write-in campaign elected Wanda to the school board while her back was turned.

Even people as important as school board members have to eat. In Comunicado, that meant jackrabbit or rattlesnake if one favored local meats. Nobody cared much for either. There was goat, if you owned one, but once the leftovers were done, you were out of goat. Tomatoes, chiles, squash, and melons were about all one could coax from a garden, and they all took water, especially the melons. It was easier to drive fifty miles to Mailpie. Maybe take in a movie, eat somebody else's cooking for a change, and wander the box store aisles. Don't forget to gas up the car, either. It's a long drive home, and the filling station's useless.

Wanda pulled into the grocery store parking lot. In the next space, a hungry van's hatch hung open like a baby bird's beak. Choo-Choo was feeding it bags of groceries, even as he maintained a running conversation with the customer. It was about trains, of course. The perpetually smiling bagger swung the hatch shut, called "See ya!" to the owner of the satiated van, and started back toward the store with the cart.

"He can give you an earful, can't he?" Wanda commented as she bumped Useta's door shut with her hip.

The man smiled. "Yeah, but it's fine. We're both train nuts. He knows his stuff, too. He's not at all weak in that department."

Something in the man's inflection rattled a synapse deep in Wanda's memory. She stopped. "Were you an Aggie?"

"That's a pretty safe guess around here."

"Band?"

"Tuba."

"Tommy the Tuba!"

He nodded but looked a bit lost. "That's me. And you're, um, but it's been quite a while…"

"Wanda Bee!"

He looked uncertain. "You're Wanda?"

"I've been remodeled."

"The twirler?"

"The same. Well, not quite the same." A different subject would be more comfortable for both of them. "So what did you do after school?"

Tommy relaxed. "More school. I started grad school at Ohio State so I could dot the I in the halftime routine, but the spot was already taken."

"Maybe you should have tried for Hawaii," she suggested. "Twice as many dots."

"Or Mississippi." He shook his head. "It didn't matter. Starvation loomed, so I took a job with the railroad. I had a business degree, and a railroad's a business."

"They had a business office in Mailpie?"

"El Paso. We're just up here for the weekend. Anyway, the job was a great gig for a train buff, and I didn't get tired of it. They got tired of me, though. They reorganized, and I was out."

She sympathized. "There's a lot of that going around."

"For old coots, anyway. I guess I'm retired. Plenty of time now to ride trains for fun, but not enough cash to do it."

"A train nut, huh? Ever hear of the Comunicado Tunnel?"

"Sure! I even drove out to take a look at it one time. It was a letdown, though, all bricked up. What are you grinning at?"

She was grinning indeed. "It is, and it isn't."

"What do you mean?"

"There's a way in."

Tommy gaped. "You're kidding! There is?"

"Yep. When you have a free day, I can show you."

"Well, I'm free most every day anymore, but-"

"Tomorrow?"

"What do you mean?" He looked dubious.

"I mean I live in Comunicado. If you show up at the first house past the gas station tomorrow morning, we'll take a look at that tunnel."

"Can I bring my wife?"

"Does she like trains too?"

"Why do you think I married her?"

Wanda frowned. "I hope you don't tell her that!"

He grinned. "She tells me the same thing. Us train nuts gotta stick together. It almost killed her when I lost my railroad job."

"Well, then, bring her by all means!" Then she reconsidered. "How does your wife feel about snakes?"

"She shoots 'em."

"Then we'll get along fine! See you in the morning?"

"Why not? I'll tell Tammy!"

"Oh! Bring hats!"

"Will do!" Tommy climbed into the cab. One hundred thirty degree air rolled out. The shifter handle was nearly too hot to touch. Behind the back seat, the ice cream was melting. It would pour like lava down the "I Brake for Trains" bumper sticker as soon as he opened the hatch at home. That's the trouble with parking lot conversations in the desert.

Wanda was halfway through her shopping before the Worrywart surfaced. What was she thinking, inviting a virtual stranger into her tunnel? Newly single and living in a town of just over zero people, was she that desperate for human interaction? What if Tommy should notice the gold? Maybe the railroad had cashiered him not for growing old, but embezzlement! Then there was his wife. As little as Wanda knew about Tommy, she knew nothing at all about Tammy except that she liked trains better than snakes. Tommy and Tammy, indeed! Did they have children: Little Timmy, tiny Tippy, and adolescent Teeny? A Tabby cat?

Those worries just about ruined her supper at the Burger Trough. They nearly cost her life on the way home afterward. Wanda was driving, but the Worrywart managed the thinking operation. It was nearly too late when Wanda noticed four headlights abreast coming at her. She slammed on the brakes. The pair of lights directly in front whipped around the left pair at the last second, and the left pair swerved onto the shoulder. In the rear view mirror, she could see the shouldered car slewing back onto the pavement. Everybody seemed to be okay, if one didn't count the effects of terror. It didn't soothe her line of thought.

Maybe she should get sick. Something really contagious would be good, so she could call and cancel. But call who, where, and at what number? She didn't remember Tommy's last name, and she didn't have a phone number for him, either.

《　》

"Tarantino," inserted Rex. "Tommy Tuba Tarantino."

"Yep."

"Somebody dropped half a cantaloupe into his Sousaphone before Thanksgiving my junior year."

She gazed into the past. "I remember. He blew on it the next Monday, and fruit flies came out like smoke."

"It didn't smell like smoke. But we digress. Continue with your tale."

《　》

Wanda did not sleep well that night. Every time she drowsed off, the Worrywart would nudge into her dreams with another scenario more disastrous than the last. They became more elaborate as the night wore on, so Wanda was almost grateful when the sun gouged her in the eye at eight in the morning. It only helped a little. The Worrywart ran a round-the-clock operation.

Wanda dragged herself out of bed and started coffee. Pausing, she doubled the usual helping of grounds. It would brew while she took a quick shower. Maybe she should skip the shower. If she smelled bad enough, Tommy and Tammy might just toddle away. Ta-ta! Toodle-oo!

Her brain was not being much help. It needed coffee. Maybe a *cold* shower would wake her up.

It did, but wakefulness is not necessarily pleasant. She more or less dried off, pulled on some almost clean clothes, and homed in on the coffeepot. She poured a mug of black, syrupy brew and threw in two spoonfuls of sugar for energy. The breakfast of champions. Or was it chumps?

Maybe they wouldn't come. Maybe Tammy had an appointment. Maybe..."

A vehicle was coming. She could hear it. Tires scrunched to a stop in front of the house. It was eight fifty seven. Surely nobody would leave Mailpie at eight in the morning to see a tunnel!

Car doors slammed, and footsteps sounded on the hard ground outside. Somebody banged on the door at eight fifty eight in the morning.

Wanda surrendered. She dragged herself, coffee cup and all, to the door. Working up courage, she twisted the knob and pulled the door open.

There was Tommy, smiling and sporting a floppy hat. Standing next to him was a woman shaped very much like Wanda, also with a floppy hat. She obviously had not been smiling but brightened when she met her hostess.

"Wanda, this is Tammy. Tammy, Wanda." Tommy nodded his head toward the appropriate person at the appropriate time but did not point. His hands held a box and an insulated jug. "I hope you don't mind if we brought juice and breakfast."

"I never pass up free food. Come in."

Tammy nudged her hostess as they passed in the doorway. "Wanda, I hope you don't take this wrong. I'm so glad to see you! You see, I was a cheerleader but kinda grew out of it. Then when Tommy told me we were going to meet a twirler from the band, I wasn't too excited. Now I feel right at home!"

"Good! Us upholstered types gotta stick together. Let's put some food on these girlish frames! You too, Tommy. Coffee?"

"I could use some," he agreed.

It was not a bad conversation for nine in the morning. The Worrywart withdrew into its lair, awaiting a better opportunity.

Eventually the last bagel went down the last gullet, and the coffeepot went dry. Tommy, full of caffeine, slid his chair back. "That was great! Now where's this tunnel?"

The Worrywart perked up, but not in time. Wanda was so highly caffeinated that exhilaration overcame caution. "Okay, let's fill up a few canteens and go! Let me grab my pistol." Not just for snakes, suggested the Worrywart.

"I have mine," responded Tammy.

"Me too," added her husband.

The Worrywart was not comforted.

They piled into the van shortly afterward. It was more spacious than Useta.

"Where to?" asked Tommy.

"The end of the road."

They admired the unfinished train station as they passed by. "We need one of those!" Tammy suggested.

"For our model train set, she means," explained Tommy to a confused-looking Wanda.

"Let me guess. Two trains."

Tammy nodded. "His and hers. Mine's pink."

They reached the turnaround. "Where now?"

Wanda pointed. "To that gate."

"The football field?"

"Uh-huh. I have a key."

He stopped the van. "Are you sure about this?"

"Yeah," added Tammy. "We can't take weapons on school grounds, can we?"

"It's okay," Wanda reassured. "It isn't really school grounds."

"What do you mean?"

The first moment of truth had arrived. "I sort of own it."

"Sort of?"

"Okay, I *do* own it! It's mine."

"A football field?"

The second moment of truth was upon them. "And a tunnel."

"*Yours?!*"

"Yup."

Tommy was uncertain. "If you say so. But I'm still half expecting the sheriff to show up."

Wanda reassured him. "It's too far out for the sheriff to worry about. We'd only get Deputy Doug, and he knows about it. Oh, yeah- I'm on the school board, so consider this an official visit if it makes you feel better. Now let me unlock that gate."

She climbed out and fiddled with the padlock. The other two glanced nervously into rear view mirrors, but no police appeared. The van edged in as soon as Wanda pushed the gate open. She swung it shut and started down the track, and they drove behind. She unlocked the field house door and stepped inside.

A gunshot roared.

Tommy and Tammy jumped out opposite sides of the van. Wanda staggered from the building with her hand to the side of her head.

"Are you all right?" Tammy shouted.

"Yeah, but my ears are ringing to beat the band. There're snake parts all over the floor. You still want to see that tunnel?"

"Why not?" chattered Tommy's teeth. "The snake is dead."

"That one is."

"We'd better remember our pistols then."

"And the water," reminded Wanda.

As soon as they were supplied, Wanda led them into the building. "You know," she confessed, "I wasn't too sure about showing you this."

"You don't have to," Tammy suggested.

"No, I think it's all right. Anybody who runs *toward* a gunshot is either real stupid or a good friend to have in your corner. I don't think you're stupid." She unlocked the inner door. Cool air rolled out as she flipped on the lights. Her guests stared.

"Come on in! You came to see the tunnel, didn't you?"

Wide-eyed, her visitors followed her to the cart. Wanda unplugged the charger. "This thing only has a couple of seats."

"I'll ride on the back," offered Tommy.

"Do you think it'll haul all of us?" Tammy asked.

Wanda suspected it had carried more than their weight in gold numerous times. "I expect it will," was all she said.

The first view inside the railroad tunnel dazzled the train buffs even more than it had Wanda. They stared, fascinated, while she drove into the mountain. Finally they reached the water passage. The cart was not as eager to ferry all three of them up the grade as it had been to take them that far. Tommy slid off the back. "I can walk this part. No sense using up the battery."

"Ditto." Tammy climbed off. They looked around.

The gold mine! nudged the unfettered Worrywart. Wanda took control. "Why don't you two walk ahead in the headlight? I don't want you stumbling in the dark."

"Oh. Sure."

Wanda and the cart took the rear guard. Tammy and Tommy squeezed back on after reaching level ground. Nobody talked while they inched through the narrow passage. Shortly they entered the large western bore.

"Look, Tommy, more tracks!" squealed his wife.

He nodded. "I've seen maps. The old line ran north before it went back west. It's all Federal land now, military stuff and national wilderness. No railroads allowed."

"Not *all* Federal," corrected Wanda. "The first section is mine. Oh, keep your hats on and your feet up. It's bats and snakes from here on out."

A tunnel entrance fascinates most people, but especially railroad buffs. Wanda stopped as soon as they cleared the archway, the better to bask in her guests'' excitement. They barely noticed the rattlesnakes just beyond striking range, but the snakes noticed. Oohs, ahs, and buzzes abounded.

Tommy longingly eyed the trestle. "It's like a model train setup, full scale! My brother would give his eyeteeth to see this!"

"Is he a train nut too?"

"Is he! He's a dispatcher in El Paso, the guy who directs trains in the switchyard and up the Mailpie line! If that tunnel had ever been finished, he'd be directing trains right where we're sitting!"

"I thought computers would do that," commented Wanda.

"Nah. The Mailpie line is all manual. There's not enough traffic or switches to justify automating it."

An idea glimmered in Wanda's brain. "You mean he could send a train right into the tunnel?"

"Out the other side too, if it was finished."

"On these old tracks?"

"Maybe. You'd have to go slow."

She turned to look into the tunnel. "Do you guys know anybody who's good with explosives?"

Tommy gaped. "You're not thinking about-?!"

Her focus was far away, in the dark behind the bats. "Mmmaybee. What would it take to make a full-scale train set?"

"Money. Toy trains are bad enough."

"I suppose. But you haven't answered my first question."

The T's looked at each other. "Rumbles!" they answered in two-part harmony.

Wanda straightened around. "Not the tympani player! The one who was always protesting something?"

"The same," nodded Tommy.

"Do you ever talk to him?"

"Sure. He's not a bad type if you can keep him off politics."

"What's he do for a living?"

"Construction. Demolition. If it makes noise, he's in."

"Do you think he'd be up to a career change?"

Tammy nodded. "It was changed for him. He sold his business but stayed on, and the first thing the new owner did was lay him off. He was getting a little too creaky to climb up and down scaffolds as fast as the kids he worked with."

"Not much climbing in a tunnel," Wanda mused. "Do you suppose he lays track, too?"

"He's good at it. He did a lot of yard work at Environmill."

"You mean the steel mill that's about to go belly-up?"

Tammy colored. "That's the one. Wanna buy a steel mill, cheap? I could use a new boss."

"You work there?"

"Only the senior administrative assistant!" boasted Tommy.

The senior executive assistant shushed him. "They used to call 'em executive secretaries before we were enlightened. Same work, different day. I still looked like a cheerleader when I hired in."

A second idea glimmered. "What do you know about the business?" Wanda asked.

"More than the CEO. I don't play golf. I don't get eight weeks' vacation or have houses in Vail and Bermuda. I pack my lunch and get out in the plant. Anything he's supposed to see comes across my desk first. If I don't think he needs to know about something, he won't. When people come in and he's out, I tell 'em what he said to do, even if he didn't."

"And he lets you?"

"Of course! I make his life easy. That's why I'm still there."

The glimmering idea fairly glowed. "Not bad. Do you do anything besides steel?"

"You name it, we can melt it. We mostly do steel, but aluminum too. Even computer guts for the gold plating."

Wanda was nearly blinded by glimmering little ideas. She had serious thinking to do. "What do you say we run down to the trestle and head back?"

Tommy doubtfully eyed the cart. "Do you think it's got enough juice?"

"Maybe we should walk. It didn't like that grade much in the tunnel. But let's get a little further from these snakes first." One had made itself comfortable in the shade of the cart. Wanda tromped the accelerator, and the snake buzzed good-bye.

It promised to be a hot day. The black bridge was already soaking up sunlight and would remain hot after sundown. Tammy inspected the structure with an ironmonger's professional eye. "The metal's not bad," she decided. "Rivets look okay, but you never can tell without a real inspection."

"The deck could stand to be replaced," observed Tommy.

Wanda broke in. "It's getting on toward lunchtime. We might as well go home."

《　》

Saturdays are made for sleeping in, and Comunicado was a nice, quiet place to do it. Usually. The exception is when somebody across the street blasts an air horn.

Slumber had been easy for Wanda after she moved her bed against the shaded south bedroom wall. Billy's snoring no longer kept her awake. Hopefully it bothered Bambee. If life were fair, Bambee also would snore.

Nine in the morning was way too early for any civilized human to be awake. Unfortunately, some people are early birds. One of them, sporting a pinstriped cloth cap, was driving a blue locomotive slowly up an ancient rail line. The engine rocked from side to side. Its nose was festooned with mesquite and tumbleweeds that had grown up between the tracks.

A second person, wearing a similar lid, rode in the other seat. "So far, so good," she observed.

"Uh-huh. Kinda lumpy, but not too bad otherwise."

"Good. Looks like we're coming up on civilization."

"If Comunicado counts," he deadpanned.

"Be nice, Tommy."

The rumbling engine squealed to a stop just past the Coyote Lounge. A wide-eyed boy on a bicycle watched from the road. Barely civilized creatures like children don't know that nine o'clock is early.

"Now?" Tammy asked.

"Go for it."

She pulled the handle. A long, treble blast issued over their heads and rebounded from the mountain. The boy's jaw dropped. He let go of the bicycle and clapped his hands over his ears. Torn between awe, a burning desire to broadcast the event to anybody who hadn't heard, and fear that the apparition would disappear if he turned his back on it, he stood transfixed. Other people began to appear even without his announcement. Children were first, followed by incredulous parents in sundry stages of dress.

Wanda's door opened and closed. She reappeared in a housecoat and flip-flops. A hand waved at her from the locomotive cab, and she tentatively waved back while scuffing across the road, leaving dual dust clouds behind her feet.

The T's climbed down from the engine. Tommy zeroed in on the wide-eyed bicyclist. "Pardon me boy, is this Comunicado station?" he crooned to *Chattanooga Choo-Choo*. The transfixed child, who had never been to Chattanooga and didn't know the tune, nodded speechlessly.

"It worked!" Tammy yelled over the thrumming engine and spitting air valves.

"Do you *own* that thing?" Wanda shouted back.

"Environmill does, but they're closed weekends. We take Old Blue for a spin once in a while when nobody's looking. Usually just in the mill yard, but Tommy's brother said nothing was scheduled on the Mailpie line today, so we figured why not?"

"Yeah, what could go wrong except maybe derailing or getting busted for train rustling?" Tommy added as he arrived with the bedazzled bicyclist in tow.

Tammy glanced nervously as curious natives surrounded them. "You don't suppose these folks'd turn us in, do you?"

"Heck, no!" called a craggy ranch hand. "Life was pretty dull here before the Crazy Lady moved in! Beggin' your pardon, ma'am, no harm intended," he addressed said Crazy Lady.

She grinned back. "No harm taken. If more crazy things happen, can it just stay between us crazy Comunicado folks?"

"Long as nobody gits hurt."

"Well, then, there might be a few more crazy things if everybody can keep quiet about it. But if word gets out, it's back to boredom."

"It's a deal!"

She turned to the railroad crew. "C'mon over! We've got talking to do!"

With regret, Tammy shook her head. "Later. We've got to get Old Blue back home before anybody notices. But we haven't reached the end of the line yet. Ready, Tommy?"

"Sure! Wanna come, Wanda? Just to the tunnel, and we'll drop you off here afterward."

"Is there room in the cab?"

"Do you mind standing?"

"Why not?" She puffed up the steps behind them. After a short toot from the whistle, Old Blue inched past the station, behind the bleachers, and by the field house. Comunicado's human population walked alongside, chattering in two languages.

Barely moving, the front coupler tapped the stopped-up tunnel. The engine's beard of mesquite and tumbleweeds crunched into a prickly mass.

"End of the line," announced Tammy.

"Not for long." Wanda had made up her mind. "Next time you see Rumbles, tell him I have a job for him."

"Will do," Tommy chuckled. With another toot, the locomotive commenced its reverse trip, stopping only long enough to discharge a passenger and deliver another long, echoing blast. The spiky beard dropped off the coupler, and Old Blue returned clean-shaven to El Paso.

《　》

The T's didn't waste any time.

On Sunday morning, the telephone jangled Wanda awake. She blearily flapped a hand onto it and hauled it to her face. "H'lo?"

"Hi, Wanda?" a male voice responded.

"Uh-huh," she mumbled.

"This is Gilbert, down the street. Did I wake you up?"

"No, I had to answer the phone anyway."

He hesitated. "I'm awful sorry. But I just thought you oughta know somebody's messin' around your tunnel."

Suddenly she was awake. "They are?"

"Yeah. A guy with a van, walkin' back and forth an' lookin' at the wall."

"Thanks! I'll get right over there!"

"Now, Wanda, you be careful!" Gilbert cautioned. "We wouldn't want nothin' to happen to you."

"I'll be fine! Don't worry. Bye!" She slammed down the phone and rounded up some clothes. "Why can't troublemakers make trouble at a decent hour?" she grumbled. This would not be a pistol job. She loaded her shotgun and started for the tracks.

It was as Gilbert had said. A rusty commercial van was parked by the tunnel entrance. A paunchy man with a bandana and silver ponytail was on his hands and knees, inspecting the base of the block wall.

"Freeze!" she shouted.

The man's head turned. Wire framed glasses perched across a bent nose above a white beard. Grey eyes blinked slowly, and the beard parted. "Wanda, you're a sore for sighted eyes!"

She lowered the shotgun. "Well, thanks! You're lookin' pretty ugly yourself, Rumbles!"

"I try. Are you still a good shot?"

"Even better."

He stood up. "Good! I'd hate for you to hit the van by mistake. It's full of dynamite."

She glanced toward it and moved the other way. "You must be pretty serious about this job."

"It's been pretty slow."

"Well, what do you think?" She jerked her head toward the blocked archway.

"It's stout, but doable. Tough enough to hold back a lake, but built for looks too. Good work."

He ambled toward Wanda.

"DON'T MOVE, MISTER!" yelled a voice from the roof of the field house.

"WE'VE GOT YOU SURROUNDED!" called the bleachers.

"WANT ME TO SHOOT HIS TIRES OUT?" shouted a clump of mesquite.

"NO!" screamed Wanda.

Rumbles' eyes twinkled as they surveyed the surroundings. "Is this your gang?" he asked *sotto voce*.

"My neighbors."

"Pretty good neighbors."

"As long as they don't shoot up your van." "IT'S OKAY!" she shouted. "HE'S A FRIEND!"

"IF YOU SAY SO!" replied the mesquite.

Wanda nodded to it and turned. "Now, Rumbles, what were you saying?"

"I think I've figured it out. We'll lose a few blocks, but the rest ought to come down pretty much whole. We'll reuse 'em somewhere. All we have to do is haul them out of the way."

"Right! Just pick 'em up and toss 'em over our shoulders!"

"Well, we'll need a little help. But I think it's about here."

A toot tooted. Wanda spun around. Old Blue edged past the station, pushing a rusty caboose and pulling a flatcar with a beat-up yellow tracked loader lashed to the deck. The train stopped with hissing brakes. The T's clambered out of the cab, and another solidly built couple exited the caboose.

"What's all this?" Wanda called.

"Junk!" Tammy yelled back. "It was all going to be melted down anyway."

"Why anybody'd scrap out a perfectly good loader is beyond me," mused Rumbles.

"And the caboose?" Wanda asked.

He shrugged. "Cabin, field office, whatever. But first, a cork. We'll slap a little plywood around it, and it'll keep people away from your gold until we get a door installed."

She blanched. "The-! How'd you know?"

Rumbles looked sharply at her. "Tammy told me, and don't you give her a hard time about it! She knows metals. She saw the ore day before yesterday, and I'd see it soon enough. You don't think I could blast the middle out of your tunnel and not know about it, do you?"

"But-"

"Gold's not my thing. Mining it, maybe. Worrying about it, no. That's your problem. We're having too much fun to get wrapped up worrying about gold. It'd just spoil our day."

Tommy edged into the conversation. "You *were* talking about a full-sized model train set last weekend, right?"

"Well, yeah, but-"

"It'd be better with a model town, wouldn't it?" interrupted Rumbles. "I can build you one!"

"*And* Environmill could, uh, launder your gold for you," added Tammy. "Those idiot bosses'll never know if we sell more gold than we get from computer scrap!"

Wanda blinked. "Is that legal?"

"Almost, I guess." She considered. "Tell you what: the company can take a commission if it makes you feel any better."

The Worrywart was outnumbered. It was too late to worry. "Okay," Wanda conceded. "At least you can cover the cost of scrap if we, uh, salvage it."

Tammy grinned. "You bet! A carload of old rails came through the south mill gate yesterday. They'll roll out the north gate next weekend!"

The couple from the caboose had wandered off toward the station. "Who're they?" Wanda asked.

Tommy answered. "My brother Teddy, the dispatcher. And his wife Tessie."

"Figures," Wanda muttered under her breath.

"He said if he was gonna play gatekeeper for us, he was entitled to take a look." He turned toward his brother and yelled. "Didn't I tell you? Whaddya think?"

"Deal me in!" Teddy yelled back.

"Me too!" shouted Tessie.

"What about us?" called the mesquite.

"You all too!" answered Wanda.

"I've got a goat that wants roasted!" bellowed the bleachers.

"I've got an ice cream maker!" offered the field house roof.

The Crazy Lady turned to the train nuts. "You have time to stay and eat?"

"Might as well. Old Blue sneaks better in the dark anyway. Moon's full. We won't need the headlight."

"You kids start cooking," ordered Rumbles. "I've got blasting to do."

Everybody in Comunicado but the goat was busy that afternoon. Lest anybody overestimate, "everybody" consisted of forty two people. Men and boys manhandled planks from the flatcar to construct a ramp. "Outa my way, guys!" ordered Tessie as she climbed up to the loader seat. After a discouragingly long whine from the starter, the engine coughed and grumbled into life with a belch of black smoke. The squealing machine clanked to the ground. Its first duty was to push yesterday's prickly mass of weeds off the track and into a clearing.

"Needs oil," observed Gilbert.

"And a set of rings," added a neighbor.

"Some people just don't take care of their junk."

"Yeah. Just because it's junk, you don't have to treat it like junk."

Children supervised everywhere except around the tunnel. "Stay way back and wait for the whistle," Rumbles ordered. "Then cover your ears." They watched curiously from a distance as he lugged all sorts of interesting paraphernalia from the van. He leaned a ladder against the stone wall, fired up a compressor, and started boring holes with an air drill.

Finally the last hole was drilled. Rumbles rammed electric blasting caps into sticks of dynamite and slid them into the holes. Wires dangled out like scraggly whiskers. Then he followed every stick with a plastic sausage of bagged high explosive. Dynamite wasn't high explosive, just what it took to detonate the good stuff.

He strapped the ladder onto the van's roof rack. After driving back to the locomotive, he kicked a spool of cable back toward the tunnel face, and it obliged by unwinding. He connected all the wires at that end and, returning to the van, attached the other end of the cable to a metal box.

He climbed into Old Blue's cab, located the whistle lever, and pulled three times. Excited children covered their ears. Equally excited adults turned to look.

It was two o'clock. Rumbles clambered to the ground. "FIRE IN THE HOLE!" he called and covered his ears. He pressed the heel of one boot onto a button extending from the top of the box. That was the charger. Pivoting his ankle, he pressed a second button with the sole of the same boot. That was the trigger.

There were four explosions, fractions of a second apart. A burst of dust accompanied the disappearance of the middle blocks in the bottom row. The second blast shattered blocks surrounding the newly created gap. The third shot expanded the hole further and split the middle of the wall upward. The last explosion shook the entire face. Stone blocks tumbled like, well, blocks.

The progression was easier to describe than watch. A boiling brown cloud enveloped the wall from bottom to top. The one-second series of blasts ended before the first chest-rattling roar reached the audience. Booms and rumbles bounded and rebounded between the granite cliff and brick schoolhouse like a mountain thunderstorm.

The cloud dissipated, revealing a black, arched void in the pink face of the mountain where an off-white stone wall had stood less than a minute earlier. A jumbled pile of stones spilled out. Forty one larynxes cheered. The forty second, a very small larynx, screamed. Around fifteen canine larynxes howled and barked.

Children started to run toward the opening, followed by slower adults. "NO! POISON!" bellowed Rumbles. They stopped. "The explosion makes poison gas!" he explained. "It'll be okay by the time the loader gets there."

The loader was in no great hurry, thanks to the blown rings, but it eventually arrived. Black smoke poured from the exhaust while Tessie expertly manipulated the machine to push, pull, lift, and dump rubble until she was able to back into the tunnel. From then on, it was easy work. Cut stones and shattered rock lined the track by the time that Tessie parked her toy to the side. A last puff of smoke accompanied the dying cough of the motor.

Tommy examined the rails. "Pretty dinged up, plenty rusty, but passable. He started for Old Blue. "Ladies first!"

Wanda and the two she-T's preceded him up the locomotive steps under the eyes of a small but envious crowd. "Everybody else into the caboose!" she yelled. The people didn't need to be told twice.

Old Blue whistled and began to rumble down the rough track. The rusty caboose, dwarfed by the high arch, rolled into shadow. The engine and flatcar followed. They stopped as soon as the flatcar was fully inside. A toot rebounded inside the tunnel, and the train crept back out.

"Next stop, Comunicado!" Teddy bawled. The passengers debarked at the weedy station platform. Rumbles ambled to the side of the engine and yelled upward. "Drop the caboose in the tunnel. I'll camp there tonight and keep an eye on things."

The goat roast was a success. So was the bonfire afterward, when they touched off Old Blue's pile of whiskers. Tumbleweeds roared into crackling flame but were gone within two minutes. The mesquite flickered and glowed considerably longer.

"I hear Easterners pay good money to cook over mesquite," commented Gilbert.

"We oughta be rich then," replied his neighbor around a toothpick. "Wonder what they'd pay for tumbleweeds."

The mesquite eventually burned down, without an Easterner in sight. Thirty seven yawning Comunicado denizens dispersed, and four T's commenced their midnight ride to El Paso. Rumbles drove his vehicle to the new old hole in the cliff. He dragged a pair of bags and an electric lantern into the caboose before making further preparations. The light blinked out shortly afterward, leaving only an arched black void in the moonlit mountainside.

It would not be long, he thought. He was correct. The lantern had not been off for fifteen minutes when rustles and whispers approached the tunnel. Rumbles tiptoed barefooted to the back platform, where he scratched a match down the rough steel wall and touched it to a fuse protruding from a stick of dynamite. "A thousand one, a thousand two," he muttered while pitching the sparking stick as far as he could into the mountain. "A thousand four …" The door swung shut between him and his creation. "A thousand eight, a thousand nine …" He scrambled up to the cupola bench and covered his ears. The back windows were shut, but one facing the tunnel mouth was open. "A thousand nineteen, a thousand tw-"

He had timed the fuse perfectly. The caboose was momentarily silhouetted against a brilliant flash. A deafening roar erupted from the hole. "Stay out of the tunnel, kids!" Rumbles called from the cupola.

The rest of the night was quiet.

《　》

« 5 »

Rex laid his pistol on the side table, but he did not release the hammer. Wanda noticed the omission, as he had known she would. She did not relax.

"So you're behind the whole thing?" he asked.

"I was."

"Not anymore?"

"Things change."

"Suppose you enlighten me."

She picked at the chair arm with her fingernail. "It started out fine. Rumbles finished blowing the tunnel open in two weeks. It turned out Tessie worked for him when there was work, so she ran the dozer."

"That's how she learned to operate heavy equipment?"

Wanda scowled. "No, that's why he hired her!"

"Silly me. Keep going."

"Yessir. Tommy and Tammy couldn't wait to start their railroad. They brought the first load of rails the next weekend, and we walked all over that valley making plans." She grinned. "A lot of snakes lost their lives."

"What about the bats?"

"They didn't care much for the blasting."

Wanda took a pull of beer. "Old Blue came every weekend. Sometimes we got a shipment of so-called 'scrap' that happened to be useful, and sometimes it was carloads of new stuff that happened to find its way to the Environmill yard."

"Bought?" asked Rex.

She shifted in her chair. "Usually."

"Uh huh."

"Honest! Mostly. The gold commission paid for it. The mill had to sell off a big electrical generator to meet their payroll about the time we got started. The honchos thought they'd sold it to the Mailpie mine, but the mine never heard about the deal."

"I wonder how that happened."

"Wonder away. Besides wiring, Rumbles plumbed for water and propane. Every so often a few tank cars come up the line."

His mouth twitched. "Propane, water, and sky blue paint?"

"Environmill blue," corrected Wanda.

"What about the original Comunicado folks?"

Her expression softened. "They figured a few things weren't quite on the up and up, but they were in. Nobody much knew about 'em, and even less people cared, so why should they care? Here they had their very own secret, and they weren't about to give it up! They were on the first train through the mountain."

"Other folks moved in, too. Old friends, by invitation. A lot of 'em had been sidelined but weren't ready for the junkyard. One guy wanted his own hardware store. A stock trader from some city or other wanted a subway station. A fishing nut fixed up the dam outlet to make a pond. The college is on the east bank."

Rex's eyebrows lifted. "The college?"

"Why not? Old professors need something to do. New Mexico State University at Comunicado. Nimsoo-C on the Nimsoo Sea. Two years, plus special classes."

"Does the university know?" he asked suspiciously.

"Almost. We have a friend in the business office. He'll put stuff in the budget for NMSU-C. If anybody asks whether he means Carlsbad or Clovis, he just looks at 'em like they're idiots, and they shut up and vote yes."

"That'd work."

"Yup." She drained the last drops from the bottle. "We moved Comunicado School across the mountain, too. The School Board forgot to tell the state, though, and the teachers don't mind. It made sense. Nobody lives on the other side anymore."

Rex frowned. "Now hold on! I saw a mess of kids around your house!"

"No, you didn't." His mouth flapped open, but she plowed ahead. "It's not really my house anymore. Well, I guess it is since I own it, but we call it the Gatehouse. Somebody's always there to give us a heads-up if strangers come around, and it's handy if a person needs to get away for a few days. It probably was a day care trip."

"Could be. But back to the schools. Doesn't the state notice they're empty?"

"Nope. They don't come any more often than they can help. Old Comunicado isn't the type of place anybody wants to visit, and that's on purpose. If we hear school inspectors are coming, we toss a load of kids and a teacher into the building. They're good actors. The kids play smart enough to keep the state from taking over, and dumb enough so we won't be worth studying. School's actually going great. We keep it interesting."

"How do the kids feel about being so isolated?"

"It's normal to them. There's no TV reception, so they find other things to do."

"Like six-man football?"

"It isn't always the same six. Same for the marching band and cheerleaders. Games are a reward for studying. If we send too many people, folks might start asking questions. Everybody rides the bus together and sits together, and they leave the other school as soon as the team is back in street clothes."

Rex cocked an eyebrow. "How did Berno get involved?"

She picked her words with care. "Berno heard about Comunicado from a band buddy. We needed a doctor, and he, uh, thought his specialty would fit in."

"Witness protection."

Wanda relaxed a bit. "So he told you. His patients' enemies are not nice people, and he can't afford to be found any more than his patients can. So he picks his customers up at some airport or FBI office, and lays it on real thick about them not needing to know where they are in case they slip up in conversation. They generally agree to take a nice long nap, and when they wake up he tells 'em they're incommunicado. Most of 'em figure they're in an Albuquerque suburb."

"They've got to be smarter than that!"

"Think again, bub. Most of 'em don't know New Mexico from the moon."

"That I can believe. But nobody's crashed your party?"

"Two," she answered sullenly.

"Who?"

"You and the Director."

Rex frowned in thought. "So who's this Director?"

"A guy named Randy, but he likes to be called the Director. Nobody ever paid any attention to Randy, but everybody *has* to pay attention to the Director."

"How come?"

"Blackmail. There was a message on my phone a couple years ago." She attempted a deep, raspy voice. "'Wanda, this is Randy. Remember me? The ugly drunk you steered clear of at the Coyote Lounge? You and everybody else. Well, I'm dried out now and starting to notice things. Like Comunicado, and trains. Call me.'"

Wanda coughed. "So I called. He hinted that the railroad might not like to hear about other trains on their tracks, and he said he wanted to see the place. We set a day. I told the T's first, and we decided to go together. Randy could like it or lump it."

"We met him at the playground. I was the only one of us who had known him, and I hadn't known him any better than I could help. He wasn't as bleary, and he'd skinnied up a bit, but he was Randy if you could stand to look hard enough. What had changed the most was his behavior. He'd always been a whiny drunk, but sober he was mean. Not snarly mean. A smiley face with fangs."

She grimaced. "You should have seen his ugly face when we came out of the tunnel! He looked like he wanted to eat the whole place. Then he said, 'I wonder how many permits and licenses this all took! Zero, I'll bet. You don't need permits when you have enough accomplices, right? Taxes are low, I suppose.'"

"We called a town meeting that night. Randy laid the same trip on everybody and said we could keep on what we were doing as long as he could play too. We could call him the Director. He might want a favor sometimes. Nothing had better happen to him. You know the bit."

"I do indeed," Rex agreed. "Berno said the Director kept my gun. Are you saying he did the shooting?

"Him or his goons."

"Why?"

She shrugged. "I dunno. Not for money. Billy got canned a couple weeks ago."

"What for?"

"Locomotives and alcohol don't mix," she replied. "Anyway, I know Billy was trying to track me down for some reason or other. Maybe the Bambee thing wasn't working out now that he was broke, and he thought I'd welcome him back with open arms. Hah! He showed up in Comunicado one day. The old one. Everybody played dumb, but the Director must've heard about it. He tends to."

Rex looked at his watch. "Well, Wanda, that was a nice story. It's one thirty. You need to get ready to go."

"There's still half an hour."

"Not for stories. You'll want some time to calm down. Otherwise they'll ask why you're so jumpy."

"I'm calm enough."

"You won't be when I tell you this was recorded."

"WHAT!" She started from her chair.

Rex retrieved his pistol from the side table. Wanda reluctantly sat back down, and he nodded. "See? You're all jumpy. I've made arrangements. If anything happens to me, like I die or get tied to a murder, this all goes public. Sound familiar? I'm your insurance. We're the only people who know about this– at the moment. Now, what're you going to say you found?"

"I hate you!" she hissed.

"Understandable. They'll believe that. But what're you going to say you found?"

She glared. "Nothing."

He tch-tched. "That won't do. They'll expect something. Tell 'em Yootibibit's gone, and-"

"Who?"

"The truck. You had Useta; I have Yootibibit."

"What sorta name is that?"

"Janet named him."

"Sorry."

"Never mind. Anyway, you found a couple Comunicado satellite pictures on the desk and a newspaper article about the murder in the trash. Maybe there's a French horn in the closet, so they'll know you were a proper snoop. Other'n that, nothing special. Got it?"

"If you say so."

"I do. And if I come up with any ideas about your problem – assuming it's real – maybe we can work something out. Just remember, I've already made arrangements about this recording."

That part was a lie. He intended to make the arrangements right after breakfast, but she couldn't know that. Her keepers would ask questions if she lost her pistol, and she could keep it only if she was afraid to shoot him.

He remembered something else. "Oh, and don't get any big ideas about hijacking your ride. They'll find you."

From the way her eyes jumped, it was clear that the thought had crossed her mind. "Why do you say that?"

"My truck picked up a tracking bug while I was boarding at Berno's. They could be contagious."

"So *that's* why they said you were gone! Where's the truck?"

"None of your business."

"You still don't trust me. Can't say I blame you."

"Likewise. But you'd better start looking for your ride." Rex retrieved Wanda's pistol, without losing sight of Wanda. "Just remember that if anything happens to me, or if anything makes me really, really nervous, you'll be famous." He handed her the gun, barrel first.

Keeping a wary eye on Rex's weapon, Wanda checked the safety on hers and pushed it into a pocket. She eyed the floor. "What about the flashlight?"

He slid it to her with his foot. Keeping her attention on Rex, she carefully retrieved it and flipped the switch without effect. It was dead.

"I'll leave the desk lamp on."

Wanda edged out of the room. Rex followed, making just enough noise so she would know he was there. He did not tell her if his weapon was trained upon her, and she did not ask. She peered out the door window. A minute later, a car without headlights sighed to the curb.

- 85 -

"They're here," she whispered.

"Watch your step," he murmured. "If you break your neck in the dark, I'm not here to help."

"You're a real gentleman, mister!"

"Only in the presence of ladies."

She deflated. "I guess I had that coming."

"Sorry. It was uncalled for. Take care for both of us."

She pulled the door open without replying. The screen door rattled, the door clicked shut, and the screen clacked closed. Her sneakers silently sneaked down the cement walk, so the next sound Rex heard was a car door opening and closing, followed by the low rumble of an accelerating engine.

The driver turned at the next corner, flipping on the headlights as they rounded the curve. "Find anything?"

Wanda stared straight ahead. "Not much. A couple satellite pictures of Comunicado. A wadded up paper about the murder. And-"

The driver interrupted. "Paper?"

"Newspaper."

"Oh. What else?"

"The truck was gone."

"Duh! Of course it was! Two hours and that's all you found?"

"Unless you count a French horn and family pictures. He's still hung up on his dead wife."

《　》

There is nothing like an armed intruder with an outlandish story to get one all worked up at two in the morning. Rex was not ready to sleep, but he would have things to do when the rest of the world awakened. He might as well prepare as long as he was up anyway.

The first item was to empty his pistol. The next was to stop the Snitch, which hopefully had recorded the entire session. Step Three involved popping a beer open. For Step Four, he popped open a box of CDs. All that was left was to burn the interview onto a CD, make sure it worked, and give the Snitch amnesia.

Two forty eight. The Snitch said it was done copying. Rex ejected the disc and slipped it into Junior. The baby computer clicked, whirred, and asked if it should play the disc.

"Of course, Stupid; why else would I feed it to you?"

The speakers came to life. Clatter. Sneak, sneak, sneak. Click! "Tell me about Comunicado, Wanda." He fast forwarded to the end and backed up a short distance. The segment was barely audible. "-break your neck in the dark, I'm not here to help." "You're a real gentleman, mister!"

That was enough. If both ends worked, the middle ought to be just fine. Rex ejected the disc and shut down Junior. Taking a marker, he christened the recording with his name and the date. Maybe he should slip it into a sleeve and tape the flap shut. Done. As soon as he was up and about, he would take the CD to Larry the Lawyer. Larry had been after him to make an up-to-date inventory of his worldly goods to go with his will. He would think Rex had listened for a change. Maybe Larry would stay off his back for a while.

It is very boring to watch a computer copy a long file to a disc. It is even more boring to brainwash a Snitch. In fact, it is almost restful at three in the morning when a beer is kicking in. Rex started for the study door and looked back at the recliner. It *was* awfully comfortable. He retrieved a fresh sheet and returned to his perch. The bed would have to do without him that night.

Morning dawned bright and fair, as always. A few puffy clouds hinted at rain, but they were the lying kind and would burn away by noon. Noon would be about the time of Rex's breakfast if he hurried.

The recliner might be comfortable, but Rex was not. Sleeping fully clothed with a comb and wallet in his hip pockets, plus a belt cinched around his middle, left something to be desired. The sheet had wound itself into a lumpy ball. A nickel on the cushion meant at least part of his change had escaped. His teeth needed combing. Beer is a poor substitute for toothpaste.

Maybe the bed was better after all for good, solid sleeping. Save the recliner for reading, midnight interrogations, and naps.

Dried-out sandwiches on the table no longer held the same appeal as at one in the morning. The pistol looked extraneous in the daylight. Had he actually heard such a ridiculous story in the middle of the night? Was it really that important?

Yes, said the gun. The CD agreed. Somewhere between Mailpie and Albuquerque, a peanut buttery chunk of black plastic made the vote unanimous.

A shower, shave and clean teeth were the first order of business. Clothes with a few less wrinkles also would be nice. Rex had slept on enough wrinkles.

He cogitated in the shower until the hot water ran out. That took less and less time as the years dragged on. His forty-gallon water heater probably held twenty gallons of petrified calcium. Eventually it would have to be replaced if he could afford it. Otherwise, showers would get colder and colder until he died.

A cup of coffee, a glass of milk, and a slice of toast later, he was ready to roll. He retrieved the disk and opened the door to the garage.

No Yootibibit.

The shock was momentary. Of course not, stupid! He needed more sleep, but that was too bad.

An Ither's leftover bicycle hung from the rafters, with a bit of air left in the tires. He lowered it and opened the garage. But what about the disc? It would get bent in his pocket. A flowered backpack hung from a nail. Problem solved.

It was hot already. There was nothing between him and broiling asphalt but sneaker soles and a few inches of air; nothing between him and the sun but ninety three million miles of cloudless sky. The street led uphill. Every pump of the pedals moved him that much closer to the sun.

Larry the Lawyer's office was on the way to the garage. Rex puffed to a halt and leaned the bicycle against the front of the building. He wobbled inside on rubbery legs. The sweat-soaked back of his shirt would dry later into crusty white salt. The receptionist looked up with her I-learned-this-in-secretarial-school smile, and her eyes grew wide. "Are you all right, Mister Albert?"

"I'm fine," he panted. He reached for the backpack flap, but it moved away when he turned.

"Let me help you!" she offered with an expression bordering on this-is-what-they-teach-in-nursing-school. "But first, would you like a glass of water?"

"That sounds good. Thanks!"

She pressed a button on her desk and hastened attractively toward the refrigerator. Larry emerged from the inner sanctum. His expression switched from a law-school welcome smile to a frown of benevolent concern. "Rex! How are you doing?"

"Fine," his client fibbed. "I brought you that inventory you've been begging for."

"Not begging, encouraging. But you didn't bring it just now so you could keel over on my carpet in good conscience, did you?" Larry turned. "Lisa, bring us some water, please!"

She hurried back, just as attractively as she had left. "Coming right up! Now Mister Albert, don't drink it too fast."

"Do I really look that bad?" Rex took a sip. It tasted excellent.

Larry did not answer directly. "This is *not* bicycle weather! If you're going to take that up, check with your doctor first and ride first thing in the morning or in the evening, at least to start."

"You make bicycling sound like medicine."

"It is. It can cure you or kill you."

"But at least you'll have my inventory."

"I'd rather not need it anytime soon. Now, you're not planning on riding back home right away, are you?"

Rex shook his head. No, first I need to get that disc out of my bag, but it keeps running away from me."

"I'll get it." The attorney drew out the contents. "Nice bag. Do you always wear flowers when you bicycle?"

"So far. I think it was Hither's."

"Whose?"

"Heather's. My daughter."

"That's right! I should have remembered." Larry switched his professional face back on. "But I can't let you bicycle in this heat."

"I'm just going to the garage. Yootibibit's being serviced."

"Who?" Larry stared unprofessionally.

"My truck."

"Oh, good! I thought you might be delirious. Lisa can drive you there. You can pick the bike up on your way back home."

"Okay. Thanks!"

Lisa drove a little red car. It was somehow in character. The engine started with a happy little rumble, and they scooted from the parking space. Lisa apparently believed that a speed limit was a lower limit.

They zipped past the police station. "You know, I used to have the biggest crush on you!" she chirped.

"Oh, really?" He unconsciously sucked in his gut. The seat belt retracted slightly in response.

"Oh, yes! Any girl would want a father like you!"

His gut unsucked, but not quickly enough. The seat belt locked when Lisa braked to a sudden stop in front of the garage. "And here we are! Don't forget to pick up your bike!" She smiled brightly while he fumbled for the button that would release him from the near-intravenous safety system. Finally the belt jumped away with a click, and the captive stomach wobbled free.

"See you!" She waved a pretty little hand with a pretty little ring on it, and the little red car sprang back toward Larry's office. *Somewhere*, thought Rex, *there is a very happy young man, or he ought to have his head examined!*

The mechanic was neither cute nor cheerful. "What's with the new tires?" he grumbled. "Aren't mine good enough for you?"

Rex felt like he had been caught two-timing. "I was out of town and ran into a problem," he answered defensively.

"All four?"

"Yeah."

"Did they tell you that?"

"Yeah."

"You were cheated."

"Probably," he conceded.

"No probably about it." The mechanic was mollified. He had stated his case. "One forty seven fifty eight for the service. Woulda been more, but I balanced the wheels in record time with an air wrench. All the lug nuts holding your fancy tires on were loose. You coulda lost a wheel."

《 》

"The Director plays for keeps!" Rex said for the ninth time in two hours. If anybody had been listening, they would have thought he had gone off the deep end, but he had divided his observations between the privacy of his garage, the solitude of his kitchen, and his singly populated study. Also the sanctity of his bathroom, once. At the moment of the ninth observation, he was in the garage for the third time. The Geezers' Bane Bicycle again hung upside-down from rafter hooks like a slaughtered animal. Would-Be Killer Yootibibit, tuned to a tee and lug nuts torqued to a fare-thee-well, awaited its next errand.

The insurance disc in Larry's office no longer seemed like sure-fire protection. It would protect Rex from Wanda, all right, but not from the real danger. The gun would disappear, probably in a pot of molten scrap iron to be resurrected as who-knew-what. The Director also would vanish, but he would not be neutralized.

Rex could not hope to lie low until everything got better. The Director was too interested in him. Unless Wanda spilled the beans, the Director would be hoping to hear about the loss of an unemployed mining engineer whose wheel had spun off his truck while he was driving north. If that didn't work, something else would. Ask Bambee and Billy.

Why had Rex been allowed to leave Comunicado in the first place? Maybe the Director played his prey like fish. Let them fight as long as they thought there was a chance of escape, and reel them in when ready. If Wanda told the truth, the Director was shielded by people ripe for blackmail. Just like Rex.

The difference was that the others were guilty.

Rex might live longer in the Comunicado valley than outside. It seemed a decent enough place with decent people and old friends. So why had he decided to leave? Ithers and Grandithers, that was why. Could he move back and leave them behind?

That raised an uglier question: Would the Director use Ithers and Grandithers to keep Rex in line? Yes, if necessary. They would not be safe as long as Grandpa was considered a hazard.

The Director would have to go.

That could not be accomplished from outside Comunicado, because Rex knew hardly anything about his enemy. No last name, no description, no nothing.

What would happen if he left Mailpie? The next round of utility bills would come due in about three weeks. The lawn would dry up or, if rain came for a change, go to weeds. The City would send a nasty letter. The kids would call and wonder why he didn't answer. They'd probably drive down or ask somebody to check just to make sure Pop hadn't died in the house. The Director would find out.

Two weeks would give Rex time to figure out the next step, if it wasn't figured out for him. First, he called one of the remaining neighbors to see if their son would be interested in caring for his lawn for a couple of weeks. Why, sure; the kid had his eye on a car he couldn't afford yet. Where was Rex headed? To see some old friends. Sounded like fun; when was he leaving? Tomorrow. So soon? Yep. Probably a lady friend, they theorized afterward. He hadn't been too free with the details.

Next he used Junior to e-mail both Ithers, telling them pretty much the same story he told the neighbors. Afterward, the Snitch got its blue cable back. Junior got its brain washed.

Should he take Junior with him? Probably not. It would be hacked if he used it. A gun? Not after what had happened with the last one.

Rex poured the milk down the sink and cleaned potential future furry things out of the refrigerator. Beer could stay. It wouldn't spoil, and he might feel like one if he ever got home again. The next day was garbage day, so he hauled the Herby to the curb. The neighbor kid could bring it back.

He opened the closet. Out came a suitcase and a French horn. Junior would go onto the top shelf, in the back. Something was in the way, though. He groped past the lip of the shelf and recognized by feel what it was: a flute case. He pulled it down and debated. It would not take too much room. Then, sadly, he set it back onto the shelf. "See you, Janet," he whispered.

Packing did not take long. He had become an expert on traveling light while still employed. It was getting late, and he had not had much sleep the night before. One of the remaining beers left the refrigerator. Twelve ounces later, Rex started for the lavatory but remembered he would not find his toothbrush there. He retrieved it and a few other accoutrements, and prepared for bed. The real bed, not the recliner.

The alarm did not go off the next morning, just as planned. Around eight, Rex rolled out of bed and straightened the covers (Why? he wondered. Never mind; just because). It was time to get dressed, in clean clothes. Yesterday's duds would be pretty ripe by the time he got back, if he got back. That was what plastic shopping bags were for. Into the outer pocket of the suitcase the laundry went. Comunicado should have a washing machine, or failing that, a dump.

He fixed a bowl of dry cereal because somebody had gotten rid of the milk. Rex had tried cereal with coffee one time when the milk had soured, but it just wasn't the same, so he crunched his kibbles and drank his caffeine in the usual manner. After pouring the rest of the coffee into an insulated container, dumping the grounds onto the beer bottle in the otherwise empty garbage can, and washing the dishes (Why? Don't ask), he took care of one last errand. Years of asking urchins, "Why didn't you do that before we left?" could not be undone. They had trained him well.

Finally, horn case in one hand and roller bag handle in the other, he started for the garage. He turned the doorknob and stopped. Setting down the baggage, he returned to the closet. The flute case went into the suitcase, between shirts and trousers.

He put the baggage into Yootibibit's passenger area. The garage door opened, the truck backed out, and the garage door closed. Rex had left home.

《　》

« 6 »

For such a momentous trip, it was short. The Comunicado Road rail crossing was marked only by a shot-up crossbuck. Useta was gone, but not regrettably so. Vultures had moved on to different smorgasbords.

It should have been a more relaxing trip this time, not being nudged along by a locomotive, but it wasn't. Rex was driving to the lion's den. He would awaken the beast with a horn that had not been blown for thirty years, and walk into its lair. It did not sound sensible.

He passed the Comunicado sign on that comforting note. An old man and woman rocked in his-and-hers lawn gliders in the front yard of Useta's house. Correction: the Gatehouse. They waved, and he waved back.

He halted at the football field gate. What was the combination: 1-8-8-8? The hasp sprang open. Good! Memory wasn't quite shot yet. He pushed the gate aside and drove in. Should he close it? Might as well. Then drive the last hundred yards and park in the scant morning shade.

The building door was locked, of course. Out came the horn. He wiggled the keys. A bit sticky. How was the mouthpiece? Not too bad, unless one counted thirty-year-old germs awaiting rejuvenation. Oh, well; they had been his germs. Maybe he still had antibodies.

He fitted the mouthpiece into the tube, slid his hand into the bell, and breathed into the horn. It wasn't stopped up. He tried a note. It was not the note he had hoped for, but it would do. The show was about to begin.

Rex played something slightly resembling *Aggies, O Aggies*. The notes were approximations, but the tempo was right.

"Not too bad," a voice creaked.

He whirled around. The old man and lady appraised his performance like a pair of contest judges. The gate stood open behind them.

"Not that good, either," added his wife, if that was who she was. "But I could tell what it was supposed to be. That's better than some."

"Aw, c'mon, Nelly, cut him a little slack. I bet he hasn't blown that thing in – how long, Sonny?"

"Thirty years," Rex conceded. He wondered when he had last been a Sonny.

"Thirty years. Just like I said, didn't I, Nelly?"

"Not quite, but you were getting there," she almost agreed.

"What happens next?" asked Rex.

"Kids!" The old man shook his head. "Always in a hurry! Keep your britches on. Your greeters'll be along. I gave 'em a heads-up when you drove by."

"No you didn't, you forgetful old goat. I did," his theoretical wife corrected him.

"Close enough. Maybe we both did."

Rex was puzzled. "You mean you knew I was coming?"

She shook her grey head. "Not really. But we always give a heads-up when somebody comes into town, and-"

"Unless somebody else is staying in the house," interrupted her husband, if he was such, "and then *they* do."

"*And*," continued she, "if they know the gate combination and try to play *Aggies*, we know they were invited. That reminds me." She dug in her handbag. "Would you care for a cookie?"

"Why, thank you!" Rex put out his hand. It had been an hour and a half since breakfast.

"Now hold on, Nellie!" the old man interposed himself. "Are you sure you got the right cookie this time?"

She sniffed it. "Yep. Here."

"Is there a wrong cookie?" Rex dubiously accepted the gift.

She nodded. "If you weren't invited, there would be. It'd conk you out long enough for the sheriff to pick you up for DWI. Pretty powerful."

"But they taste good," volunteered her probable husband.

"You'd know!" she snipped.

"Aw, now, Nellie, I've seen you dipping into the cookie jar yourself!"

The discussion was abbreviated by the field house door clicking open.

"Howdy, Mister Albert!"

"Charlie!"

The young man grinned. "They said you was comin'! I couldn't wait! Oh, howdy, Mister'n Miz Culpepper. I got your groceries." He set a sack onto the ground. "Need me to haul the bag to the house?"

Miz Culpepper smiled a grandmotherly smile. "Why, thank you, no, Choo-Choo. Edgar'll take it for me if he's a gentleman. You run along with your friend now."

Rex's eyes followed the bouncing conversation. "What do I do with the truck?"

"Don't you worry about that!" old man Edgar assured him. "I'll store it with the others."

"Then you'll need a key." Rex reached into his pocket.

"Nah, I'd lose a key. I'll just hotwire it."

"Now, Edgar," warned his for-sure wife, "Don't go and run this one into the arroyo like you did the last one!"

"You'll never let me live that down!" grumbled her husband.

"Got any bags, Mister Albert?" Charlie asked.

"Just one, plus the horn. I'm traveling light."

"That's all you need." The bagger retrieved the bag while Rex returned his horn to its case. Yootibibit's door slammed shut. "See ya, Mister'n Miz Culpepper!" The grinning host held the field house door open for his guest and pulled it closed behind them. A solid "click!" sealed them from the eastern world. Rex finally could enjoy his cookie in peace without having to track multiple conversations.

"Don't eat that, Mister Albert!" warned Charlie.

"But she sniffed it!"

"Then her smeller don't work. That cookie's yellow. The right ones are green."

"Then why didn't she just look?"

"She's color blind." Charlie opened the second door. The tiled tunnel stretched ahead of them. Another door blocked the far end. A very solid door, by the looks of it.

Turning right, they clicked through the turnstile and crossed the platform toward a recycled El car. Chicago's El and subway systems are one and the same. It is only a matter of context. The "CTA" on the car's side might be Chicago Transit Authority or Comunicado Transit Authority. It was all in the context.

There was one difference. Chicago motormen do not jump off the train to personally greet their passengers.

"Teerex! Long time no see!"

"Tommy! Is this your train?"

The rounded motorman patted it fondly. "One of 'em. It's Wanda's, actually, but that's close enough. Now Charlie's helping us out. He's picking it up real well!"

Choo-Choo Charlie beamed.

Rex eyed the roof of the car. "I never saw an El car with a pantograph on top."

"We modified 'em. A third rail's too dangerous where people walk across tracks. There was room for smokestacks, so there's plenty of room for overhead wires." Tommy checked his watch. "Oh, well, back to business. Charlie, why don't you keep Teerex company while I drive?"

"Sure will! Pick a seat, Mister Albert. I'll just set your stuff across from us. Can't keep it in the aisle. Rules." Rex seated himself by the window, and his companion settled into the aisle seat after stowing the baggage.

The car began to move. The compartment was lighted, but the train's headlight was not. Reflection from the windows rendered it impossible to see out. The world had diminished to a rocking, rumbling metal tube. Conversation was difficult.

"How'd you get here, Charlie?"

"Old Blue. First time I saw it," he reminisced as if recalling a favorite date, "I was home watchin' train videos. There was a lotta sirens across town, but the freight yard was quiet like usual since the mine shut down. Then I heard an engine outside an' went to look. I thought maybe they was firin' up the wreckin' train, but huh-uh! There was a blue locomotive runnin' with its lights out an' pushin' a crane, a couple flatcars, and a gondola. Some guys jumped out an' started cuttin' up the track, so I went outside to watch. Another guy but it turned out it was a lady got in the crane an' started pullin' up rails an' pilin' 'em on the flatcar. Another guy got on the dozer an' dug up the ties an' dumped 'em dirt an' all in the gondola. They got a water pipe, too."

"Then the engineer saw me. He watched me for a while an' I waved. Then he got outa the cab an' came over to see me. It was Tommy, but I didn't know him yet. We talked for a couple minutes an' then he asked if I wanted to ride back with 'em. 'Sure!' I said. So here I am! I flip switches, help work on the engine, an' haul groceries an' stuff to people who need it." Charlie was in his element.

That explained much, thought Rex, but not all. "Was there a semi, too?"

"Oh, yeah, but it didn't do nothin' but sit by the yard all day with its engine runnin'." Charlie had little interest in trucks. "The dozer guy drove it off."

Red herrings apparently also came in white. It was more of a chameleon, really; probably not even white any more. Nobody would think to look for a blue train if they were tracking down a white truck. A train could only go one direction from Mailpie. A truck might go anywhere. It was a brilliant scheme, especially when somebody tossed in a so-called drug deal with salvaged heroin to keep police and reporters occupied elsewhere.

The western portal of the tunnel grew progressively larger through the windows in the end of the car. The noise level dropped immediately when they emerged from the mountain.

The Transit Authority rolled through the toy town and across the trestle. It swung left, rumbled the length of the western street, and halted at Cognito Station. The car doors hissed open. Charlie retrieved Rex's luggage and started for the exit. "This is your stop, Mister Albert! I gotta go help Tommy park the train soon as you're off!" He set the cases on the platform. "See ya!"

The CTA rolled away, leaving Rex alone only long enough for the clinic door to click open. Berno waved him inside.

The door clicked behind them. There was a lot of clicking in Comunicado. "You guys are big on locks, aren't you?" Rex commented to Berno.

"Yeah, but I don't know why. Crashers get in anyway," answered a female voice. Wanda glared at him from the couch.

He set down his suitcase. "I have the same problem. But at least I knock."

"Honk, you mean." She patted the arm of a chair. "Sit. Why'd you come back?"

He sat. "So I can keep an eye on my enemies." His chameleon eyes were nearly green.

"Me, you mean?" Her eyes flashed back, electric hazel, if such a color existed. Her bulk tensed like a bull in the ring. Well, not quite like a bull.

Berno warily watched his visitors. "Should I alert the Emergency Room?"

"Only if she shoots."

Wanda took a deep breath and slowly released it. "Not yet. It depends on which enemy you mean."

"*That* depends on whether you were in on booby-trapping my truck while I was here."

"That bug? Forget it. Not me."

Rex faced Berno. "The wheels."

"Replacing tires is booby-trapping?"

"Leaving all the lug nuts loose is!"

The doctor stared incredulously. His face darkened. "Oh, no! The guys told me your tires smelled burnt, and I said you'd never make it back to town that way if you decided to leave. Somebody must have passed it on. I know who. No wonder the Director offered to have them changed!" He leaned forward, voice shaking. "So it's my fault, but I swear I didn't do it."

Rex's eyes blended back to blue. "I believe you." He swiveled to Wanda. "Now you know why I came back."

"So we're on the same side, after all."

"Far as I can tell."

She tensed again, and Berno broke in. "Calm down, Wanda. He's got a lot to process." The doctor parked himself on the edge of the couch. "Teerex, I hope you don't mind holing up awhile in the clinic."

"As long as you don't try to turn me into a nun."

Wanda looked puzzled.

"Never mind," Berno more or less explained. "Inside joke. Tommy'll be back in a few minutes, and we can have a nice working lunch without anybody leaning over our shoulder."

"Like the Director?"

"Or his goons," nodded Wanda. "They stay up the canyon a ways, but they keep an eye on things."

"Apparently."

The doctor glanced toward the hallway door. "We know most of the spies. You may notice my charming nurse Lew didn't meet you. He suddenly came down ill right after breakfast. Worst case of diarrhea I ever caused."

Wanda snickered. "That'll teach him to stay out of Nellie Culpepper's cookies!"

Rex's mouth twitched at the corner. "One of the yellow ones?"

"No, a brown one. Her gingersnaps'll snap the ginger right out of you."

"Now wait a minute! Berno, how did you cause Lew's, uh, indigestion if Nellie's cookie did it?"

He chuckled. "We help her out. She doesn't see well enough to read a recipe any more, and she's just ornery enough to make a batch wrong on purpose. Remember Lars, the chemistry major on bassoon? He's a chef. We get the best hospital food on the planet, and Nellie gets assorted cookies for unexpected visitors. There just happened to be a box of them here on the table this morning for Charlie to deliver to her. Maybe the gingersnaps were on top. Nellie probably came up one cookie short after I sent Lew in here on some excuse. He doesn't catch on half as well as he thinks."

"Won't he figure it out?"

The doctor shook his head. "He's worried about dysentery. Why, just this morning I mentioned reading an article about it making a comeback."

"Is it?"

"Not that I know of."

"But why today? You didn't know I was coming yet." His eyes worked their way back to green. "Or did you?"

Wanda put up a hand. "Simmer down, Teerex. No. The working lunch was already planned. You just crashed it."

A chime chimed. "That must be Tommy." Berno pushed a key fob button. The lock buzzed, the rotund engineer let himself in, and the lock unbuzzed. He eyed Rex, then Wanda.

"It's okay, Tommy. If Teerex gets to be a problem, we'll just shoot him." She redirected her attention. "I'm kidding, Teerex."

"I'll bet."

"You're on." She shifted. "Okay, Tommy, did it happen?"

"Right on schedule," he replied.

"What?" Rex blurted.

Wanda looked sharply at him. "Are you in?"

"In what? Trouble? Yeah."

She relented. "Close enough; you're in. Tell him, Tommy."

"Tammy just called. She says the bank ran out of patience."

Wanda translated. "Environmill's going belly-up. We depend on it. How much, Tommy?"

"Two point six million. By Friday."

"Is that all?"

"Yeah. The chuckleheads put the whole place up as collateral. They must have been desperate."

Wanda snorted. "Or something. Don't forget the controller skipped. But never mind that. What bank?"

Rex stared at her.

Tommy named a name. Your author won't tell you what it was, because he doesn't feel like being sued by any thin-skinned bank with a similar name, if there is one. Wanda recognized it, though. She doesn't dare sue the author.

"Good! They're in trouble with the Feds for shady investments. We'll help 'em shed one. Have Tammy tell 'em Environmill got a purchase offer for four million dollars cash on the barrelhead, but the deal has to be closed this week. Then she can tell her boss."

"He's on vacation."

"As usual. Who's in charge when he's gone?" Wanda knew the answer. Teerex might as well know.

Tommy played along. "Well, since the Plant Manager was indicted and the controller skipped for the Bahamas, Tammy's it. She has signature authority if none of the others are around."

"Tell her to limber up her signing hand. The bank will have her signing lots of papers this week."

Rex interjected. "Isn't that insider trading?"

Wanda sighed. "You're a party pooper, Mister Albert! What's the choice? A plant shuts down and a bank maybe gets seized, or somebody out of the blue offers to buy a blue steel mill and keep everybody from singing the blues."

"I was only asking!" he protested.

"Sounds like a country music title," mused Tommy.

"No, blues," Berno corrected. *"I Got Them Old In the Red Blue Steel Mill Need Some More Green Blues."*

Rex experimented with a tune.

Wanda groaned. "Enough already! Okay, Teerex, I'll tell you what. You're almost an outsider. You trade. You'll be an agent for AOA Enterprises. There's a phone. Here's Tammy's number. Have fun."

His brow wrinkled. "Could they trace the call?"

"Don't worry about that," soothed Berno. "Our geeks are sympathetic and highly experienced. They have to be. The phone company doesn't know about this line."

"No surprise there." Rex punched appropriate buttons on the inappropriate telephone.

His eyes tilted toward the upper corner of the room, looking for inspiration. He took a breath. "Hello, is this Tammy Tarantino? ... I'm Rex Albert, representing AOA Enterprises. ... Yes, Ma'am, I am. ... Likewise. Anyway, I've been authorized to offer four million dollars for the purchase of Environmill with the proviso that the sale be completed this week."

The handset squawked. Rex moved the phone away from his ear. "Yes, I'm serious. ... You would? Certainly, I understand. Just a minute."

He handed the phone to Tommy. "Ms. Tarantino would like some verification," he whispered.

Tommy nodded. "Hi, Tammy? ... Yep, it's on the level. ... She's right here."

"Hi, Tammy!" shouted Wanda from the sofa.

Tommy returned the phone to Rex.

"Hello again. Was that suitable? ... Very good. If you will be so kind as to relay the offer to the appropriate persons, we will be grateful. An agent can be in El Paso as early as tomorrow with a cashier's check for four million dollars. ... A mutually known intermediary will communicate with you later today." He winked at her husband. "Thank you. It's a pleasure doing business with you. Good-bye."

Dazed, he hung up the phone. "Did I do that?"

Wanda nodded. "You'll fit right in. We'll keep you under wraps until the deal is done. We'll slip you out to El Paso soon as we're ready to close the deal, and-"

"*Me?* Why not you?"

"Nobody knows you. You were right the other night; the Director would track me. He probably doesn't know you're here yet, he doesn't know about AOA Enterprises, and he doesn't need to know about this deal. I'll get you a limited power of attorney. We have a few lawyers here."

"Then what?"

"You'll officially move into Comunicado when you return. Everybody'll think you're just one more wrinkling refugee from the cruel world across the mountain. Except for us and the Director, but he won't know the half of it."

Berno protested. "I'll have you know that wrinkling refugees are my bread and butter! Once it was wrinkles; now it's refugees."

"I'm both, but not ready for your business," Rex interrupted. "Speaking of the Director, I'm surprised you guys don't just call him Randy out of spite."

"It's habit, I guess," replied the doctor. "I didn't know Randy before. We could call him something else, but it'd be unfair to body parts."

"Or fertilizer," grunted Tommy.

"Or horses," finished Wanda. "I never really thought about it. Randy was only a pitiful drunk. Now that he's the Director, he's just plain nasty."

The repartee was broken by the arrival of a food cart laden with covered dishes. Scented steam swirled outward. As the orderly whipped off the lids, Berno asked, "Did you run that cart past Nurse Lew's room?"

The orderly assumed an innocent expression. "Oh, yes. I parked it right outside his door while I took him his broth."

"You don't think he'll decide to come out here for real food, do you?" asked Wanda.

Berno ladled something tasty onto his plate. "Not a chance. He's on clear liquids until his, uh, condition clears up. Besides, his scrubs are in the laundry being sterilized, along with his street clothes. All he has is a hospital gown. Pink, with rosebuds."

《　》

Two days later under the early afternoon sun, a shiny sedan with a Bernalillo County plate waited outside the field house like a faithful steed, except that steeds as a rule are not burgundy colored and don't have multimillion dollar cashier's checks sitting on their saddles.

It was a perfect day for non sequiturs, Rex thought. Here he was, wearing a suit and not lying in a box. The suit fit well, which he would not have noticed if he were deceased. A wrinkled refugee tailor, not a mortician, had fitted him the afternoon before. An agent for AOA Enterprises must dress the part to be credible.

He slid the check into an inner coat pocket. Maybe it should have gone into that new leather briefcase, but he preferred to keep it within touching distance. Wanda would be unamused if he lost a four million dollar briefcase.

Image was important for this job. "Run through a car wash before you get to the bank," she had ordered. "You can't look like you blew in from the middle of nowhere."

"Even if I did," he replied.

"*Especially* if you did." She inspected him from top to bottom. "You polish up pretty well. I'd almost think you were on the level if I didn't know better."

"Thanks. Maybe I should be a con artist when I grow up."

"Whaddya mean, 'should be'?"

Edgar and Nellie waved as he drove by the Gatehouse, and he returned the gesture. The wine-colored steed traveled as smoothly as anything could travel on the rutted road. As soon as it turned right toward El Paso, it virtually floated down the pavement.

Rex gassed up and nosed into the first car wash in the city, right where the nice Australian lady in the GPS had said it would be. Why Australian? Exotic, but decipherable, he supposed. Nobody had yet stuffed a New Mexican into a GPS. Against a background of spraying water and the "slup" of carpeted rotors, he reviewed travel instructions to the downtown bank. Five minutes later, washed, waxed, and shined, the car returned to daylight and dusty pavement.

The Australian lady led them to a striped barrier arm by a booth in a downtown parking garage, where she promptly lost her bearings. She must have been an outdoorsy type.

A college-age attendant in the booth looked up from his textbook to see a driver flashing a brand-new business card.

"Rex Albert, AOA Enterprises. I'm expected."

"Just a minute. Let me check my list." The student/attendant did so. "Here you are, Mister Albert." The gate swung upward. "You get the spot right by the elevator."

"Thanks." Rex could get used to this. He slipped the she-Aussie into his briefcase as soon as he was parked. There was no need for any car thief to track her back to Comunicado.

Two minutes later, a spiffy middle-aged-plus businessman with an equally spiffy briefcase handed his business card to a well-groomed receptionist. She was more pleasant to look at than the garage attendant. No calculus book interfered with the picture.

"Good, morning, Mister Albert! They're expecting you. Please come this way." Leading him into a paneled elevator, she touched a manicured finger to a two-digit button. Up they went, and up and up. The car stopped just before it went through the top of the building. The door opened to daylight from glass walls and a solarium roof. The view was spectacular, if one liked cities and mountains. Rex liked mountains.

The receptionist escorted him to a walnut door with a brass peephole, and knocked. The door opened without a squeak.

"Mister Albert?" A suit-clad person twenty years his junior shook his hand. Similarly suited people milled suitably around a refreshment table near the window, like a herd of MBAs milling around a stock tank. Stifling an unprofessional grin at the image, Rex allowed himself to be introduced. Nearly all of the livestock were of the bull persuasion, or at least prime steers. There was one other, a previously prime heifer in a she-type business outfit. She and Rex were careful not to recognize each other. The last time they had met, both had been proportioned differently.

Your author is not familiar enough with high finance to act like he knows how to write about it. Maybe someday. Probably not. Suffice it to say that the check changed hands, lots of papers were signed, and expensive refreshments disappeared down necktied, bolo-tied, and necklaced gullets. Hands shook unrelated hands, the room emptied, and the elevator went back to work. Less well-paid office scavengers polished off the leftovers after the alpha feeders were gone.

"Back to reality," Rex said to himself, guiding his steed into city traffic.

A couple of hours later, he passed a young couple washing a sports car in the yard of a house by a defunct service station, and they waved as he drove past. He parked the dusty sedan by the striped shade of the bleachers. Briefcase in hand, Aussie in briefcase, and four million dollars less valuable than that morning, he disappeared into the field house.

« »

Chief Executive Officer Ralph Fox's vacation came to an unpleasant end. Jet lag built up on Saturday and Sunday, from Molokai to Honolulu to Los Angeles to El Paso. The last lumpy leg bounced over mountains and desert thermals.

Come Monday breakfast, the television showed nary a show, not even a commercial. The phone also was on strike, thus sparing the cable company a complaint. Not all problems were electronic, either. Some prankster had stuck a "For Sale" sign in the lawn.

The drive to work was no better.

"10:01" "10:01" "10:02" Environmill's flashing digital sign by the plant entrance aggravated his headache. So did a smoky, decrepit taxi crawling through the parking lot. Fox leaned on the horn. His head objected to that, too. The cabbie digitally saluted but did not yield. Several lungfuls of oily smoke later, both cars reached the executive lane, where a self-appointed chief executive backhoe perched in the CEO's parking space like an overgrown scorpion. The Controller's space was taken by a pickup truck with a red "Semper Fi" bumper sticker. Fox furiously pulled into the Plant Manager's slot, stepped into a water puddle the sprinkling system had left for him, and harrumphed into the building.

If the Chief Executive Officer was going to have a bad day, his Senior Administrative Assistant would have a worse one. Her chair was empty, though. Her desk was nearly so, sporting only a computer (off), a phone (flashing), and two photographs: the Fox children but not their mother, and the soon-to-be new Mrs. Fox.

Then Ralph Fox saw something even worse. His office door was ajar. It was never to be left open unattended.

It was not unattended, though. Male and female voices flowed from it into the reception area. The female one he recognized. Blood boiling, he flung the door wide open.

Tammy Tarantino was seated at the CEO's desk, discussing a stack of papers with a muscle-bound fiftyish gentleman. She looked up. "Oh, hi, Ralph! I'll be with you in a minute." She returned her attention to a file folder.

His first urge was to leap across the desk and throttle her. A glance at the stranger tempered the urge. "What's this, 'Hi, Ralph', Tammy?" he rumbled. "What happened to, 'Good morning, Mister Fox'?"

She sighed and turned to the other man. "Excuse me, Oscar."

Oscar Somebody sized up the Fox in the doorway. "Want me to stick around?" He moved so no furniture separated him from either of them.

"Thanks." Tammy faced the simmering CEO. "I figured if Tammy was a good enough name for me, Ralph would be fine for you. Your mother must have thought so. But if you prefer, I can call you Mister Fox and you can call me Mrs. Tarantino."

The urge reasserted itself. The stranger watched. *Down, urge!* Ralph decided. *Take a deep breath, and then let her have it.* He took his breath. "Well, then, Mrs. Tarantino, you and your pet gorilla have one minute to clear out of my office. In fact, you have five minutes to clear out of the building!"

"Wrong. Have a seat."

The urge broke free. "I sure will! Mine!" He started around the desk. The gorilla moved toward him.

"If you touch me, Ralph, I'll have you arrested for assault!" snarled Tammy. She pushed a button. "Now sit! There!"

There were three types of seating in the office: a truly luxurious executive chair, currently occupied; overstuffed leather chairs for favored guests; and a plastic one reserved for inquisitions. Tammy's fingernail pointed toward the plastic thing.

The gorilla did not smile. "Better do what she says."

Mister Fox reluctantly seated himself on the ergonomic disaster. His hipbones complained about the lack of upholstery. He set his computer bag on the floor. Every pound of additional weight in his lap was that much more cruelty for his hindquarters. Mrs. Tarantino's hindquarters were quite comfortable on their sumptuous perch, and her palms and forearms rested easily on a small percentage of mahogany desktop.

She leaned forward, sphinxlike, and bored her eyes into his. Sphinxes seldom blink. "Didn't your vacation end a week ago?" Her quiet voice was like a knife in a silken scabbard.

"What business is that of yours?" His growl was like a chainsaw in a sack.

The sphinx's lips moved, but not the eyes. "You didn't answer my question. Try again."

"You didn't answer mine either."

"I'll get around to it. Now quit stalling!"

He felt like a fighter pilot in a war movie, on the wrong side. At the twelve o'clock position, a sphinx. At ten, a gorilla. Unseen at six o'clock, boot steps and a walkie-talkie could only mean Security had arrived. Below, two painful hips. On top, a pounding head. The Fox was surrounded.

"I took comp time last week," he growled.

"Oh, really? How many hours did you have available?"

"I don't keep track of that! That's your job!" He instantly regretted it.

"Negative ninety three." Tammy leaned back. The sphinx was gone, but its replacement was no better. "Here's something else I keep track of: Seventeen times this year, you broke your own order that says, 'All members of management are to be accessible at all times.' Senior administrative assistants have to know how to contact the boss in case something happens. Well, something did, and I couldn't. There's been a couple of changes. First, meet Oscar, our new controller. Oscar, meet Ralph."

"Hi, Ralph." The gorilla's expression was dour, but his eyes gave him away. He was enjoying himself.

"What do you mean, our new controller? I didn't hire him!"

"Of course not. I did," Tammy retorted. "That's the other thing. You're fired."

He emphatically, succinctly, and metaphorically compared her statement to organic fertilizer.

Head shaking, she turned toward Oscar. "See what I mean? Totally unfit to be an administrative assistant."

The controller nodded, unsmiling. "Imagine what he'd say if I sent him for a banana."

Tammy giggled. Ralph goggled. She savored his reaction before resuming an in-charge expression. "Environmill was sold last Wednesday."

He gasped.

She waited for his face to finish changing color. "We couldn't locate you, so I signed everything that needed to be signed. We're part of AOA Enterprises now. They named me CEO because they could find me and I know the business. I figured you could be my administrative assistant, so I even fixed up your new desk. But you remember your rule about the assistant being here by eight. Well, here it is ten fifteen and you just showed up. Not only that, but you're swearing and you smell like you had a Bloody Mary for breakfast. That's not the image we want, so you're fired."

"That Bloody Mary was pretty light on the tomato juice," observed Oscar.

She sniffed. "Could be, but we'll let him by this time. He'll be using his own vodka from now on. Besides, he might be homeless. I made a reservation at the Y in case he needs it tonight."

"What do you mean, homeless?" Ralph roared.

"Inside voices, please. The house and living expenses are CEO perks, remember? That was your idea. My house is paid for, and I don't feel like moving. So last Friday we listed the company house, along with the Washington suite and those condos around the country. And other places. Somebody was staying in the one in the Bahamas. He's been arrested for trespassing. I have a pretty good idea who it is."

The beginning of Ralph's day began to make sense. He opened his mouth to protest, but Tammy overrode him. "But back to you. 'Your'"– she made quotation marks with her fingers – "home security system was reprogrammed. As soon as you unlocked the door yesterday, we knew. A lot of things happened right after that. Unhappened, actually. We cancelled a mess of so-called job-related memberships and travel reservations. Your corporate credit card is cancelled. Your phone's dead, cable's disconnected, and Internet is blocked. Your passwords were reset. Speaking of passwords, leave that laptop where it sits. It's ours."

"I have personal files on that!" he interrupted.

She tch-tched. "On a company machine? You know the rules: if they're on our system, they're our files. Tell you what: we'll look through 'em and see if there're any we want to copy for you."

Ralph turned white.

Tammy continued. "Your term insurance just termed out. You won't get unemployment because you were fired, but you can buy COBRA health insurance at your expense. And you have three days of pay coming."

"Three days?!"

"Last Monday through Wednesday, when you were still CEO. It was your business if you wanted to overlook the excess comp time while you were still in charge, but I put you on unpaid leave for being AWOL first thing after taking over. You've always been quick to give people time off, so I thought I'd try it."

"I'll sue you and your new owner for everything you have!" Ralph growled between gritted teeth.

"I doubt it. We took your attorney off retainer." Tammy drummed her fingernails on the mahogany. "You owe the company a hundred two thousand dollars in personal advances, plus all that comp time. You sue us, we bill you. If your tax returns are anything like your expense reports, all it would take would be a tip to the IRS and they'd eat you alive. I know where plenty more skeletons are buried. If our Bahamas squatter is who I think he is, the FBI may wonder how much you know about it. Try anything and you might get to share a cell with him or the ex-plant manager. You can laugh about old times over prison grub."

"But not over Bloody Mary's." The controller tapped a folder. "Before you go, I have a few questions if you don't mind. These files are pretty interesting. I'll get 'em all figured out eventually, but you could make it easier if-"

The former CEO bolted for the door. Oscar beat him to it and held out his palm like a bellman waiting for a tip. The difference was that a bellman would have let Ralph pass.

"The car keys, please."

"I will not!"

"They won't do you any good. There's a backhoe parked behind it. It's a company car, just like your other four. They're for sale, if you'd like to keep one. Otherwise, we'll have you arrested for auto theft the minute you start the engine. A cab is waiting for you. Your office things are in it, except for the ones AOA owns."

Tammy slid an envelope across the desk. "You can hand over your keys at the house if you prefer. I want you out of here. Here's your check, your separation papers, and a twenty for cab fare. When you get to the house, you can help the movers and the cop figure what to load into the van. We've rented you a storage unit. No charge for the first month. Just in case you don't remember what's yours, there'll be an accountant with an inventory of company property."

"The cop?" asked Ralph in a small voice.

"There's usually a cop if somebody's being evicted."

He started to retort, but his quivering jaw betrayed him. He snatched the envelope and hurried toward the door. Oscar stepped aside.

Two guards in the outer office flanked the former CEO. One scooped up young and future Fox photos as they passed the desk. Ralph hurried; they hurried. He broke into a trot; so did they. He dashed out the exit and pelted down the sidewalk with a running guard on either side. He nosedived though an open taxi door. One guard slid the pictures onto the seat, and the other guard closed the door. The rusty yellow sedan chugged away, leaving a cloud of blue smoke behind.

"BYE, RALPH!" "BYE, RALPH!" "BYE, RALPH!" The digital sign flashed, and Ralph Fox disappeared from Environmill.

Two people watched out the window of the executive office.

"That was fun, until he started crying," CEO Tarantino said quietly.

The Controller glanced at her. "You said he enjoyed driving people to tears."

"If it was wrong for him, it's wrong for me. I don't enjoy it, anyway."

"Then there's hope for you, boss. But he had to go one way or the other. We've stopped up a couple million dollars' worth of holes already."

Tammy turned toward her desk. "We'll have Wanda's investment back before quitting time. You haven't seen all the skeletons yet."

《　》

Rex wandered down the eastern street of West Comunicado. He might as well get used to it. Only by acting as though this would be his new home, could he ever hope to have his old one back.

He had bedded down for three nights at the clinic. Thankfully it had not involved hospital gowns or bloodletting. The food was good, and Lew was not a problem. Still weak from "dysentery", the nurse avoided anybody who might harbor a communicable disease. Rex tended to cough whenever Lew came around.

Wanda offered Rex his choice of unoccupied houses. He selected one partway up the western side of the canyon, a quarter mile upstream from the dam. It would be in shade during the hottest part of the day. He would check it out a little later, but first there was exploring to do. The key waited in his pocket. His paltry baggage would be waiting in the house when he arrived.

Just before he left the clinic, Wanda handed him a cell phone. "Everybody has one. The directory is programmed in."

He pushed buttons. "I don't see my name."

"Learn to spell, mister. Teerex doesn't start with an A."

"Huh! Is everybody's like that?"

She nodded. "Sure. Those are the names we know. I'm a W."

"Makes sense."

"And a C."

He looked up. "Crazy Lady?"

"Of course."

The local grapevine relayed the news that another refugee had come through the mountain. Refugees often were not strangers, but old acquaintances sharing an archaic collegiate dialect. A surprising number had never worked in their fields of study. Less surprising, they no longer were considered prime commodities in their fields of expertise. They were moved out of the job market as effectively as they had shortened their predecessors' careers.

If any interest group was overrepresented, it was the musical sector. Wanda the twirler had indeed been a people person.

"Do you still play horn?" How often had Rex been asked?

"It looks like I'm about to take it back up. You'll be sorry." How many times had that been the reply?

"Don't worry! We're all going deaf. We're in it for fun. See you tonight!" That was the stock rejoinder.

The umpteenth trolley of the day was coming up from behind. Rex moved away from the tracks and waited for it to pass, but it did not. Brake shoes squealed against steel wheels. The conveyance jerked to a halt with its steps directly in line with him. He shook his head and kept walking. Tommy Trolley bumped forward and kept pace.

"Hey, Albert!" an unfamiliar voice called. "Get on!"

"No, thanks!"

"I'm not asking. I'm telling. The Director wants to see you."

His heart lurched into second gear. Two unsmiling men in grey fatigues scowled at him. They were a bit young for classmates. He doubted he would have chosen them as friends.

The show had begun. What was the correct reaction? Fear, probably. That shouldn't be difficult. Reluctance? It would be in character. Obedience? A good act, if he could pull it off. How about resistance? Better not.

He turned toward the trolley. It banged to a stop. On board, the scowling heads continued forward until their necks stopped them. Each head bobbled on its respective neck.

"Sit here." Unsmiling Man Number One pointed to the seat beside him. Unsmiling Man Number Two settled himself across the aisle. The car lurched ahead. The Director apparently did not have the best motorman working for him.

The trolley rattled up the street and across the bridge. Then, instead of taking the western street back toward the dam, it switched rightward. Rocking up the old roadbed, it bypassed a string of docked white tank cars ("POTABLE WATER", said the stenciled sides), a string of black ones ("PROPANO"), and an assortment of other cars. Shortly afterward, it passed through a security fence surrounding a cheerless compound of cinder block buildings. The car bumped to a stop at an unmarked platform adjoining a yellow stucco house.

U.M.N.O. stood as soon as the lurching ceased. "Off, Albert!"

U.M.N.T. called out to the motorman. "Stay here!"

"How long?" groused the operator.

"Till we tell you not to stay here."

"So this one's coming back out?"

"Shut up!"

Maybe Rex should have been comforted by the motorman's comment, but he wasn't. He gripped the handrail and stepped to the ground. U.M.N.T. had already opened the building's steel door. U.M.N.O. followed Rex inside. The door squeaked shut.

The Director liked nice things: nice furniture, nice artwork, and photos of nice-looking models not wearing nice clothes in not-so-nice magazines. Rex was not asked to sit in any of the nice chairs. "Nice" was only a veneer, though, failing to conceal cracked plaster and flickering fluorescent lights.

"Got him?" a voice rasped from the next room.

"Yessir," answered U.M.N.O.

"Send him in."

"You heard him." U.M.N.T. jerked his head toward the door. "Move." The Unsmiling Men stayed put.

The inner room was meant to impress. The strongest impression, though, was made by the greatest flaw. Seated on a chair upholstered with the hide of a formerly endangered tiger, was one of the ugliest humans Rex had ever encountered. There was nothing structurally unusual about the body, but the face more than made up for it. One sagging jowl advertised long-time use of chewing tobacco, at least a can at a time. It looked like half of a bulldog. The Director either had given up that particular addiction or was doing without for the moment, or he would have resembled a squirrel with half a load of nuts. Be he bulldog or be he squirrel, he barely looked human.

A lopsided, oversized nose separated drooping eye pouches. The left eye drooped more than the right, as if to offset the bulldog cheek. The right earlobe might have been bitten off at some time or other. A lumpy red forehead scar could be from an unconscious collision with a curb. An ill-fitting toupee completed the picture.

"So you're Teerex." The Director's smile did not improve the picture. Snaggled black teeth bespoke long acquaintance with jowl juice. Straight whiskey had done a number on his voice box. "Want a drink?"

"No, thanks."

"Afraid it'd be poisoned?"

"No, sir."

Eyes flickered between sagging lids and drooping pouches. "You should be."

"Yes, sir."

"Never mind. I'm dried out, so you'd only get pop anyway. Without poison, this time." The Director shifted in his seat. "Now tell me, why are you here?"

"Your men brought me."

The lids dragged their way upward. "Don't play stupid! You know what I mean."

"Yes, sir. You have my gun."

"Want it back?" The Director's jowl wobbled when he barked.

Rex gulped. Maybe he should crank up the fear a notch. "Not since you sent me that e-mail."

"And?" His eyelids drooped again.

"And I figured if you wanted me to stay quiet, it'd be safer where you could keep an eye on me than by trying to hide."

The bulldog grunted. "Smart boy! I'd find you. Now get back to town and make yourself at home. No funny stuff. Understand?"

"Yes, sir."

"All right, boys! Let him out!"

Unsmiling Man Number Two opened the squealing door between the rooms. Unsmiling Man Number One opened the squeaky outside door. They neither spoke nor followed him out. The door banged shut. Rex hurried onto the waiting streetcar. It eased away from the station with nary a lurch.

"You're still alive," commented the motorman.

"Are they not sometimes?" his passenger asked while settling into the nearest seat. His knees were wobbly.

"Sometimes I go back empty." He cleared his throat. "A couple months ago, I brought a volunteer."

"Oh, really?"

"Yeah. He had a Bible under his arm and banged on the door soon as he got off the tram. They opened up, looked at him funny, and hauled him inside. I waited an hour or so, until a goon came out and told me to get lost."

"Any idea what happened to him?"

The motorman fixed his eyes on the tracks ahead. "I don't think they were looking for a chaplain. Least, they haven't improved much. Now, where're you headed?"

"West Street, by the bookseller."

"Are you staying up the hill from there?"

The motorman could be a spy, but one couldn't avoid everybody. They all would know where he was staying soon enough anyway. "Yeah."

"Rumbles had fun with that one. Nice view. Not too many snakes, usually. See you at band practice tonight?"

"Yep."

"I'll be by at a quarter to."

"Thanks."

The trolley came smoothly to a stop a few minutes later. Rex stood up. "You're good with this thing when you want to be."

The motorman grinned. "Thanks! The goons'll never know that. I keep hoping they'll get whiplash. ¡Adiós!"

Rex clumped up the hill. The asphalt trail zigzagged from the street to a shelf fifty feet up the side of the canyon. Maybe he would have done better to pick a place a bit closer to the bottom. His legs complained about perambulating prior to recovery from the Mailpie bike ride, and now a walk up a mountain. He promised them a ride in the recliner if they'd get him home. Wanda had said there would be one, "with a little table beside it for snacks and pistols."

The trail finally reached the ledge. He had chosen well after all. The first view of the house was of a trellised patio on the near end. Behind it, the building was wide but shallow, built hard against the canyon wall. A nearly four-foot high stone parapet, with crenellations, ten feet from the front would keep him from crashing down the cliff if he ever took up sleepwalking. It also would afford some privacy from all but buzzards. Side yards stretched north and south. The back yard was vertical for the first forty feet, where another ledge and another parapet would interrupt falling boulders from upper reaches. A footpath led up to it in case his legs ever forgave him.

The town stretched below him from left to right, rail yard to Nimsoo Sea. Across the canyon, the tunnel's black mouth emitted a pinprick of headlight, and then a streetcar. The jagged profile of Comunicado Ridge defined the eastern horizon; the flat line of Comunicado Dam the southern one. To the north, nondescript Goonville huddled between the rail yard and the next bend of the canyon. Wizmer was out of sight.

He opened the door and stopped wide-eyed. Rumbles must have had time on his hands when he built the place. The entire back wall was polished granite, part of the canyon itself. A glass-ceilinged foyer displayed the cliff above. A southbound hawk overhead banked toward the sun-warmed face of the rock and, catching a thermal, diminished to a black dot before sailing into the western wilderness.

The house followed the curvature of the cliff. Through an archway to the left, a living room beckoned with the promised recliner and a side table with snacks, but no pistol. A couch and coffee table awaited guests.

He would work his way back to the recliner, but the right half of the house beckoned first. A skylighted hallway followed the back wall past a small bedroom and bath, ending at a bedroom nearly the size of the living room. His suitcase rested on the floor. The closet and dresser were stocked with new clothes.

There was one problem, though: one should never give a rock wall to a geologist. Something will catch his eye. In this case, it was metallic yellow tracery meandering between irregular granite crystals. Not all of the gold was on the other side of the canyon.

He worked his way south, examining the hallway, foyer, and living room walls. No gold there; only in the bedroom. The kitchen was past the living room and opened onto the patio. A pantry and utility room were blasted into the back wall.

Five pounds of coffee beans, purchased green from a Nicaraguan farm and roasted that morning in Comunicado, awaited him in the kitchen. They were accompanied by a coffee grinder, coffeemaker, and, just in case Rex was the type, an espresso machine. Maybe, he decided, he would become the type.

What was in the fridge? Food. Ice. A pitcher of cold tea, unsweetened. It was the real stuff, lacking the sudsy appearance and old tire fragrance of reconstituted powder. Four assorted bottles of local beer marked "for testing" stood at attention on either side of the pitcher. One bore a taped message: *"Room Service. Don't get used to it!"*

It was too early to test beer. Glass of iced tea in hand, he settled onto the recliner. His legs approved. No sooner had they relaxed, though, than his brain kicked into gear. There would be no peace for Mister Albert this early afternoon. The Director was to blame, of course.

Or was he? He knew about the rifle; had, in fact, before Bambee and Billy were shot.

Or had he? Could he have taken credit for the killing after the fact? It depended upon who really did it. That hinged on who had access to the .22. It could be anybody who had been around Yootibibit from the time Rex was captured until he drove away.

Berno. The train crew. Wanda, who seemed to be everywhere and had a good reason to do the dirty deed. His old friends topped the list of suspects.

Or did they? Toss in people who could have confiscated the rifle later. The Director, for example, or his goons. The list actually was anybody who could have touched the gun.

Or was it? Had Rex's gun actually done the killing? He only had it on the strength of an e-mail that a .22 had been used at all. All it really proved was that somebody knew Rex had lost possession of his rifle at a convenient time.

Regardless of the weapon, the Director could have pulled the trigger, he could have ordered it done, or he could have taken credit for somebody else's action.

So much for deductive reasoning. Rex had pared the list of suspects down from everybody to everybody. There had to be a better way to solve his problem. Maybe sustenance, like that box of goldfish crackers on the side table, would help. Fish were supposed to be brain food.

He crunched his way to a couple more deductive dead ends before the food reached his brain. His problem wasn't really that some unknown person had murdered Bambee and Billy, but that Rex Albert was in danger.

In danger of what? Blackmail? That wasn't really a danger, only a threat of danger. Being framed for murder? Definitely dangerous. Getting himself murdered? The lug nuts said yes. Harm to his family? There was no proof, but it was a strong persuader to stay in line.

Okay, there was the real problem: Somebody thought Rex was dangerous. Conclusion number one. Brilliant.

It's funny how fish can make your mouth dry. His glass was empty, and the goldfish supply was dwindling. Maybe there was a connection. He swung his aching legs from the recliner and visited two rooms. One had more tea, and the other had a place to put used tea. There was sort of a symbiosis.

He ferried the sweating pitcher of tea to the table, along with a summer sausage and a knife. Deduction was hard work. Now, where was he? Oh, yeah; he was dangerous.

To whom? Knowing the murderer would help, after all. Failing at that, he must look for other clues.

The Director made no secret of his threats. He was afraid of what an unfettered Rex could do.

Or was he? Could he be shielding somebody else? Was he a lumpy red herring, or maybe a red flounder? Flounders were uglier, and lopsided to boot. The Director looked like a nightmare from Central Casting. Whoever had cast him, if he had been cast, had cast plenty of goons, too. That would cost money.

Wanda had money. She feared somebody enough to risk sneaking into Rex's house. She claimed to be afraid of the Director because he could expose her screwball town. So could Rex. In fact, he had threatened to do just that. Then again, it had become to her advantage to keep him safe. Threatening him via the Director would be counterproductive.

The sausage was getting shorter, the brain food was gone, the pitcher was half empty, and the bladder was full again. The stomach questioned how much more sustenance it could handle.

It was time to pick a villain. The Director would do until a better one came along. Anybody that obnoxious had to be guilty of something.

Rex would decide what to do about it later.

《 》

« 7 »

The trolley arrived punctually at a quarter to, full of people and instrument cases. A pickup Dixie band noodled in the back while the assemblage rumbled to the community hall by the Nimsoo Sea. There they disembarked, motorman and all.

A volunteer community band takes musicians wherever it can find them. Third cornet players and bottom-feeding clarinetists dusted off old instruments, if school band hadn't squashed their musical ardor. Long-ago first chairs could rebuild their lips without embarrassment. Ages spanned from eleven to "eighty two and proud of it!" In the front row, a tenth grade girl from Old Comunicado struggled with a beat-up school flute. Rubber bands substituted for long-missing springs. Plastic wrap and tape held frayed pads together.

Rex and Janet's gridiron wedding naturally came up during long-time-no-sees. He would force a smile to replace those the other persons lost, and he would say it was okay while wondering if it ever would be.

Practice finally ended. "See you Saturday?" How many times did people ask him that?

"I hope so." About that many.

Eight hours later, an orange sun dawned across jagged Comunicado Ridge like the top half of a Jack-o-lantern. A square beam of dusty daylight slanted through the window. This is a back-handed gift from the desert: the ability to see the shape of a sunbeam. Rex slouched in an armchair and finished the morning's first cup of coffee, while the bottom edge of the beam slowly crept across the floor toward its place of origin. The upper shadow line imperceptibly crawled down the granite wall.

The brew was delicious, but even the best coffee could not ease a fresh collection of facial aches. It would be a while before he could play without pain to himself and others. Nobody had complained. They were happy to have anybody who dared try the horn parts. Musicality would come. At least he hoped so.

He shuffled through the sunbeam toward the door, swirling up little eddies of dust. When he had been a boy, he would pick a silvery speckle and watch it meander up, down, and sideways in the light. Sometimes he would puff a bit of air just to create chaos in Dust Land. His children had done the same thing at the same age. It was cheap entertainment for young eyeballs. Older eyeballs mostly wished the dust would stay off their glasses.

He stepped onto the front porch. What were the Ithers doing at the moment? Probably wishing they could snatch a bit more sleep before getting the next generation ready for the day.

It was calm. The only breeze was the still air he cut through on his walk down the hill. The sun was not yet strong enough to wash the deep blue out of the high desert sky. A jumping fish marked its position with a bull's-eye of ripples in the equally blue pond. A roadrunner stalked a lizard in the empty street. A body could get used to this.

First, though, there was damage to be done. Either he or the Director would be out of commission before it was over. But how? It was nothing they taught in geology class, and he had never been drawn to violence.

Another person wandered down the street toward him. The beard, wire-rimmed glasses, and ponytail had not changed shape since college. Only the gut was rounder. A gnarled hand waved a couple of truncated fingers at him. Something else had changed shape, after all. *There's somebody who enjoys rebellion. Why not him instead of me?*

"Whatcha up to, Teerex?"

"Nothing."

"Huh! You never were a very good liar. Whaddya think of the house?"

"Great! That back wall was made for geologists."

Rumbles peered over his glasses. "See anything special?"

"Aside from the gold in the bedroom, naah."

His friend grunted. "I was going to put the living room there before that showed up. Thought it'd be better to keep it in private space. You had breakfast yet?"

"Just coffee."

"Not good enough. Remember any Shakespeare?"

"A bit. Why?"

"'Yond Cassius has a lean and hungry look. He thinks too much. Such men are dangerous.'" Rumbles had been a drama major, learning too late that drama seldom paid the rent.

"*Julius Caesar.* Tenth grade," Rex recalled.

"So you need breakfast if you aim to take on the Director."

He jolted. Was he that easy to read? "I'm not lean!"

"But you're hungry and you think, so you're dangerous. There's a bakery across the bridge. We can talk our way there."

Rex studied his uninvited companion.

Rumbles did not turn. "You're thinking again: Can you trust me? Not necessarily, and that's good. And I'm an actor, meaning I specialize in fakery. But listen to my lines anyway."

"Okay."

He kicked a rock down the road. "I always root for the underdog. Now Wanda's a millionaire, maybe even a billionaire, but for all that she's the underdog. She could keep everything for herself, but she doesn't."

He was silent for a moment. "You missed quite a show the day Randy found the gold. Tommy was lugging a bag toward the locomotive when the guy came up and said, 'That looks like an awful heavy sack. Lemme help.' Tommy went white and kept lugging. Then Randy pulled out a knife and slit the bottom out of the bag. Gold all over the place!"

"'I've got friends outside,' Randy said. 'You wouldn't like 'em. But it looks like Wanda could afford to support my friends as well as hers. Up the canyon where nobody'll bother us. Tell her that.' Then Randy made Tommy drop him off at the other end of the tunnel."

They reached the trestle, where a foot lane had been added to one side. The wooden walk thumped beneath their shoes. "Tommy was a wreck after he got back from El Paso that night," continued Rumbles. "He said when he and the Director pulled out of the tunnel, better'n a dozen guys were waiting behind the bleachers. Not a smile in the lot, but if guns were grins it would've looked like Happy Hour. They were lucky he drove a train. He couldn't run over 'em."

He slowly shook his head. "I had to build Goonville. There's never been a job I hated worse. I wanted to booby trap the place, but Wanda wouldn't let me. She said if they found out, it'd be curtains for all of us." He winked a watery eye. "There might be one or two things she doesn't know about. Plumbing's not too good, and the wiring's cheaper'n it oughta be."

"Don't they complain about that?" asked Rex.

The beard split into a grin. "Naw, they just think I'm a lousy contractor. Nobody invites 'em into other houses where everything works and the doors don't squeak."

They were back on solid ground. Yeast and bacon smoke enticed lean and hungry thinkers into an alpine style building with gingerbread trim. *"Comunicado Coffee Klatch and Terrorist Society"*, announced the sign in German Gothic script.

"No politics, no plots," warned Rumbles. "The sign's so the Director's snoops'll come here looking for secrets instead of running all over town. We toss 'em a bone once in a while, like a boxcar in El Paso they might like to look into."

"What about Lew at the clinic?"

"Dumber'n a box of rocks. Unsneaky as a moose. Ol' Randy thinks he's got the place covered, but Lew might as well honk a horn to say he's coming." Rumbles reached for the door. "Enough plots. Now it's all howdy, chew and jabber."

There was plenty of that. It was one of those places where whoever had the coffeepot refilled everybody else's cups. Rex met a few old friends and made some new ones between bites.

His host finally pushed his chair back. "I've got it today." He had barely made the six-foot hike to the cashier before a young man with a plate of food took his place at the table. "Young" was a little shy of forty.

"What do you think of the Director?" the youngster asked as he settled into the chair.

Rumbles' back stiffened.

Spy, Rex decided. "Pretty good. One hold was a bit too long, but otherwise he's easy to follow."

The stranger eyed him quizzically, and then laughed. "Not *that* director. "I mean-"

Dumb spy. "You mean the kid who led a couple marches? He'll make a good director someday." Rex smiled, all innocence. "What part do *you* play?"

"Uh, horn."

"Really? Too bad you weren't there last night! I could've used the help. Maybe tomorrow?"

Caught dumb red-faced spy. "Probably not. Awful busy. See ya!" The chair scraped away from the table, and its occupant hurried out the door.

Rumbles commandeered the abandoned plate. "Poor guy forgot his breakfast. Want another cinnamon roll for the road?"

"Why not? But first, let's eat his bacon before it gets cold."

They left five minutes later. The dumb spy was out of sight. "Was that a test?" Rex asked in a low voice.

"Probably." Rumbles turned to the left. "We'd better split. Little Nosy might still be around. Besides, I've got work to do for the Director."

Rex chilled. "You work for him?"

"We all do, like it or not. Tell you what. When you run across Stan Chess, ask him how his satellite killer is coming."

"Rocketman's still at it?"

"Yep. Thirty two years at Wizmer. He's hooked. So long." The gray ponytail bounced north.

Rex wandered the other direction, cogitating. He must have been crazy to think he could undo the Director. There were thugs and guns on one side, and cowed townies on the other. How was he any different? Well, he might the only adult in town who wasn't a lawbreaker- yet.

He hiked up the track to the tunnel. The big ventilation fan whined and thrummed deep inside. There had to be another opening somewhere for the exhaust. It would be on this side of the mountain to prevent detection, probably high up one of those slit-like crevasses. Once a mining engineer, always a mining engineer. Maybe someday they would let him have a look at the gold mine, if he lived long enough.

This would not be the day. A rough road meandered from the tunnel toward the top of the dam. Originally used to ferry blasted rock from the tunnel to the construction site, it had been resurrected as a haul road for blue paint and airplane chunks.

What did a blue dam look like?

He started up to see, watching for snakes. It was a good time to get away from the tunnel anyway, as a streetcar full of men zipped up from town. He had never seen a streetcar zip before. Would somebody yell at him to stay off the trail? No, they were too busy zipping.

He puffed upward, wondering how good his heart really was. Better than his legs, he hoped. It had been bad enough hiking up the hill to his house, and this was worse. Comunicado would either put him in shape or out of service.

The dam's concept was simple. Find a ditch. Add rocks until plugged. For most of its height, it was a steep-sided, stone-faced causeway across the canyon. A twenty foot high cement wall crowned it. Wider at the base and tapering toward the top, the cement ridge bore a vague resemblance to the Great Wall of China marching across Mongol hills. A spillway made a ten foot deep notch in the top of the wall, at the head of a cement chute.

Scuff, puff, scuff, puff: the tired sound of the open road. Then other noises intruded. First, a rattling streetcar zipped out of the mountain. Next were sounds from the downstream side of the dam. Neither screeching hawks nor hissing wind, but voices.

Friend or foe? Stay or go? It would be a shame to get so close to his destination and not see what was beyond. The world south of Comunicado was beginning to take shape, working its way down, puff by puff, from the rim of the canyon to the top of the dam. He would go on, but more slowly. *That's nice*, agreed his aching calves.

The road reached the crest. The top was just wide enough for a service road with a three-foot concrete parapet on the downstream side and a foot-high curb on the other to keep vehicles from tumbling off. The difference, he supposed, was because it would be a long way to the valley floor on one side and a short drop to the water on the other. The parapet was fractured a short distance ahead, likely by some airplane that almost – but not quite – avoided impact. Rather than contribute to the skyline, Rex crawled to the gap and looked down.

A broad, sloping face spanned the canyon, about as steep as a pile of broken rock could be without collapsing. Decades of dust storms had silted into the chinks. A crumbling cement-lined channel ran down from the spillway to a concrete apron that fanned out at the base of the dam. There was the shadow of a passage entrance, just over man-high and about as wide, where the spillway chute met the apron. That marked the outfall of the discharge tunnel from the floodgate by the Nimsoo Sea. A stream trickled from the passage and watered a tiny bosque of cottonwood trees at the edge of the apron. The bosque was as far as the water got. Downstream, the channel was dry. It curved to the west a quarter mile further south. That would account for low-flying smugglers not seeing the obstacle until it was too late. Turn the corner, see the dam, and boom.

All told, it didn't look that different from other old dams, except for one thing. Between bosque and crest, it was as blue as the sky above.

There were exceptions to the blue rule. The dam's face was scarred partway down by a black smudge, shattered fuselage, crumpled wings, and scavengers in grey coveralls. They were a bit too agile for old Aggies, but just about right for a gang of hoodlums. Neither retrieving bodies nor salvaging metal, they pulled bag after bag from the broken airplane. The bags went into a basket litter at the end of a rope in the spillway chute. The litter began to skid up the incline…

Toward a passenger van parked at the spillway's edge…

Not two hundred feet from Rex.

The scavengers would haul the bags to the top, and they would see him. It was time to go.

He could hurry when he put a mind to it, downhill at least. Putting even more mind to it halfway down when the truck engine rumbled to a start, he reached the mouth of the tunnel in what surely would be record time in the Old and Out of Shape class. Panting, he detoured into the shadow.

"BUZZ!"

Maybe he should look for snakes.

A healthy-looking one was coiled on the rail, four feet away and probably five feet long if it unwound. Rex had heard they could only strike one third of their length. *Let's see; five feet times twelve is sixty; divided by three is twenty inches is less than four feet.* Had the snake heard the same thing? Neither one moved. Maybe the rattler was calculating.

The van clattered by. The clattering rattler stayed. Then a light blasted from deep inside the tunnel.

Which would hurt worse: snakebite or getting hit by a train? The only way to know was to experience both. He was not interested enough in the answer to experiment.

It was quiet for a train. Narrow, too. A tram not seven feet wide eased to a stop, rendering the rattlesnake nonfunctional. The door slid open.

Rex clambered gratefully aboard a car full of grimy miners. Some watched him curiously. Others were catching a few Z's. One worked a crossword puzzle by the light of his cap lamp.

"Howdy, Mister Albert! Whatcha doin' in here?

The new passenger smiled nearly as broadly as the motorman. "Boy, am I glad to see you, Charlie! Are you driving now?"

"Yep, long as I'm careful. But why were you in the tunnel? It ain't safe in here. Trains. Snakes too." Charlie carefully moved the lever for the door, and then the throttle handle, one at a time.

"I was hiding," blurted Rex. A few passengers perked up.

"From what?"

"Watch the road, Charlie. I don't want you to lose your job."

"Oh, yeah. Thanks."

A miner leaned over from one seat behind. "I saw the Badmobile go by. Can't blame you for hiding."

"The Director's gang?"

"Who else? There's more money in heroin than gold, 'specially if he gets it free. But he'll take both." He was silent for a minute. "Did you work at the Mailpie mine?"

"Uh-huh."

"Mining engineer, right?"

"Yep."

"We could use one. Some of that rock's not too good."

"I'll see what I can do."

"Thanks!"

The tram stopped by *Lucky Gulch Grub and Bath*, a false-fronted building with batwing doors. "They git an hour for lunch," Charlie explained. "I can take you someplace else if you want."

"How about that bookstore by my house?"

"It's a good one! The guy got me lotsa train books." The tram began to move, and Charlie spoke over his shoulder. "You like train books?"

"I like lots of kinds of books, but the thing is to find a bookseller who'll get you what you want."

Rex looked back toward the tunnel. Something didn't add up. "Where'd you come from, Charlie?"

"Mailpie."

"No, I mean in the tunnel. I saw a trolley go in and out, but I didn't see this tram. Were you in front of it?"

He kept his eyes forward, watching for pedestrians. "Naw. I was parked on the spur. You cain't see no trolley from there."

"A spur? In the tunnel?"

"Sure. The one in the mine."

Of course. Choo-Choo Charlie had out-thunk a mining engineer. Who woulda thunk?

Rex laughed. "Charlie, you've made yourself right at home here, haven't you?"

"Uh-huh, Mr. Albert! Folks're nice. I only been away a couple times since I got here. Once was when I picked you up."

"What was the other time?"

"Tommy thought I'd like a run in Ol' Blue to El Paso one Saturday, but we didn't git there. Ol' Billy the Engineer Flaherty got so plastered he forgot it was his day off, an' he drove Number Seven Twenty Nine an' a string of empties from Mailpie till he run outa Number Two Diesel on top o' the Comunicado switch!" He stopped for breath. "We come around the bend an' there it was! I said, 'Must be Billy, drunk again!' I bagged his booze enough times to know! We had ta back alla way back through the tunnel!"

Charlie decelerated. "We're here, Mister Albert. Bye!"

It *was* a good-looking bookstore. Dusty, faded covers outnumbered paperbacks. Armchairs and floor lamps shared the room with shelf after shelf of two-deep books. The proprietor, sporting an appropriate beard and a sweater with leather elbow patches, looked up not from a computer screen, but a collapsing hard-covered volume of *How I Found Livingstone,* by Stanley.

"Mister Teerex, I presume?"

"George, you look right at home!"

Bright eyes sparkled over the beard. "Indeed I am. No more weeding library shelves of the very volumes that attracted me to libraries. Now I rescue those weeds and give them new lives." He inserted a bookmark into Stanley's tome and closed the cover.

"You know, you delighted a young man recently with some train books."

"Ah, yes. Charlie. Limited in scope, but he more than compensates with zeal. Those books were bound for a dumpster in Deming." George sized up his old friend. "What's your literary taste these days? Subversion's two aisles over."

Rex grimaced. "Have you been talking with Wanda?"

George nodded.

"I'm an engineer, not a revolutionary!"

"Exactly. You're an unknown quantity to our friend up the canyon. From what I hear, you have a better sense of the danger than most folks here do."

"Probably. But what am I supposed to do?"

"I wish we knew." He brightened. "I have an idea. Can you look menacing?"

"What do you mean?"

"Something happened a while ago. I need another henchman."

Rex hesitated. "You lost one?"

"No. We have a prisoner. He should be menaced."

"I'm not quite ready for violence."

"Violence and menace aren't synonyms. All we want at the moment is menace." Casting a regretful look at the book he wasn't reading, George led Rex between the stacks to the back of the shop. "Remember," he whispered, *"Menace!"*

An old, varnished five-panel wooden door opened into a back room. The setting beyond the door did not maintain the woody ambience of the public area. Cinder block walls rose from a slab floor to a steel roof supported by open trusses. The space was piled with books that hadn't yet made it to the front. A seedy, probably comfortable desk chair was drawn up to a wooden table that supported more books, an impressive array of electronic equipment, and a gooseneck lamp. The goose, though, was not hunched over the tabletop at the moment. Rex knew what gooseneck lamps were good for.

A terrified middle-aged man was tied to a steel post, facing the business end of the light. It wasn't one of those wimpy fluorescent twisty bulbs, either, but 150 blinding watts of Edison's incandescent finest. The prisoner couldn't admire his stark shadow on the back wall, but he could sense the presence of a menacing captor behind him. To his right, another one paced the floor and growled. How many more might there be?

George and Rex lumbered through the door. Rex slammed it shut. Crossing his arms, he stood to the right of the lamp where the captive could vaguely see his form. Sparkling residents of Dust Land, shaken from repose by the slamming door, settled slowly downward from the trusswork, blundered over the hot lamp, and shot back up aboard the Thermal Express.

Grand Inquisitor George seated himself behind the table. He cleared his throat portentously. "Where are you from? Santa Fe? State Police?"

The cowering prisoner shook his head.

"DC? FBI?"

"Huh-uh."

"Okay, then. Where?"

"Jal."

George's forehead wrinkled. "Where?"

"Jal."

"Spell it."

"J-A-L."

"You lie!" The inquisitor transferred his attention to the captor in the background. "Tell him where you're from, Sammy."

"Am from Jail!" The prisoner could not see Sammy's grin.

Now, anybody unfamiliar with Southeastern New Mexico might think that Sammy had said, "Am from Jail," but of course he hadn't. Any Southeastern New Mexican could tell you that's how you say, "I'm from Jal," if you're from Jal.

"We don't like spies," hissed George.

"But I'm not a spy!" protested the captive.

"Then what are you?"

"Just a reporter."

The room went deathly still. The leader broke the silence. "That's worse!" More silence. One could have heard a watch tick, if they hadn't all been digital. "From where?"

"D-Dallas…"

The captors glowered. "A Texan!" the growling one growled.

"A Texas reporter!" snarled Rex.

"A Texas Big City reporter!" expostulated Sammy.

George slammed his hand onto the table, stilling the hubbub. His eyes were like slits. "What's your name?"

The man stared speechlessly. Sammy spotted a rectangular pocket bulge and fished out a wallet. Flipping it open, he studied the driver's license. "Texas, yep. Says here his name's Jack."

George glowered at the hapless journalist. "You're a dead man, Jack!"

Jack fainted.

He was safe enough. There would be no crash to the floor. Trussed to the post, he only sagged. Sammy shook his head. "Huh! Thought Texans were s'posed to be tougher'n that." He emptied all remaining pockets. "Hmm! What's this?"

The Growler leaned over to see. "Looks like reeds. Big ones."

The prisoner groaned. His eyes fluttered open, and he gazed around the room. Spots were all he saw. He considered fainting again, but George would have none of it.

"You listen to me, Mister Jack Texas Big City Reporter. Before you conk out again, suppose you tell me what these are for." He flexed the business end of the reed, close enough that the reporter could see it.

"B-bari sax."

"I thought so. Maybe I should just break all of these, slowly!"

Jack jerked upright, nearly braining himself against the post. "NO! Do you know what those cost?"

"I have a pretty good idea. That's why I stuck with alto. Now tell me, are you TV or newspaper?"

The reporter released a bitter chuckle. "Newspaper. I have too many miles on my mug to be a pretty-boy anchor."

"Maybe there's hope then. Untie him, Teerex."

"Yessir." Remembering to scowl, he circled behind the captive and undid the knots.

George bent the gooseneck down to a position more suited for reading, but the grilling continued. "Don't get any ideas, Mister! Tell me what you were doing in our tunnel, or this reed goes!"

Jack licked his lips nervously.

The inquisitor's face softened, just a bit. "Would you like a beer? You look pretty sweaty."

"Well, thanks, I wouldn't mind."

"Two, Sammy. You know what kinds."

Sammy scuttled to a refrigerator. The light within briefly brightened the room while brown glass bottles clattered across clear glass shelves. He scuttled back, grinning until he remembered his duty to glare. It was hopeless. Sammy was born to grin. He could not glare for more than two minutes at a time.

George leaned across the table. "You should know, Jack, that this beer is locally brewed. Some of it's really, really good, and some is awful. If we think you're telling the truth, you get the good stuff. If we don't, well..." He pried off a lid. "Taste?"

The reporter tilted the container. His nose wrinkled and tears started down his face, but it was too late. Some had already passed his lips. He spat it onto the floor. "Thanks, but I'd rather go thirsty."

"I can't blame you. That's what we give to Texas big city reporters we don't like." The inquisitor popped the other bottle. "It's your choice."

Jack suspiciously sniffed the new offering. His tongue warily extended between his lips, accepted just a drop, and retracted into his mouth. Facial gyrations accompanied the introduction of the drop to the palate. Palate, meet beer. Beer, palate. Pleased to meetcha. Likewise. Jack took a good swallow and smiled a blissful smile. "For this I'd read you the encyclopedia!"

George retrieved the bottle. "You wouldn't make it halfway through A. Just stick with what you were doing in our tunnel. But please, take a seat."

Rex took the cue, sliding a chair behind Jack like a waiter.

"Thank you. I'd be happy to." The prisoner settled onto the proffered perch. "Well, I do the environmental beat. The newspaper bosses are all younger than me, and they think environment is a young people's game, so they wouldn't mind if I was recycled. I needed a good story and thought maybe the Environmill ruckus would work. You know, protests, recycling, the whole ball of wax. There'd be plenty of people begging to be interviewed. But I got down to El Paso and the company wouldn't talk. I interviewed a few protesters and neighborhood folks, but that was about it. Pictures of the mill didn't come out too well, either. The blue paint job washed out against the sky. All I got was pictures of scrap iron waiting to be melted down." He nervously eyed his inquisitors. "But then I started to wonder if it all was scrap."

"What do you mean?" George's tone was ominous.

Jack's mouth went dry. "Can I have a swallow of the good stuff?"

"Will you keep telling the truth?"

"Yeah, but you might not like it."

"You let us decide that. Here."

He swallowed one swallow and handed the bottle back. "I'd better let it last. Anyway, there were tank cars that looked too new to salvage. And a drill rig on a flatcar. One went missing down around Houston a while back, so I began to wonder if Environmill was all it was cracked up to be. I drove around early the next morning, and what should I see but a sky blue yard engine coming down the tracks from the north! It didn't belong on somebody else's railroad in the first place, and in the second place it wasn't just hauling scrap. It was pulling a track crane, a flatbed with a loader and cutting torches, another flatbed full of rails, and a gondola with old ties sticking out."

"Then at lunchtime, I saw on TV that somebody had done a number on the Mailpie rail yard, and I got even more curious. I-"

"Just a minute," George interrupted. "Do you think anybody else noticed that train?"

"Not that I know of. It was pretty early."

"Good! For that, you get another swallow."

"In that case, nobody saw it." He sipped. "I decided the environmental angle would have to wait. Conspiracy sells better." His listeners glared, even Sammy. Maybe Jack should faint, but he didn't feel up to it. They might revive him with the bad beer. "Wrong word, huh?"

"Let's just say it's not politically correct in present company. Go on."

"Yes, sir. I had to fly back to Dallas that night, but the Environmill thing kept nagging at me over the next week or so. So I took a couple sick days and drove back down to El Paso. Dumb. Six hundred miles plus."

He took a big breath. "Anyway, I thought I'd see what I could see in Mailpie as long as I was around, even though that story had been pretty heavily mined already. Pardon the pun. The difference was that I had a hunch. Then on the way up I saw a sign pointing to Comunicado. 'Hmm,' thinks I, '*there's* an angle!' Skullduggery on the Mailpie line, railroad to broken dreams, starting with the ill-fated Comunicado tunnel, and ending with a budding ghost town named Mailpie. Melodrama sells even better than, uh …"

"Conspiracy," finished George. "Have another drink."

"Don't mind if I do. So I decided a picture or two of Comunicado would be in order, and I turned west. That was a bad idea, except for this beer." He took a gulp and smiled.

"Maybe. Pray continue." George retrieved the bottle.

"Comunicado was everything I could ask for. All dried up, an adobe train station reverting to the soil from whence it sprang, and behind it all, a big black tunnel to nowhere. So I climbed over the fence and went to look. I hadn't expected tracks, especially shiny ones. I followed them into the tunnel, and what do I see but a subway station! About that time, my brain started connecting conspiracies and subway stations where they don't belong, and I decided I'd rather be elsewhere. But it was too late. Next thing I hear is a streetcar bell, and it looks like half of the Keystone Cops are on board!" He hesitated. "Uh, scratch that last remark."

"You're lucky we like the Keystone Cops! Here, finish that beer." George slid it across the table. "Then what?"

"Yeah," piped in Sammy. "What was that about Jail?"

"Just a minute," replied Jack, taking time for a swallow. He wiped his mouth on a sleeve. "I had to be from someplace when you asked. Dallas didn't seem like the right answer under the circumstances."

"Y'all got that rat!" Persons from Jail would know Sammy did not refer to rodent hunting.

"So Jal came to mind. I saw it on a map once. Short, sweet, and to the point. How could I go wrong?"

George slowly shook his head. "Now you know. Well, Jack, you have a topnotch article, but you realize you can't publish it."

The reporter paled. "Dead men tell no tales, and all that?"

"Not necessarily. How tied are you to Dallas?"

"What do you mean?"

"Do you have family there?"

"Just my wife and me now. The kids left town as fast as they could leave."

George nodded. "Sensible tykes. How would your wife feel about moving west?"

"Are you kidding? She hates cities! She's a ranch girl."

"Good! Call her and say you got a job in New Mexico, effective immediately. Tell her she's moving, all expenses paid, first-class; bring the sax but don't worry about the house. As soon as she says yes, call your newspaper and quit. Or go AWOL; it's up to you. But don't say why, or we drown you in bad beer."

Jack stared, incredulous. "A job?"

"Bari sax player. We need one. We like storytellers too, and you'll do."

"But-"

"Consider the alternative."

Jack gulped. "Okay. I think I'll quit. The paper might not notice if I just went AWOL. Where's the phone?"

George raised his hand. "First, one more thing. Don't you breathe one word of this story to anybody, not even here! You'll meet the Director soon enough, and then you'll understand. If he thinks somebody from the outside is starting to figure out the situation, he'll do more than just drown you. If he hears about somebody leaving the tunnel door open so a reporter could wander in, we're all cooked! I'm serious. Got it?"

"Then is it safe here?"

"Is it safe anywhere? Consider the alternative."

The journalist sighed. "Put that way, it sounds safe enough. But maybe I shouldn't try to put away an encyclopedia's worth of beer."

"Probably not. Here's the phone."

Two calls later, George leaned toward his latest henchman. "He looks a bit giddy. Why don't you run him over to the clinic? Keep an eye on him."

Rex guided Jack to the street. *A Streetcar Named Doris* jingled to a stop, and they found a pair of empty seats toward the back.

The ex-reporter did a 360-degree study of the valley, like a barn owl inspecting a new barn. "What *is* this place?"

"Asylum."

"I don't follow you."

"It's a hideout for has-beens. Throwaways can finally do what they dreamed of. George'll die happy someday in his pile of books. You're riding on Tommy and Tammy's train set. Ned the Nerd brewed your beer. Band three times a week, and no tryouts. And so on, and all paid for."

"There's got to be a catch."

Rex nodded. "The place is secret. If word gets out, it's over. Then there's the Director. He's the snake in the garden."

Jack watched the linear world roll past the window. Without turning, he commented, "They called you Teerex."

"An old nickname."

"I could tell. You know, I have pretty good ears yet."

His diffident tone put Rex on alert. "Oh?"

"Uh-huh. I heard you and George talking before you came in playing gangster. I'd bet good money you haven't seen each other for years. He's been here long enough to set up shop, meaning you just arrived. And," Jack faced him, "you've talked about everybody but yourself."

Rex reddened. "I'm a washed-up mining engineer. Is that good enough?"

"Not when you're that color, and especially not when you say it like that. We Texas big city reporters are trained to be nosy. I can't turn that off. You're hiding something."

Rex's quiet voice shook. "Somebody said I was a lousy liar. All I really know about you is that you carry around big sax reeds, so I'll just shut up."

The other man nodded. "Smart move. I don't blame you. Maybe we'll find we're on the same side."

"I hope so." What could he say that would help if they were "on the same side" but not be dangerous if they weren't? Maybe share a secret that everybody but newcomers knew.

The clinic platform hove into view. Rex pulled himself to his feet. "This is the place. Berno - he's the doctor – is good for everything from snakebite to facelifts. He's okay. But there's a giraffe in there named Lew who calls himself a nurse. Watch out for him."

"What do you mean?"

"Never mind. Just watch out. And if anybody asks how you got here, just say you're an old friend of Wanda's."

He would talk to Wanda later. In the meantime, he would try to keep one eye on the stranger and the other on his own back. If only he had been born a bullfrog...

《　》

Two men stood on the clinic platform. One, an engineer by trade and temperament, was mentally stepping through a plan. Ring doorbell. Admit stranger. Assess the situation, meaning said stranger. Adjust plan as needed.

The second, a reporter by personality, studied his surroundings. Observe. Interpret. Report when able. Oh, yes, forget the last part.

Lew cracked the door open. He looked a bit pale yet. "Yeah?"

Rex gestured toward Jack. "My friend has a stomach problem." He nudged him in the ribs.

The reporter was a quick study, working up a good grimace.

"Well, I don't know..." hesitated the nurse.

Rex rolled his eyes. "Aw, for crying out loud, this is a clinic, isn't it? Sick people come here all the time!"

"But-"

Jack moaned.

"You better let us see the doctor quick, or my buddy's likely to dump his guts all over your porch. Berno'll have you clean it up!"

That decided it. Lew swung the door open. "Doc! Come quick!" he yelled and hurried for a wheelchair.

Berno hustled into the lobby. "What's the problem?"

Jack doubled over, howling. His guide grabbed the doctor by the arm. "Quick, Doctor, you've got to help my friend! I think it's dysentery!" He winked.

The nurse, his back to them, stopped in his tracks.

The physician returned the wink. "I see. We'll need to take a blood sample right away. Nurse!" he called. "Bring me a syringe. A big one!"

"*Me?*" Lew's voice broke.

"Who else? See any other nurses in here?"

"I'll find one." He turned toward the hall.

"Oh, no, you won't! There isn't time. I can hear the patient's intestines from here! Aw, never mind! I have a needle in my pocket. Just come over here and support my patient."

Wild-eyed Lew inched their direction. Berno withdrew a monstrous syringe from his lab coat with a flourish. He popped the cap off, licked the pointer finger on his off hand, and felt the end of the needle. "Sharp enough, I guess."

The reporter's eyes were nearly as wide as Lew's. The doctor squinted and stuck his tongue between his teeth. He drew back for a good jab, and-

And Nurse Lew crashed to the floor in a great linear heap.

And Jack whimpered.

Berno slipped the cap back onto the needle. "He's afraid of blood," he whispered to his patient and slid the syringe back into his coat. "Do me a favor and flop on the couch. Look half dead."

The relieved reporter complied, just as the nurse began to stir. Berno leaned over. "Lew," he suggested in his best bedside voice, "I think you're having a relapse. Why don't you drive that wheelchair to your room?"

Six feet ten of near-zombie crawled to the chair, positioned himself in the seat, and slowly rolled away. The hallway door opened automatically. He passed through like an automaton, and it closed with a hiss and a click.

"Can I get up now?" the Texas Big City Reporter asked.

"Certainly. You're healed."

Jack swung his feet to the floor. "I hope so. You don't really use that needle, do you?"

"Sure, for Lew repellent."

"If he's that bad, why don't you fire him?"

Berno hesitated, and Rex answered for him. "The Director might object. Better the devil you know than the devil you don't." He turned to the doctor. "Berno, this is Jack, who might be a reporter or a devil."

"Is there a difference?"

"I don't know. George sent him over with his compliments, although for the life of me I can't figure how George'd get mixed up in business like this."

"Maybe he read a detective novel." Berno did not tell the real reason. Not all information in the bookstore came from books. The tunnel was alarmed, and it was unlikely the Director's men would frequent a bookstore. Not that kind of bookstore, anyway.

The reporter studied the doctor.

"Bernardo Cognito, once Surgeon to the Stars, since dropped off the face of the earth?"

The doctor hesitated. "I wouldn't put it quite that way."

"The gossip columns did."

"I'm just in Comunicado. And you want to know why."

"I'm nosy. It's my job. Was. But I'm gagged now. George says gossip would be unhealthy."

Berno swallowed. "He's right, so here's your non-gossip. I was married. She was an eyeful already, but always wanting an upgrade. I finally upgraded her to the point that she didn't want a middle-aged plastic surgeon hanging around. People might talk, and she was looking for a husband upgrade anyway. I got cynical. When you're in my business, you can tell if somebody's had body work. Beautiful people start to look like lab specimens. Little scars nobody else would notice, and so forth." He leaned forward. "Even the Director's had it done."

Rex's eyebrows rose. "That's a facelift?"

"Something like that."

"I hope he got a refund."

"Don't count on it. He must've been *really* ugly before. Probably checked the mirror after the bandages came off and thought he looked better than he had in years."

"If you say so."

The doctor resumed his tale. "So I married my surgical nurse. She's plainer than a mud fence and couldn't care less. Neither do I. No more making perfect people. Now I fix broken ones. I'm just your average hick doctor with a witness protection sideline."

Rex interrupted. "Berno, are you sure-?"

Berno nodded. "If Jack is the Director's man, he already knows. If he isn't, he needs to know. There's more, too."

They waited.

"The Director is sending me business."

"What kind of business?" asked Rex.

"He came to the clinic a couple of months ago. Not for treatment; he doesn't dare. He said a customer would be coming the next day. I might recognize him, but he had better not be recognizable when he left. Then he added a warning. 'You'd better keep him healthy! This is strictly business. I don't want to upset my customers, understand?' The next day, three men were at the door. They spoke barely enough English to get by. Two bodyguards, and one man who's in the news a lot. The more corpses, the more likely he's in the story. Now, if his picture shows up in the paper, you can be sure it's an old one."

"Who?" asked the reporter.

"You don't want to know, in case anybody asks. He had aortic aneurysm trouble while he was here, though, and I operated. Now the man is aneurysm-free, unrecognizable, and gone. There have been a couple others, too. After I'm done with them, they're smuggled to different airports, or maybe across the border. The Director doesn't tell me where, and that's fine with me. If his customers find out where the work is being done, he won't be a middleman anymore."

"Or alive," grunted Rex.

"Any of us," agreed Jack.

Berno sighed. "It's not if, but when. Somebody'll figure it out one of these days."

Thousands of miles away in a dusty camp, men were adjusting to their commander's new appearance, even as they released blurbs with his former appearance to the media. The blurbs had been prepared in advance to coincide with a preplanned newsworthy event.

The blurbs did not discuss the aneurysm that had nearly undone the commander.

If things went as hoped, the organization eventually would introduce his new appearance along with the revelation that it had been done in the heart of the enemy's realm. He had passed undetected through five airports after the change. That would add to his mystique.

Something else had passed undetected through the same airports. Deep inside the commander, a plastic scalpel was cocooned in multiple layers of fabric sheathing. An outer layer of surgical gauze was wrapped to hold the working edge of the blade toward a perfectly good aorta. The cocoon was slowly dissolving.

《 》

« »

Saturday night was band night. So were Tuesday and Thursday. Comunicado was out of the social orbit, and the absence of television left time for other activities.

Gracie, short for Graciela, was late. She had not wanted to come at all, but her parents had insisted. "Stop your moping! Every teenager does it once."

"But they'll laugh at me!" she had whined.

"If they laugh, it's because they remember. Laugh back."

"It" was the previous night's diligent effort to scrub her acne away once and for all, with plenty of strong soap and a good coarse washcloth. Come morning, her face felt like fire and looked like it had been sandpapered. The pimples were still there.

She had finally decided to go. The band couldn't give her any less sympathy than her parents. Her seat was in the front row where only the conductor would see her face. His visage was so cratered, he surely would understand.

Face turned downward, Gracie hurried into the hall during a swing piece. She heard rather than saw a new instrument growling like a musical chain saw. She ducked in front of the conductor and sat down. He nodded without missing a beat.

Her shoulders drooped as soon as she snapped open the instrument case. A broken rubber band lay in the bottom. A pad that should have been closed, wasn't. There would be no music for Gracie.

Something tapped her drooping shoulder. She turned, and her eyes widened. Last Thursday's new French horn player held one end of a narrow leather box. He looked like he was trying to smile, but it wasn't working. Wondering, Gracie reached for the box. He nodded. She took it, mouthed "Thank you," and turned back around. For three whole seconds, she had forgotten her face.

The flute was a deep silver-blue. Fifty years of student fingers had not worn it down to brass. There were no rubber bands. The pads were pads instead of plastic wrap. She assembled the instrument, fitted her fingers to it, lifted it to her lips, and found her place in the music. She blew.

Real notes came out. The keys responded immediately when she moved her fingers, instead of when they got around to it. Suddenly music was fun. She had thought about dropping band, but maybe she wouldn't after all.

The horn player wasn't very good, she thought. His notes chopped in and out like he was laughing, probably about her face. Let him laugh. She would play. His horn gave a last squawk and went silent.

- 136 -

The music ended. Gracie turned to thank the man again, but her smile evaporated. Tears dripped onto the horn in his lap. His shoulders heaved, and his neighbors pretended not to notice.

"Do you want your flute back?" she asked in a small voice.

He shook his head. "Just keep playing. Please."

It was difficult to keep her mind on the music at first. The flute did its part to make her comfortable. Not only did her sound improve, but the horn player was getting better, too.

Finally, though, the last tune was over. Talking and laughter replaced music, and instruments settled into their plush beds until the next session. Gracie offered the little black case to the horn player. His eyes were dry, but still a bit red.

"No. It's on loan to you. Just treat it well and tell me if it needs anything."

She hugged him. That was undoubtedly a violation of some rule. He briefly patted her shoulder and let her go. She hurried outside to the tram and looked for a seat in the darkest corner.

"Gracie, sit here."

"Yes, Ma'am." It was the Crazy Lady. Was she going to make a big deal about the hug?

"You take good care of that flute. Make it sing. Mister Albert has just done more for you than you can imagine."

"What do you mean?"

"That belonged to his wife."

"Oh. What happened?"

The Crazy Lady's voice caught. "She died."

"Oh." Gracie was quiet. "Did you know her?

"Mm-hmm."

"Now I'll cry every time I play it."

"Don't do that, honey. They were happy. That's what he wants to remember."

《　》

Rex tested a beer at home, and it passed. Already this was home? For the moment it was, even if he and Janet had raised their family elsewhere. She would have liked the place, although it was one bedroom too small. Now the kids were gone, and so was Janet. Even her flute was gone.

He wondered how the girl would treat the instrument. Had that been a wise idea? He hoped so. It had been nice to hear it again. Yes, it hurt, but the good memories came with the bad. He was not sorry.

《 》

« 8 »

He awoke to pounding the next morning. Grumbling and pulling on the nearest pair of pants, he stumbled down the hall to the front door. It was so early that the coffeemaker had barely begun to gurgle. Anybody banging on the door like that before the first cup of coffee ought to be shot. He pulled back the curtain.

Four eyes scowled into his two. If there was to be any shooting, it probably would go the other way. Two goons stood on the porch, looking as fatigued as their fatigues. The younger one could have been one of Rex's kids, if he'd let a kid like that live. The older one could have been, too, if Rex had started early.

"Open up, Albert," ordered the senior goon. "You have work to do."

"Not till I've had my coffee, I don't. Want some?"

The startled villains looked at each other. "Why not?"

"Okay, hang on." Rex started to turn, but reconsidered. They might suspect he was raising an alarm. He opened the door. "Aw, c'mon in. It'll be a few minutes."

Surprised, they stepped inside and gawked. The pot burbled in the kitchen. Rex retreated to the bedroom for a few more clothes and shut its door. He pressed his ear against the wood.

"The Boss's place suddenly doesn't look so good," the younger goon quietly commented.

"Serves him right, considering the dump he's got us in."

You think this guy can really pull off Old Ugly's pet project?"

"He'd better."

Rex grabbed the nearest articles of clothing and returned to the hall, pulling the bedroom door shut behind him. There was no need to advertise the filigree in his wall. Ahead of him, the goon cub stroked the granite with his fingers while his superior surveyed the cliff through the ceiling.

"So what's the job?" their host asked, pulling on a faded "Aggie Dad" sweatshirt as he passed them. He hoped it stank.

They trailed him into the living room. "You're a miner, right?" Alpha Goon asked.

"Mining engineer, geologist, whichever."

"Then you should know something about drilling." He pointed out the window toward the valley floor, where Old Blue was pushing a flatcar across the trestle. Chained to the deck was a drill rig that barely cleared the streetcar wires.

A crackly radio news report came to mind. Jack would have been amused. Rex certainly was.

He chuckled. "That's a whole 'nother game. A rig takes a crew, and I'll bet the Director forgot to kidnap one. Anyway, what's he think he's gonna find? Oil? Forget it. There isn't any. Not here."

"Gas."

"None of that, either. Wrong geology. Why?"

Alpha gestured toward the rail yard. "He's tired of propane cars. Afraid somebody'll blow one up."

"Why? Does somebody not like him?"

Goon Cub snickered. His senior was more reserved. "There are rumors."

Not about me, I hope. "Pat him on the hand and tell him not to worry his ugly head about it. If one of those tankers blew, it'd take out everybody, not just the bad guys."

"You mean us?"

Rex shrugged. "Whoever you want. We'll all be gone."

"You think it could find water?" asked the youngster.

"None you'd want to drink. Not unless you like radium." He was guessing. An old spa named Radium Springs was not too far away, down by the Rio Grande. "Not too far" in New Mexico can be a hundred miles.

"How would you know that?"

"I'm a geologist." *And I can bluff better than you,* he thought to himself. "Want that coffee?" He started for the kitchen without waiting for an answer. He could overhear them from there.

Problems replaced geology on the bad guys' agenda. "What'll we do with that thing?" worried Alpha Goon. "The Director wants gas by the time he gets back from his trip."

"Then he'd better take a *long* trip," their host called while gathering cups. "Drilling takes weeks even when there's something to find, *if* you have a crew." He started into the living room with coffeepot and paraphernalia.

"That's your problem, not mine." Alpha Goon held executive promise. Give orders. Drink coffee. Problem solved.

"Huh-uh. Can't." Rex handed cups around.

"And why not?"

He poured. "Where's the stem?"

"The what?"

"Drill stem. Pipe. You can't drill without pipe."

The goons stared at their one-car train, and swore.

"No bits either, I'll bet." Rex set the pot onto the table. "Or drilling mud." He sipped. Good coffee, better than mud. It was a shame to waste it on goons.

"Shut up!"

"We're toast," Goon Cub said somberly. He scuffed a shoe on the floor. "What're we gonna do?"

"Might as well send it back," suggested Rex.

Alpha Goon whirled toward him, sloshing coffee over the rim of the cup. "Albert, I've about had it with you!"

Rex backed up. "Easy, there. I'm serious. Maybe I can help."

"Whaddya mean?"

"Let's think about this. Take a seat." He parked in the recliner before one of them could claim it. The goons sat at opposite ends of the couch, but not before Alpha Goon replenished his mug.

"Nobody in your outfit comes out good if the Director gets riled, right?" Rex took a long, slow sip. "Does he know the rig actually got here?"

There was no answer.

"What if he hears that somebody got suspicious back around El Paso and you had to ditch the thing?"

The goons exchanged glances. "Might work," Alpha decided.

"Is there anybody in your bunch who'd spill the beans?"

"Not if they've got any brains."

All three men thought up snappy rejoinders, but nobody used them. Rex took a quiet, leisurely drink instead, and the goons' eyes did not move from his face. Finally he set his cup onto the table with a theatrical thump that would have made Rumbles proud. "Well, then, you let your buddies know it never got here, and I'll make it disappear. Deal?"

Goon Cub was suspicious. "Wait a minute! Why would you do this for us?"

Smart cub. Rex gave him a pitying look. "What makes you think I am? It doesn't do *anybody* any good to have the Director mad. I'm worried that he's getting wilder and wilder ideas. You gotta admit the drill rig thing was pretty half-baked. Sooner or later he's gonna get us all in trouble."

"How do you know it was his idea?"

"I put myself in your shoes. I wouldn't sell him on any scheme I couldn't deliver for sure. This one has too many holes. It could only come from a total idiot or somebody who was used to getting whatever crazy thing he wanted."

"Watch your mouth, Albert," warned Alpha Goon. He drained his cup and set it onto the floor. "We gotta be going. Do your magic."

Rex locked up as soon as they left. He was about to close a window that had been left open to admit cool night air, but voices floated in with the warm morning air. He would wait.

"Wait'll he hears about the rocket." Goon Cub's comment wafted inside. There was a lot of head shaking as they hiked down the hill. The heads bobbled to a fare-thee-well when the waiting tram lurched to a start.

Rex closed the window. Returning to the living room, he mopped up spilled coffee and turned his attention to the couch. One never knew what one might find beneath the cushions. There were twenty six cents where Goon Cub had sat, and a black plastic device stuffed deep between the base and armrest at Alpha Goon's end. The coins went into his pocket, and the bug into the garbage disposal. Somebody would not enjoy that.

"Why should I be the only person rousted before coffee?" he asked himself and punched Wanda's number into the phone.

Alas, it was too late. She was already up, and not happy about it. "Whaddya think you're doing, Teerex, letting those goons into your house?" she yelled.

He pulled the speaker away from his ear. "Sowing seeds of dissension. Why?"

"Watch yourself, stupid!" she whispered fiercely. "They probably bugged the place while you were playing waitress."

"Probably, nothing!" he blurted. Then his eyes widened. "And how would you know what I was doing?"

There was momentary silence. "Never mind. But you're a fine one to complain!"

He smiled. "Touché. But to change the subject, I may need a new garbage disposal."

"That *is* a new garbage disposal."

"It sounded pretty bad when I ran their bug down it."

She chuckled. "You rat!"

"Comunicado's crawling with 'em."

"Rats or bugs?"

"Yes. But to change the subject back, I made a suggestion to our friends. You probably know what it is."

"Not yet."

"But you will, right?"

"Could be."

"Good enough. Bye." He hung up.

Wanda pushed the cradle button, released it, and punched in a different number.

"Hello?" A male voice, expecting the call, answered.

"George?"

"Speaking."

"Do you think he's on the level?"

"I'd say so. Everything we heard this morning lines up."

"Did you hear his suggestion?"

"It makes sense."

She relaxed. "I'll be by in an hour. You can fill me in. Oh, one more thing."

"Yes?"

"Kill his bug."

《 》

The sweatshirt did stink. Rex selected some new duds he would probably fit into and headed for the shower. The water had that slippery water softener feel that never quite rinses the soapy feeling away, but it gave him plenty of time to think. His first stop would be the clinic.

Half an hour later, a pleasant nurse with a face like a mud fence admitted him. She dropped him off in the head office and left to hunt down her husband. Rex had barely thumbed through *Neurosurgery Today* and *The Monthly Urologist* when their subscriber arrived.

"Good morning! Have you had breakfast yet?"

"No, but your magazines didn't leave me hungry."

Berno shrugged. "They're to keep Lew out. Today's omelet will make you forget even that article about bladder infections."

Rex grimaced. "Thanks for reminding me. Okay, I'll eat, but business first. What do you make of Jack?"

"If he's a spy, he's a good one. We loosened his inhibitions a bit last night to see what would happen. Nothing except he's happy to be here."

"Truth serum cookies?"

The doctor frowned. "A most unscientific suggestion."

"No doubt."

"In the beer."

"That'd work. I'd like to talk to him."

The reporter arrived in five minutes, pushing a food cart. "Lars said I could have seconds if I drove the wagon." His bright expression faded when he noticed the magazines.

Berno slid the offending periodicals across the desk and onto the floor. "Is that better?"

"As long as I stay over here."

"Just remember, Lars puts only the tastiest parts in his omelets," assured the doctor. "And none of them are human. Now dig in and talk with your mouths full." He poured himself a glass of orange juice.

"Mm, these *are* good parts!" Rex mumbled around a mouthful of omelet. "Jack, did you see the train that came in this morning?"

"Conspiracy Special with a runaway drill rig?"

"Yup."

He shook his head. "Nope, sure didn't. The windows are too high to see out."

"Huh! Then how'd you know?"

"You just told me."

Rex laughed. "Nice trick. I'll have to remember it. Do you think you could find out whose rig it is?"

"I already know. I checked it out before I left Dallas. Why?"

"It's homesick."

"Already?"

"No oil, no gas, no nada."

The office door opened, and the chatter stopped.

Wanda sniffed the air. "What do you mean, having breakfast without me?" she chided.

"We aren't," replied Berno. "You're here."

"I guess I am." She helped herself to a plate and started heaping food onto it. "You must be Jack."

He nodded. "And you're Wanda?"

She stopped piling. "Who told you?"

"You did."

"Wise guy! Welcome to Comunicado, I hope." She turned to Rex. "What else does he know?"

"Far as I can tell, about as much as I do, except about me."

"Teerex, sometimes you're a little difficult to decipher."

"So's this place."

Wanda chewed and nodded. "By design. Anyway, I talked with George and Tommy about that idea of yours I might know about. That monstrosity can roll out tonight. The Mailpie line's busy till then."

"Moving what?"

"Mine equipment."

Rex cocked his head. "What kind?"

"I'm not a miner. Trucks and stuff, I think."

"We need a roof bolter."

"A what?" asked Jack.

Reporters are bad about listening, so Rex tailored his explanation. "It's used to keep the tops of tunnels from falling in."

Wanda caught his drift. "It *is* a pretty old tunnel," she mumbled around a mouthful. "You must know every contraption in the Mailpie mine. Is there anything else we could use?"

"Plenty."

She pumped a cup of coffee. "Well, then, I'll get hold of Environmill. The gear'll park in their yard for a day, and you can look at it. The mine just might get a higher bid for their junk."

"But if they already sold it…" interrupted Jack.

She sighed. "You're as much of a party pooper as Teerex. Just watch! Those mine guys are in it for the money, honey. It's all for sale until they have cash in hand."

The doctor selected a croissant. "Too bad they aren't poker players. You could cheat."

"They wouldn't go for it, not unless they cheated better." She snagged the last orange muffin. "I tried that with the Director once, but he wouldn't bite."

"Why not?"

"He's sober. Randy used to play poker with anybody who'd stick around, and he always lost. No strategy. A chimpanzee could outcheat him. *And* his jowl'd wobble every time he thought he had a good hand. Trouble is, he figured it out after his brain unpickled, and he gave up cards."

"Pity," said Jack, scraping up the last of the omelet.

Wanda agreed. "Yep. But enough Director talk. Does your wife have a horse?"

He shook his head. "You have to own an acre of Dallas to keep a horse in town."

"Does she want one?"

"Oh, yeah." Jack had heard that often enough.

"Are you horsy too?"

"That's sort of personal, but I used to be."

"We have treatments for that," offered the doctor.

Wanda snorted. "Sorry I asked. I'm about to get a horse, and company'd be good for it. There's a nice little house with a paddock at the foot of the west wall. You two and a couple horses will fit just fine. When's she coming?"

"If I tell her that, maybe yesterday!" Jack replied, stunned. "She'll wish she'd shipped herself with the sax."

"She should've. A van'll pick her up tomorrow morning. We'll round up some horses as soon as she gets here."

He gaped. "Begging your pardon, Ma'am, but are you crazy?"

She wiped her mouth with a napkin. "Sanity is overrated. Call your wife and tell her to start burning bridges. You can say she's getting a horse, but nothing else about Comunicado. We'll be in the lobby while you call. C'mon, guys!" She led them out.

After the door closed, Rex asked her, "Are you sure you can trust him alone on a phone?"

"As much as I trusted you this morning."

"I get it."

"But you're off the hook now."

"That's nice. Say, Wanda, where's Rocketman's place?"

She stopped. "Why do you want to know?"

"Rumbles said I should ask him about something."

"Well, then, it's probably okay. Way north, east side of the canyon. Nothing around to catch fire, and as far from horses as I can keep him. No stampedes allowed."

"Same old Rocketman, then."

Berno grinned. "Brilliant, not a lick of common sense, and half a bubble off plumb. I've put him back together a few times."

《 》

Abner Crombey waved his boarding pass at the security officer at Logan International Airport. It was late. His back ached, his head throbbed, and he needed sleep.

His keepers seemed to be carrying secrecy a bit far. He had slept, drugged, on the floor of a van, all the way from – from - from wherever he had been, to Denver. Then there was that wretched motel, an envelope full of tickets on the pillow of the last bed he was to have in America, and six hours later, a cab to the bus station. Nobody should have to ride a bus 3,000 kilometers, especially after surgery, and then fly a nonstop redeye to the Mediterranean. Abner never slept well on airplanes.

Where had they ever come up with that ridiculous new name? He also was not thrilled with his new body, seven inches bigger around than the old one. The doctor had promised it would not really make any difference in his agility. "It's foam, not fat," he had said. "Skin stretches. If you get a few stretch marks, they'll just look normal for your size."

The doctor had not mentioned that stretch marks hurt in the making, or that the patient's midsection would feel like it had been scrambled. Abner learned all of that while awakening from the anesthesia. The doctor also failed to mention that part of the new persona was not foam.

Abner stepped into the body scanner.

Beep!

"He's got a gun!"

The next thing he knew, he was on the ground. Handcuffs and ankle cuffs clicked. They did not ask if he would consent to a search, and they were very thorough.

"There's something in there."

It would take a pretty special search warrant to retrieve the something. X-rays indicated a very small pistol just above the base of Abner Crombey's spine, accessible only by scalpel. Thus he was granted what he no longer wanted: a bed.

While the warrant was being sought, he had the run of a special hospital room. The frosted window was unbreakable. There was nothing substantial to hang anything from, not even a prisoner. Even the monitoring equipment was special, keeping an eye on the patient instead of reporting on the state of his innards.

The door clicked open at nine the next morning. A policeman looked in. "Your attorney is here. We'll shut down the monitor for privacy." Across the hall, a second policeman kept watch on the first one and a stranger in a suit.

Crombey's eyes widened when the suit walked into the room. The door clicked shut.

"You're no lawyer."

"And you're no assassin if you can't get through airports. You won't be state's evidence, either."

The attorney left fifteen minutes later. His client slumped quietly in a chair, mouth sagging open, sightless eyes facing the Boston skyline through the frosted window. The consultation had only been long enough to establish that legal assistance would not be necessary.

《　》

Rex stopped off at the Terrorist Society for a coffee, a sandwich, and a canteen full of ice water. A bit of fortitude always helped before calling on Rocketman. One never knew quite what to expect from such visits.

Amply fortified, he dropped a twenty onto the table and started out the door. It wasn't bad for an unemployed mining engineer. Wanda had stuffed a handful of bills into his paw before he left the clinic. "Prepayment for services to be rendered, we hope," she had called it. Jack got "an advance on the first story we'll let you tell."

East Street followed the streetcar tracks from Nimsoo to the trestle. Pedestrians and trains could cross the stream to West Street without getting their feet or their wheels wet. Horses, urchins, and leashed dogs followed a sloppier route beneath the bridge. Unleashed dogs were not welcome in the valley. They tended to become cougar food.

The east side of town pretty much ended upstream at the bridge. A narrow asphalt road wound north from there, mostly used by hikers and bikers to get away from it all, however little "it all" was. The pavement ended at a branch in the trail. The left fork meandered across the stream toward the rail yard and, just upstream from there, the Director's compound. That path looked as unwelcoming as its terminus, zigzagging down one rocky bank and up the other, between patches of catclaw and quicksand. Hummingbirds and cactus wrens called the area home. So did snakes. Coyotes came to call every night, ears perked and nostrils flaring.

Rex was in an exploring mood. Either his legs were getting used to exercise, or he was becoming numb to pain. The right-hand fork cut across rocky outcrops, through broken stone from the cliffs, and on to the eastern edge of the world as West Comunicado knew it. Rocks crunched and shifted underfoot, threatening to slide an unwary walker into lechuguilla spikes that laughed at jeans and would go right through the sole of a boot. Lechuguillas are mean, clannish little creatures, like artichokes with an attitude problem. Maybe a foot high, they don't attract much attention until a hiker runs out of spaces to step between them. They especially enjoy bicycle tires.

The trail dead-ended at the cliff, by a cement table in an overhung grotto perfumed with the coal-tar tang of creosote bush. A bit of morning shade lowered the temperature just enough to make a desert picnic agreeable. Rex had no picnic basket and made do with his canteen, as he looked back into the valley. The sparse foreground made West Comunicado seem a city by contrast.

A small house and a slightly larger shed huddled by themselves a hundred fifty yards to the right of the trail. He had not previously noticed the buildings or anything resembling a path to them, probably because he had been too busy listening for rattlers and watching for thorns.

He retraced his way more slowly and finally spotted a northbound dry wash, oddly lacking in cactus. Black scuff marks on an outcrop decided the matter. One of the ubiquitous electric carts had gone that way. So would Rex.

He had not gone far when he began to hear music. Beethoven's Fifth. "Ta-ta-ta-bumm!" was long past, but the Beethoven flavor permeated the air. Stan Chess had always been a classical buff.

Rex scrunched onward. It was unlikely Rocketman would hear him over the music, which was coming from the shed. The door was halfway open, and the lights were on. That was as good as an invitation.

Old Ludwig Von B. was not alone. Somebody inside was keeping up one end of a conversation. Rex looked through the doorway. A round man with thick glasses and thin hair was waving a screwdriver and arguing with a rocket.

The rocket, twenty five feet long and nearly three feet in diameter, rested on a pair of steel cradles. It was temporarily decapitated. Wires dangled from a polished nose cone on one end of a brightly lighted workbench. A CD player occupied the bench's other end, pumping music into speakers at opposite ends of the gable.

Rex waited for the arguer to catch his breath. "Who's winning the argument, Stan?" he called.

"WHA-!" The rocket man whirled to face the intruder. He drew back the screwdriver like a throwing knife.

Rex ducked back outside, away from the doorway. "It's Teerex, Stan! Rumbles told me to stop by."

"Teerex? From State?" He sounded dubious.

"The same."

"Well, I don't know... Okay, what's your real name?"

"Rex Albert."

"What was your freshman dorm?"

"Garcia."

"Majored in geography, right?"

"Geology."

"And music for fun, uh-huh. What part did you sing?"

"I can't sing. French horn." That was four questions down; sixteen to go?

"So far, so good. Stay put. Lemme check."

Rex could hear a muffled phone conversation against the orchestral backdrop, followed by a shouted, "C'mon in, Teerex! Rumbles says you're okay."

"You still have that screwdriver?"

"Nah!" laughed Rocketman. "I had to put it down to use the phone."

No further invitation was necessary, because an air conditioner competed with Ludwig for noise rights. Rex stepped inside. The shop was spotless, obsessively so, except for a pair of sneakers standing by the doorway. Rocketman's feet wore only white socks.

"Do you want me to shed my shoes?"

"If you don't mind."

"That must be your satellite killer," Rex commented while pulling off the last boot.

His friend froze. "Who told you that?"

"Rumbles."

The rocket scientist looked down toward his socks. "I wish he wouldn't."

"I don't think he makes it common knowledge," Rex soothed. "He told me to ask you about it."

"Is that all he said?" The eyes came back up.

"Yep."

He relaxed. "He must think you have a need to know."

"Seems to. So what satellite is it killing?" The killer rested quietly on its cradle like a sleeping dragon. There was not a dent in its finish. Three perfect tailfins sprouted from what would be the lower end as soon as the dragon stood up.

Rocketman stood proudly by his creation, disregarding the names he had called it only minutes earlier. "It's *supposed* to kill a German mapping satellite."

"Why?"

The round man frowned. "The Director heard the Europeans had launched one. We can't doctor their pictures. He's afraid they'll find Comunicado, so he got me everything I'd need to build a rocket."

Rex whistled. "He must have pretty good connections. You don't suppose the Germans will object, do you?"

Stan laughed bitterly. "Of course! International incident, an act of war, the whole ball of wax. No better way to put Comunicado on the map!"

"Uh-huh. But it won't happen, I take it. You said, '*supposed*' to kill a satellite. Can't it?"

"Sure it can!" The rocket man patted his dragon. "It has enough fuel to reach anything in geosynchronous orbit or below. Twenty two thousand miles of gas in the tank."

"Plus a warhead?"

"It doesn't need one. A plain old head-on collision'll do just fine. But that isn't what's going to happen." He grinned archly. Noticing a handprint where he had patted his pet, he pulled a rag from his pocket and wiped the finish clean.

"What will?"

Rocketman stuffed the rag back into his pocket. He closed his eyes, happily playing out the scene he had composed, accompanied by the final movement of Beethoven's Fifth. "Some Wednesday, this rocket will lift off from a pad just north of here at Wizmer. It'll burn for five seconds, and the engine will stop. The rocket will turn over about six miles up, low enough it shouldn't attract too much attention, and the engine will restart ten seconds later after it gets a bead on its target. About a minute after it leaves the ground, it'll hit it again at 2,400 miles an hour..."

He waited for the symphony's multiple false endings to pass. During the last, long chord, he finished his dream with a blissful smile:

"...in the Director's living room."

The shop was quiet except for the hum of the air conditioner. The dragon lay silently in its nest. Its creator sighed. Rex stared, transfixed by the scenario, and shook his head violently to clear the cobwebs.

"That ought to tear the place up."

"Better than that," grinned Stan. "The rocket has enough fuel to go 22,000 miles, remember? Six miles up and back won't burn much. The rest will decelerate from twenty four hundred to nothing in seven thousandths of a second, compress like crazy, superheat, and explode. The crater will be bigger than the house. There won't be a thing left standing in the Director's camp."

"Or a window left in Comunicado." Rex was thinking of his foyer.

"Maybe not. If the explosion doesn't get 'em, the sonic boom might."

"What about the train yard, Stan?"

"It's pretty close."

"And the propane cars?"

Rocketman opened his mouth but reclosed it without speaking. He looked upward, seemingly focused on something at geosynchronous distance. "That could be a problem. Let me think about it."

"Happy to. But why on a Wednesday?"

His concentration broken, the inventor snapped, "This isn't Wednesday!"

Rex held up a hand. "I know that. But you said the launch would be on a Wednesday."

"Oh, that! Wizmer only staffs that site on Mondays and Thursdays any more. I have some friends who are going to help me. But Arnie's got church on Sunday. Ben says Saturday's the Sabbath. Muhammet says if they're going to be that way, there's no way he's going to do it on a Friday. Band's on Tuesdays, so that leaves Wednesday."

"I see. So you're just going to cut the fence, drag in the rocket, stand it up on the pad, and let 'er rip."

Stan cackled. "Nothing so crude. I've got more class than that. We're taking the train."

"You what?"

"Look out there." He led Rex to a window in the back. Outside, four modified golf carts were coupled end to end, mounted to opposite ends of a cradle, with flanged wheels that could be lowered like those on a railroad pickup truck.

"One cab, four motors. Wizmer's tracks run right under the launch pad. It's an old mobile launcher they don't use any more. Wizmer pulled up the track to the north, but they never worried about the rails to the south. After all," he nudged his old friend, "everybody knows they stop at an unfinished tunnel. Nothing to worry about, they *think!*" He chortled the Rocketman chortle that hadn't changed in thirty-plus years.

Rex desperately hoped he could find an excuse to stymie the plan. "Won't they notice the fence is cut?"

"Nice try, Teerex. It won't be. There must be some rule in some book somewhere that if you have a secret site and a train track, you need a gate you can lock. Can you believe it? I have a key."

"Of course, you realize somebody'll catch on. A footprint, some mesquite broken along the track, something."

Rocketman had always been remarkably single minded. "Sometimes you have to take a risk."

"It's called premeditated murder, Stan."

"Nah. He got me the stuff. The way I see it, it's assisted suicide. He just doesn't know it."

"Courts don't like that either."

His friend suddenly became serious. "Look, I may be crazy, but I'm not stupid. I know all that! But I also know it's only a matter of time before somebody notices this place anyway. So do you. I might as well have a little fun and get rid of the Director on the way there! Look at me! Heart's half shot, hearing's going, eyes not far behind, hardly any friends; what've I got to lose anyway?" He softened. "I must sound like a paranoid old nut. But you're new here and don't know how dangerous that man is."

"Oh, but I do; trust me."

"I always did, Rex."

It tugged oddly at his heart. To be trusted by the campus joke was akin to earning the devotion of the ugliest puppy in the pound. Rex had not always welcomed Stan's friendship. It was embarrassing at times and earned him some criticism, but he could never bring himself to kick the puppy. That had not changed.

"I appreciate that. But if we can come up with a better way to deal with our problem, would you consider it?"

"Of course! I don't want to lose it all." He looked fondly at his rocket. "But I *would* love to see my baby fly."

Rex smiled. "Even if it ends up in smithereens?"

The grinning old puppy ran his hand through what remained of his hair. "You don't buy fireworks to leave on the table. You light the fuse."

"You're right. Well, Stan, I need to get back to town."

Rocketman pumped his hand. "I'm glad you stopped by. Tell you what: I'll let you know before my baby gets its ride. Maybe you'll want to watch."

"I might just."

Two minutes later, Rex was reshod and outdoors. He had not gone a hundred feet before strains of Vivaldi caught up with him. Rocketman must be feeling calmer. Rex wasn't.

《 》

Airports seldom are relaxing places, but some days are worse than others. It was Tucson's turn to have an especially bad day.

Gaylord Jones had just shed his luggage, shoes, pocket contents, et al, into plastic trays. The TSA officer beckoned him through the detector portal.

Beep!

"Step back, please."

He stepped back.

"Do you have any more metal? A belt buckle, maybe?"

Jones unbuckled. Another officer at a console shook her head.

"Metal's not his problem, Ted."

"What is it, then?"

The console officer addressed the passenger. "Have you had any recent medical procedures?"

He flushed. "No. Why?"

"Nothing involving radioisotopes?"

"No!"

"Would you step over here, please?" a third officer asked.

Impatient passengers behind Gaylord Jones checked their wrists before remembering they had removed their watches.

He hesitated, and reentered the monitor.

Beep!

He ran. Guards shouted. Alarms chimed in. Then he realized he would be trapped in the concourse. Belt flapping and socks slipping on the floor, he reversed course and dashed back through the monitor. It complained afresh, as did passengers in his way.

Automatic gates slid shut. Unbelted trousers slid down Gaylord Jones. A detail of security officers with high traction boots rapidly caught up with the hobbled, skidding fugitive.

The Tucson Airport was locked down. Wherever people were, that was where they would stay until it was certain that Mr. Jones acted alone.

Fifteen minutes later, the terminal police station was considerably quieter than the public areas. The would-be passenger sat handcuffed to a chair in the far corner of the room, as far away as the police could position a radioactive prisoner and still keep an eye on him. They approached him long enough to introduce his reluctant fingers to the fingerprint scanner. It was all electronic. No ink, no muss, but plenty of fuss.

The desk officer examined the prisoner's identification. "It's a pretty good driver's license, but not quite good enough."

Another policeman at a side table studied a computer screen. "No problem. Here he is."

"Already?"

"Yep. These new machines are fast. His name sure isn't Jones. Probably never had a Jones in his family tree. Washington wants this one. Moscow and London'll just have to wait in line with everybody else."

The cornered prisoner forced his tongue against one tooth, a false one, and it rocked out of line. Mouth closed, he jockeyed it between an upper and lower molar, and bit down.

The nearest officer heard a crunch.

Washington, Moscow, and London would not be asking Mr. Jones any questions.

《 》

Ten forty three, said the clock on the stove. P.M., added the black sky. There had been a time when ten forty three was early, before the days of seven-to-four employment. What goes around comes around, though, and early ten forty threes had come around again after the mine closed. Rex could sleep as long as he wanted, but he no longer needed as much sleep. That left quiet evenings for reading, thinking, or whatever.

"Whatever" the night before had been a train ride...

« »

Rex rocked from side to side in the fireman's seat. Diesel locomotives don't have fires, but they still have firemen. Tommy was in the engineer's seat (Diesels do have engines), piloting Old Blue without lights at thirty five miles an hour, backward. The full moon, just above the horizon, cast stark shadows from east to west. The view down the track was impeded by a drill rig directly ahead of them, rolling south.

They crawled into El Paso, stopping at a V-shaped "Yard Limit" sign where the track was blocked by a string of freight. A silhouette in coveralls waited with an old signal lantern.

The cars bumped together, and the silhouette connected air hoses before walking to the engine. Tammy climbed onto Old Blue's nose and gripped a handrail. The locomotive, working harder, towed the cars from the El Paso yard to just short of the south Environmill branch.

"Aren't there yard police?" Rex asked the T's over the rumble of the engine.

"They got a tip about prowlers on the other side."

Tammy hopped to the ground and swung the switch before climbing back onto Old Blue. The train clacked sideways and pulled a few minutes later onto an empty track between lines of rolling scrap. The engine halted. Two minutes later, Tammy climbed into the cab. Rex yielded his seat.

The Environmill CEO drove her engine and the drill rig, but nothing else, to the north mill gate. It was Tommy's turn to get some exercise. He swung the switch and then the lantern. The train pulled back onto the Mailpie line and halted as soon as the lantern swung back and forth. Tommy switched the switch one more time and climbed back into the cab, and Tammy started past Environmill.

They halted again at the other end of the mill to realign the tracks, and the engine thrummed south again.

They braked as soon as the flatcar cleared the "Yard Limit" sign. Tommy uncoupled and resumed his post on the step. The lonely locomotive started north.

"Isn't that a strange place to leave a car?" asked Rex.

"That's where the dispatcher said to put it," replied Tammy, keeping her attention on the road.

"Any dispatcher we know?"

"Yep."

The engine stopped after clearing the north Environmill branch. Tommy swung the lever, and Tammy backed into the yard. As soon as the last set of steel wheels finished clattering across the switch, Tommy flopped it back to the main line and climbed into the cab. Tammy backed Old Blue to a convenient parking spot by a parked automobile, and parked the engine.

Rex spent the night in their guest room. He spent the next day hiking up and down a trainload of mining machinery, shopping list in hand, picking out familiar equipment he had never expected to see again. It all looked very different by sunlight instead of the eternal nighttime of underground.

A full day was shot by the time he drove a truck, not a train, back to the Comunicado tunnel, but he was wound up. The long drive was not quite long enough to decipher his dilemmas.

《　》

So there he was at ten forty three: barefoot, cup of decaf in hand, and restless. Wall sconces reflected off the foyer's glass ceiling, and he switched them off. Much better. Laying his fingers against the cool polished granite, his eyes wandered upward, up from his personal piece of cliff, up through the ceiling, and up that same granite to a jagged line across the sky. Left of the line was formlessness and void. To the right, starlight twinkled through the ceiling and spattered off dust on the glass.

The sun had been down long enough for the temperature to drop into the low eighties. That which Easterners called "a dry heat," southern New Mexicans pronounced "cool, finally." It was perfect weather for sitting in the yard, where nothing but a few miles of high altitude air would impede his view of the heavens.

He slid flip-flops onto his feet and pulled open the front door. It was quiet after hours of train and truck rumble. Crickets serenaded each other, while lizards silently stalked love-struck crickets. Coyotes howled, not as loudly as when his ears had been younger, but they still howled.

Comunicado's lights, designed not to shine into the sky, dimly illuminated the valley floor. The town disappeared behind the parapet as soon as he settled into a lawn chair in the north side yard. The tattered black profile of the cliff above was echoed by Comunicado Ridge across the canyon. The sky between them was not black, but innumerable points of light against the backdrop of the Milky Way. A shooting star flashed greenly across the scene, split in two, and went out. Less spectacular ones followed.

There were hardly any mosquitoes. Maybe he should just fall asleep in his chair. First, though, there was another show, brought to you by the Moon. Its upper edge peeped over the eastern ridge. Apparently liking what it saw, it climbed free from the horizon and bathed the western canyon wall in silver-grey light. Black bats, short and blocky, zigzagged after insects. Shrieking nighthawks with bull's-eye wings hunted more gracefully.

Pebbles rattled near the end of the yard. A sleek feline shape, with erect ears on one end and a heavy tail on the other, leapt eight feet from the cliff to the parapet wall. Pausing to survey the area, yellow eyes reflected the moonlight before the cougar continued down the hillside. The tip of its tail burned an image into Rex's memory.

Maybe he should sleep inside after all.

He climbed out of the chair and started for the door. Glancing over the wall, he could not see the itinerant predator, but a quick canine yelp announced its location. Comunicado's loose dog population had just decreased by one. Rex walked a little faster.

The "shuff" of the front door's weather strip welcomed him into his shelter. "Thump" and "click" followed. Mountain lions presumably had not learned to operate doorknobs. Humans had, though, so he also locked it and secured the safety chain. People were a different breed of cat.

Rex stopped, his hand still on the knob.

He had just deciphered part of the puzzle.

« 9 »

The Director leaned over the hotel sink, shaving with an electric razor. It didn't shave as closely as a blade, but neither did it threaten to cut his face off. Between his jowl, little scars, and the cragginess that comes from highland sun, he could bleed to death in an effort to look presentable.

"Presentable" was a relative term. There were advantages to being ugly. People didn't bother you, but you could bother them. The ability to intimidate was a plus with his type of customers. He had scored a few new ones and expected one or two more by the end of his trip. Some were very big in their fields.

New Orleans is a good city for ugly people. Anything goes. No matter how beautiful, ugly, or oddball one is, somebody else is more so. Nobody stands out. It was one of the few places away from home where the Director ever dared to get out in public. Even at that, though, he generally took meals in his room.

Television news babbled around the corner. The pretty anchor shifted to her frowny voice to discuss troubles at the Tucson airport. Although the TV was out of sight, he had seen her often enough to know this was when she would raise her eyebrows.

A man had crashed through security after setting off alarms, and the airport was locked down. He was captured but committed suicide during questioning. Then (her forehead would wrinkle) he had been identified as an (exclamation points) International Criminal named-

The Director nearly cut himself with the electric razor. He rushed into the other room in time to hear, "Police are withholding further comment." The scene flashed to a commercial for a pill with one benefit and a hundred serious side effects, followed by a human interest story about roller-skating cats.

The razor, hanging from the lavatory by its cord, buzzed.

His cell phone jangled on the breakfast tray. It could wait. His customers did not know where he was, and vice versa. Voice mail messages helped keep it that way.

The eighth jangle jingled. Only the perky newscaster and the razor buzzed on. The Tucson event would not come up again for thirty more minutes. The Director pointed the zapper at the TV, and it zapped off.

How had they recognized his customer? Berno had changed him completely, ... except ... the ... fingerprints. "You can't change fingerprints," he had explained. "They're in the genes."

It was odd, though, that a professional would set off an alarm. His career depended upon not being noticed. "Everybody gets one chance at being stupid," grunted the Director to himself.

The phone jangled again. Somebody was awfully impatient. The Director finished shaving while the ringer rang itself to death. There was a fine line between customer service and subservience.

Two phone numbers were displayed. Neither one meant anything to him, of course. His customers were as cautious as he was. He pulled up the first message.

"Hello, Director?"

His heart jumped. That voice had been his go-between with a recently deceased International Criminal.

"We have a warranty claim. Call me."

He quickly advanced to the next message.

"Meester Deerectoar."

A foreign voice, last heard regarding another client.

"Our friend is home. Ve vish to conduct more beesiness vith you. Plees call."

That sounded more promising. Maybe he should use more buses and fewer planes in the future to deliver finished goods. He clicked the call off and punched the number back in.

Boop, boop, boop, boop. *"Plees leef a message."* Beep!

"This is the Director. Call me." Click.

He might as well do something useful while waiting. No sooner had he squirted toothpaste onto the brush than the phone ordered him back to the bedroom. Around the corner he went, a slave to electronic noisemakers.

"Hello?"

There was no immediate reply. The caller might have been distracted. Yes, he was. A faint voice in the background growled, "When you get him, don't forget to trace the call."

"Shot opp, eediot! He vill hear!" the caller whispered to his invisible coach.

Indeed he vould. The Director snapped his phone off. A trace was a serious breach of protocol, appropriate only when a person had to be physically contacted unaware. Business could be conducted long-distance. Money could be transferred by wire. Murder, though, still called for the personal touch.

Something must have happened to so-called Abner. The "home" where he had arrived was undoubtedly permanent. Could it be related to the Tucson debacle?

How could it not? The less-than-satisfied organizations would know each other as enemies, if at all. All they had in common were socially unacceptable behavior, the Director, and a plastic surgeon. They were in philosophical agreement only on the benefits of violence and, for the moment, doing in the Director.

Speaking of enemies...

The surgeon was not fond of the Director. Had he booby-trapped anybody else?

There was only one other customer, so far. The Director's mouth went dry.

The mouth was not all. A promising line of business had dried up, too. He phoned home, briefly. One instruction, nothing more. Ten seconds, tops.

Just in case there was a way to track his phone, the SIM and memory cards went into his pocket. The battery went down the toilet. The phone itself got a nice hot, soapy bath in the sink, with a vigorous scrubbing to clean off any fingerprints.

His new enemies mustn't find where he was, where home was, or anyplace in between. They would be watching the airports. Some other mode was in order.

The bus had not spared Abner. Besides, too many bus passengers liked to visit.

He could buy a car, cash. Registration might be tricky with out-of-state ID, especially from New Mexico. Some folks never quite learned that the gap between Texas and Arizona was a real, live state.

The train. It ran straight from New Orleans to El Paso. A cab could take him from the El Paso station to his truck in the airport lot. His customers would have to watch five hundred stations to catch him, if they even thought about trains. Probably they wouldn't, not in America.

He called Amtrak from the room phone. Yes, he could get a reservation on the Sunset Limited at 11:55 Monday morning.

"Monday?"

"Yes, sir. It runs Monday, Wednesday, and Friday. Today is Saturday."

That was too long to hang around town. "Do you have anything else?"

"To El Paso?"

"Anywhere. I feel like a train ride."

"New York left already. There's Chicago."

"Can I get to El Paso from there?"

She laughed. "You can get anywhere from Chicago!"

When would I reach El Paso?"

"On Tuesday, same as if you wait here till Monday. On the same train, in fact."

"When does it leave?"

"1:45 this afternoon."

"Can I get bedrooms?"

"Let me check… Yes, sir, both trains have rooms available."

"I'll do it."

The Director would disappear for three days. First-class lounges in New Orleans and Chicago were off-limits to the general public. He would hole up on board in his own room with private bath. The car attendants might deliver his meals if he acted sick.

Within thirty minutes, he checked out by TV, breezed past the desk, and whirled out the revolving door. The lifeless phone, wadded inside his unread morning newspaper, went into the first trash barrel. One of the state-by-state blurbs would have interested him:

MASSACHUSETTS: Two Boston police officers have been suspended following the murder of a suspect under their watch in a hospital.

Knowing something is different from knowing what to do about it. Rex's theory kept him up longer than he would have liked, and he could not find any holes in it while awake. Asleep, all sorts of problems showed up. It made for a restless night.

It also was a short night. The eastern sky was indigo going on magenta when he was awakened by pounding on the front door. Two goons had been on the porch the last time that had happened. Grumbling and pulling on a pair of jeans just like before, he scuffed to the foyer. He was not surprised to see a goon. Again. Maybe he was only dreaming.

No such luck. Baby Goon pounded even as he fearfully looked over his shoulder. Alpha Goon was not around. Rex cracked the door open as far as the safety chain would allow. "You're too early for coffee. Go away."

"No, Mister Albert!" The goon was almost crying. "You gotta let me in! It's life or death!"

"Whose? Mine, or yours?"

"The doctor's!"

He could hardly disengage the chain fast enough. Then he pulled the door open and stuck his head out to see if it was a setup. His fuddled brain questioned whether that was really wise, but nobody showed except one panicky goon rushing past him and whimpering, "Close the door!"

Rex did so. "What's this about?" he demanded.

"Quiet!" whispered the young man. "It's- it's-" His head jerked toward the living room.

"The bug is gone. Now tell me what's going on!"

Baby Goon gawped like a fish, trying to calm down. He closed his mouth, exhaled loudly through his nose, and took another dose of air. "The," his voice shook, "the Director called yesterday. The Doc double crossed him, and we're supposed to-"

"When?" Rex interrupted.

"This morning. Mr. Albert, I'm a bum, but I have my limits. You gotta help!" The panic was returning. "They-"

He was talking to the air. Rex was already in the living room, punching numbers into the speakerphone. Four rings and a message. It was no time for that. "Berno, if you hear this, answer me. Now!" he yelled.

The line clattered. The doctor seemed to be locating his phone by Braille. "Teerex," he mumbled, "do you know what time it isn't?"

"Same as here, but too bad. The Director's on the warpath, and they're coming for you this morning."

The line was quiet for a few seconds.

"Berno?"

"I'm here." He no longer sounded tired, only resigned. "It had to happen sooner or later."

"What are you talking about?"

"I broke my oath. I've done harm. If I die, I've earned it."

Baby Goon ran to the phone. "He's not gonna kill you! They're gonna skin you alive!" he sobbed.

There was a hiss of indrawn breath. "That's a bit much. It kills, by the way, but not fast enough. When and where?"

"Nine this morning, on your operating table! The Director called it plastic surgery."

"He would." A frantic, whispered conversation, half female, half male, issued from the speaker. "Okay, I have a plan. My wife insists on helping, and I wish she wouldn't, but she'd be next anyway. Who am I talking to?"

"Mike," replied Baby Goon with barely a shudder. The doctor's calming voice had done its stuff. "Just Mike. One of the bad guys."

"Not all bad," corrected the phone. "Teerex, maybe you and a couple of buddies could stop by the clinic around tennish if it looks safe. Use Sister Clarisse's exit. Bye."

The call clicked off. Rex punched the "End" button and leaned heavily on the table. Pounding and yelling of only a few seconds earlier were already history in the quiet room. The salmon sky over the mountain, oblivious to the crisis in the valley, was trying on vermilion stripes with turquoise splashes and gold piped clouds, but it would eventually settle for blue, as usual. Mayhem is only a little thing, except to those touched by it.

Mike Just Mike stood frozen in the archway, staring fearfully at the window.

"Coffee?" asked his host without turning around.

"Uh-huh. I mean yes, please."

"It'll be a couple minutes. Why don't we go to the kitchen?"

The erstwhile goon scuttled low across the living room, as close to the back wall as he could get. He relaxed somewhat upon reaching the kitchen. Rex pushed the "Start" button on the coffeemaker. If he had to get up early, so did the coffeepot.

"Shouldn't you be doing something?" asked Mike, fidgeting. Young men are not made for waiting, unless a deer blind or fishing rod is involved.

"I am. I'm getting breakfast." Older men are seldom hurried. Rex unclattered a pair of clean bowls from the dishwasher and clunked them onto the counter.

"I mean about the doctor."

"There's time." Two spoons jingled after the bowls. "Berno has some sort of plan. He didn't tell it to me, meaning I'd get in the way. I'll call a couple of buddies like he said when it's a decent hour." He pulled a carton of milk from the refrigerator with one hand and a jug of orange juice with the other.

"Sorry."

Rex seated himself on a stool. "Don't be. You did the right thing at the right time. Now, what are you going to do?"

Mike commandeered the other stool. "Eat, I guess. After that, I dunno. I can't go back. Not much anywhere else, either."

"Did you finish school?"

He smiled ruefully. "Valedictorian at Springer Boys' School."

"Hmm! Tough school."

"In its way."

Rex poured cereal for himself and slid the box down the counter. The coffeemaker was making enough noise that the brew should be close to passable. It sputtered like an old hen when he stole a cupful before it was finished.

"Have you thought about college?"

Mike poured milk onto processed food flakes. "Oh, yeah, I've *thought* about it, but they didn't exactly break the juvie door down to pass out scholarships."

"I'll bet not. It'd be a tough door. But there may be options."

The ex-goon set down his spoon. "Mister Albert, you're trying to make me feel better, and I appreciate it, but let's get real. I'm a squealer, I've got a record, and nobody cares about me. If I walk out that door right now, I'm dead before nighttime. If I leave the valley, I'll be on the street until I'm dead or in jail. If I go to college and manage to stay in, they'll find me and I'll be dead anyway."

Rex sighed. "Okay, Mister Mike, I'll get real. If you go about life like that, you're dead already. But you've still got a conscience, and you don't know everything. Not yet; not ever. None of us does. It's a little early for you to give up. We'll find someplace you can hide out long enough to screw your head back on. Now eat your cereal."

"Yes, Dad." The slightest sparkle glimmered in his eye.

"That's better."

They ate in silence until the phone interrupted. Rex glanced at the display and picked it up.

"Hello, Wanda." Mike froze. "Yeah, that's about right. ... Not much choice, really. ... Uh-huh. ... Rumbles? ... That sounds good. ... He's here.

... Mike. ... Scared. ... I think so. ... If he wants. ... Just a minute." Rex glanced at his guest. "It's for you."

Mike took the phone. "Hello? ... I-I had to. ... Really?" His face registered hope for the first time, followed by fear. "No, Ma'am, he didn't say. ... Yeah, I guess I can. ... Wait, they won't know for a while. Except for the, uh, skinners, everybody's gonna be cleaning up that plane that hit yesterday, starting at nine. With the Director out of town, it'll be a party. ... Yeah, that kind. Guess I'll miss it. ... You're right. ... I'll get him." He handed the telephone over.

"Teerex, did you hear that?" Wanda sounded pleased.

"Half of it."

"Mike'll be one of your hands. Then we just have to figure out what to do with the rest of 'em."

He looked over the sink toward the shadowy dam. "There'll be time. The party animals won't be fit for much of anything for a while. If we cater, they might hang out a little longer while we cook up a long range solution."

"If there is one," grumbled the Worrywart.

A recent sermonette jumped to mind. "Wrong answer. Do you have a better idea?"

"No."

"Then try to be a charming hostess until we get the Berno thing straightened out."

"You think you can?"

"He seemed pretty sure of himself."

"He always does. Okay, I'll put on my frilly apron and toss munchies off the dam."

"Lovely. Bye." He set down the phone. "Well, Son, am I doing enough yet?"

"I'd say so, Dad."

《 　 》

Three men waited by the bookstore. One, a generation younger than the other two, wore relaxed fit jeans that more than relaxed - they slouched - on his unrelaxed frame. A plaid shirt and borrowed felt cowboy hat topped his wardrobe.

"I haven't worn a hat like this since I was a kid," the young one commented.

Rex let the obvious reply slide, saying instead, "Good. Your friends won't recognize you if you see you. Wear it low."

"You look better without fatigues anyway," added George.

"Long as I can keep my pants up."

Tommy Trolley dinged to a stop, and they boarded. The only other passenger, portly with a ponytail, waved a hand in greeting. Mike looked where a pair of fingers should have been.

Rumbles acknowledged the stare. "That's what stupidity does. Glad you're being smart for a change."

The bell rang, and Mike automatically stiffened his neck muscles to avoid whiplash. It was a Pavlovian response. To his surprise, though, the car eased to a start. It glided to a stop a short distance before the clinic.

"We're here," said Rex. "Stay close to the wall so they can't see us through the windows."

They skulked around the building to a trail that led up the side of the canyon toward the wilderness. Mister Pierce, almost Sister Clarisse, was up there somewhere. His/her memorial exit was to their left, locked.

"Say the password," called a voice from inside.

Rex's brow furrowed. "Password?"

"Try one."

"Aggies, O Aggies?"

"The hills send back the cry," answered the voice, and the door swung open. "Come on in!"

Berno and the Missus met them in the hallway. "You must be Mike," said the doctor. "I can't thank you enough! Okay, let's take our wagons and go."

Four carts with basket litters were parked in a line. The Cognitos took the first one. Rex started for the second with Mike in tow, and George and Rumbles appropriated one each. The procession rolled toward the lobby. "It'll smell," warned Berno as he whacked the door button with his elbow, "but it's safe."

They all held their breath as long as practical, but it only made the next breath that much stronger. The doctor led the way to his office, where a hose ran under the closed door. A fan hummed inside. He turned the doorknob and pushed, but the door did not budge. Rumbles leaned into it with his shoulder, and it slowly opened to reveal four men crumpled on the floor.

The erstwhile fifth villain gaped at the scene. "Are they dead?" he whispered.

"No," reassured Berno. "Just feeling no pain." Uncoordinated limbs moved, and uncoordinated throats emitted bovine noises. "Lew'll have a nasty bruise, thanks to Rumbles, but he deserves it. He let the others into the lobby, and they charged into my office. Claire had made up a doctor dummy in my chair. The real dummy doctor was hiding under the counter out here. Soon as they were inside, I locked the door and turned on the gas."

NITROUS OXIDE, USP, said the bottle behind the receptionist's desk. Mike whistled. "Our salutatorian was in for stealing laughing gas from a dentist's office."

"As it should be," editorialized Claire. "Let's get moving. The fan's cleared the air long enough, and we need to hogtie these guys before they come around."

Grunting and tugging, the conspirators stuffed the incoherent villains into the litters and strapped them down. Lew was a bit too long, so they bent his knees, taped them together, and strapped his feet where they would fit.

Mike was getting into the spirit of things. "They might call me hurtful names when they learn to speak. Can we gag 'em?"

Berno shook his head. "They might vomit. Nasty way to drown. They won't use any words you haven't heard anyway. Now let's take them to the party."

Good guys hoisted bad guys onto carts and rolled the cavalcade to the station platform, where a flatbed car was coupled to the back of a tram. They lashed down the litters like freight.

The winners rode first class, inside the tram. Behind them, back in baggage class, eyes began to flutter open. "A bit of fresh air will do them good," observed their nurse.

It did, if "good" is finding oneself immobilized on an open car, nauseous, rocking from side to side and bound for an unknown destination. They clacked over the switch, rumbled across the bridge, and rolled toward the tunnel, drawing attention like a parade band.

Four golf carts with fringed tops, and one Wanda in a frilly apron, waited at the foot of the dam road. The horizontal commuters resisted transfer, yelling drunkenly. Wanda pulled a pistol from one apron pocket and a limp, dead rattler from the other. She aimed the gun and a poisonous glare at the goons. "Shut up and calm down, or we leave you for the snakes!"

Shortly afterward, the carts and their quiet cargo arrived on top of the dam. Music and shouting resounded from the downstream side. The Badmobile was parked by the spillway.

"Nobody wanted to miss the party." Wanda reached into the van and pulled out a rifle. "Can you shoot, Teerex?"

"I used to be pretty decent."

"Okay, but no killing unless you have to. Skedaddle about fifty feet that direction."

The rest of them undid the passengers, who stared stupidly around. "Okay, boys, you're invited," Wanda announced, herding them toward the spillway. "Anybody who doesn't go gets shot."

"How?" mumbled a goon.

"I pull this trigger."

"Not that," he slurred. "Too buzzed to fly down."

Wanda pointed to the top of a ladder. "You can sit on the spillway till you're ready to go down the rope. There's ice water and pizza to tide you over till then. Now move!"

They somehow managed to descend the ten rungs. The pistol may have helped. Rumbles pulled up the ladder after the last man was down.

Three grey-clad goons and one in green scrubs perched on the spillway like woozy sparrows and an inebriated parakeet, muzzily watching a dozen grey compatriots clustered below the wreckage of an airplane. Drugs had been carried down, not up, the dam for a change, and the inventory was diminishing.

A skinner flailed for a pizza box, but he bumped the stack over the rounded rim of the spillway. Three boxes slid neatly to the base of the dam, but the fourth tumbled end over end until it flew open. The clumsy goon swore and pushed the cooler off in frustration. Bouncing and clattering, it made it halfway to the bottom before the lid came off.

Heads popped up below, to note four silhouettes against the blue sky. One man, sweet smoke swirling below his nose, pulled a pistol and fired their general direction, but his aim was rapidly deteriorating.

A gunshot resounded from the top of the dam, splattering lead off a rock. A kilo bag five feet from the would-be assassin exploded into white dust two seconds later. Partiers scattered toward the bosque, contraband in hand.

"Forget it, boys! We can still shoot straight!" Rex shouted.

"The next shot's for keeps!" roared Rumbles, unarmed but not unvoiced.

"I never thought I'd be shootin' to guard goons!" muttered Wanda. She turned to the spillway. "You guys have sat long enough. Git!"

The four gingerly descended one by one, hands gripping the rope, feet shuffling down the cement chute. Lew was last.

"Did you get that skin?" a voice called from the bottom. The descending team did not answer.

"I'm still wearing it!" shouted Berno.

Rumbles hauled up the rope as soon as the last goon wobbled away. Wanda leaned over the parapet, making sure her pistol was visible. "Okay, guys, it's like this! You like that side of the dam so much, it's your new home. Everything north is ours. Food and drink are coming. Tents, too. Don't try to come back!"

"Food and drink?" asked Mike.

She turned. "Bread and water."

He looked dubious. "We got more than that in Springer."

"I didn't run the place."

Curious townspeople were puffing their way up the road. As a reward, they were assigned shifts to monitor the Great Wall of Comunicado around the clock.

"Mister Albert?" Mike Just Mike asked.

"Hmm?"

"If I was down there, I'd come back through the water tunnel."

"Good point! It has a grate, but we should watch it anyway." A round-the-clock guard station with a lawn chair and fishing gear subsequently went up at the outlet of the pond. Emergency instructions were posted:

"In case of invasion, open valve two turns."

A toy company ought to be a happy place. It should be brightly colored and surrounded by trees and birds.

So one would think.

Amalgamated Recreation Devices occupied a putty-colored steel building in a row of putty-colored buildings beneath a putty-colored Houston sky. The only trees in the neighborhood smoldered in a pile across the street, making way for more buildings. The only birds were sparrows.

It was not a happy place. One only had to look at the face of Nancy Fitzbottom to see that Monday had come with a vengeance. Phone in hand, she glowered out an open roll-up door named "RECEIVING C-3". Factory workers in putty-colored coveralls, who would never be mistaken for elves, kept their distance. She was shouting at a railroad.

"I ordered toys, not oilfield equipment!"

"Yes, Ma'am, I see that on the manifest," agreed the voice of the railroad. "Two containers of plastic ducks from Dijia Yazi, Ltd., in China. They were delivered FOB your dock this morning."

"They were not!"

"You mean the car's not there?"

Ms. Fitzbottom groaned. This was the fourth railroad voice she had spoken to already. "What *is* here is an oil rig on a flatcar."

"Have you opened the containers to make sure?"

She released an exasperated sigh. "There is nothing to open."

"You can't open them?"

"Nooo!" can be enunciated between gritted teeth.

"Then how do you know there's an oil rig inside?"

"There is no inside! No containers! Only a drill rig." She pointed, as if the voice could see.

"No containers?"

"Not a one."

More non-elves gathered, taking bets on when Miz Fitz would lose it completely.

"You're sure?" asked the railroad.

"Positive!" replied the factory.

"The manifest says two containers."

"I don't care what the manifest says! It isn't."

"What does your copy say?"

Ms. Fitzbottom read it for probably the fiftieth time. "Two containers, ten thousand plastic ducks each."

"Then it's ducks."

"IT ISN'T!"

"Begging your pardon, Ma'am, but I'd appreciate it if you didn't yell. I have headphones on, you see. Tell you what: can you tell me the number painted on the side of the car? It'll be down low."

"Just a minute." She sent a laborer scurrying to write down the number. He reappeared a minute later. She snatched the paper and read aloud.

"Thank you. Let me check something. It may take a minute or two. I'll be right back."

After three minutes of funereal music, the railroad voice returned. "Ma'am, I checked that number against our rolling stock. It's a container car, not a flatcar. Do you have anybody who can tell ducks from drill rigs?"

A cell phone sailed through Receiving C-3, shattered against the rig, and showered pieces onto startled sparrows.

A non-elf reached into his coverall pocket. He had just lost a bet to the only smiling person in the factory.

Ms. Fitzbottom could not know that three miles to her east, a receiving agent was picking up his phone to ask the railroad what a drilling company was supposed to do with two containers full of rubber ducks. He had worked up some suggestions, replete with adjectives commonly employed in his industry.

Eight hundred miles to the west, dispatcher Teddy Tarantino hummed to himself. This should be the day. Amalgamated Recreation Devices once had sold him a piece of junk. Their delayed container shipment would be blamed on a tropical storm barreling in from the Gulf. The new tempera paint numbers would wash right off both cars. Houston Dispatch could straighten it out afterward.

Meanwhile, back at the dam, fourteen out of sixteen goons woke up on Monday morning. The other two had underestimated the heroin's strength. Lew could do nothing but stare helplessly at their bodies.

An electric booster pump, connected to a spigot in the Nimsoo lawn, filled a collapsible polyethylene tank on top of the Great Wall. A green garden hose ran down the blue dam to a brass-colored nozzle. The water would be warm and plastic flavored by late afternoon.

Two small loaves of bread per goon appeared at eight in the morning. Unlike manna, it did not grow overnight like hoarfrost on the ground. It flew from the top of the dam, thrown by winners of an impromptu drawing. Some tried for distance, some aimed for targets, and others experimented with form. First prize went to a miner who managed to impale a loaf on a Spanish dagger stalk.

Wanda scowled at the lethargic lot at the bottom. "Those characters need something to do besides dope," she decided. A case of playing cards, assorted board games, books and magazines accordingly slid down the spillway. It was not a rousing success. The recipients would have preferred other literature that she refused to provide. The first knifing over cards occurred at eleven. Lew fainted when he saw the victim, who had terminally fainted.

Free drugs remained the recreation of choice. One goon with more vigor than sense decided to climb hand-over-hand up the water hose to the crest of the dam. He would have done better not to announce his intention first.

Rumbles loosened a can lid with a screwdriver. "Ready?"

"Give him ten more feet," suggested George.

"Got it."

Ten feet later, he lobbed. The can crashed in front of the would-be escapee and flew open, lubricating the environs with a gallon of fresh paint. The target slid and tumbled down the slope. Although not severely injured, he was blue.

"How long are we gonna have to watch these clowns?" Rumbles asked.

George observed the men below. "At the rate they're doing themselves in, not too long."

"And if any of them wise up?"

"We'll take it on a case-by-case basis," Wanda replied, coming up from behind.

The old rebel surveyed the town. "Speaking of which, where's our young friend Mike?"

Wanda nodded toward the tunnel. "He's having a rough time. Those guys were his friends. Some folks in town don't trust him either. I told him he could stay a few days at the Gatehouse if he needed time to think. Doug dropped him off this morning."

Rumbles looked worried. "That could be dangerous if he gets too down on himself."

"We're keeping an eye on him," George reassured. "The bugs are on."

Gilbert drew fishing duty Monday night. He lounged in the lawn chair, sneakered feet up, with his fishing pole stuck into a tubular socket by the right armrest. He was only drowning worms so far, but that didn't matter except to the worms. Fishing was a socially acceptable excuse to enjoy solitude.

The stars were bright. Water gurgled over the weir into the black discharge tunnel to his left. Coyotes yipped, and once he glimpsed a mama raccoon and three young'uns lumping through the moonlight on the opposite bank. Essence of skunk wafted from another direction. Moths silently sipped nectar from saucer-sized century plant blooms eight feet overhead. Bats silently snacked on moths.

Then he heard different wildlife. First came the haunting cry of carefully stacked aluminum cans becoming carelessly unstacked in the discharge tunnel, followed by whispered swearing. Gilbert quietly left his chair and tiptoed to an eighteen-inch handwheel.

Righty tighty, lefty loosy.

Two revolutions, counterclockwise.

Water roared hollowly into the drain. Yelling roared out but rapidly diminished as panicky goons scrambled for the other end. There was not really enough water to be dangerous, but more than enough to be discouraging in a hundred yards of slippery, echoing passage. They had not thought to take flashlights to their party.

Gilbert checked his watch. Three minutes should be enough time for them to clear out.

Two revolutions, clockwise.

The noise ceased. There was little appreciable change in the level of the Nimsoo Sea, but the bobber had drifted closer to the outlet. He reeled in and recast.

« »

« 10 »

The Battle of Comunicado Dam occurred on Tuesday. You will not read about it in your history book.

The day started much like Monday. Another heroin user failed to learn from his friends' examples. The winner of Monday's card competition did not get up either, thanks to a knife in his back. Lew fainted again. One goon was blue, and two were muddy. They all groused about their bread but ate it anyway.

Wanda and George drew early afternoon guard duty. "Is Doug doing a shift on the wall?" asked the bookseller. "This should be right up his alley."

"Huh-uh," Wanda replied, without taking her eyes off the bosque. "He's running his motorcycle south along the outside foot of the ridge, looking for any way our guests might get help."

"He won't find any."

"No, but it made a good excuse to go off-roading."

"As if he needs one."

The 1812 Overture, complete with tinny cannons, resounded from George's pocket. "Huh! That's the emergency ringtone." He retrieved it and answered. "Hello?" His forehead wrinkled. "Hang on," and he handed the phone to Wanda. "Doug."

"Hello, Doug?"

"We got big trouble, Wanda," announced the phone. "There's a power line across the ridge, fifteen miles south."

"You went that far?"

"Yep. Now listen. I was runnin' down a fence line when I found it. Then I seen dust come up from the east, so I laid down my bike an' myself behind a clump o' mesquite. A couple crew cabs that could take on most anything come up to the fence an' stopped. Seven tough hombres got out to take a leak, an' they was talkin' about findin' out why their airplanes keep disappearin'. The way they talked, they could take on an army."

"Oh, Lordy!" Wanda pivoted to look down the canyon. Nothing was changed.

Doug continued. "Only good thing was one of 'em tried to phone back to their bosses, wherever they were, but no signal of course. He was so mad he flung his phone. It's mine now. Then they shot the lock off the gate and in they went."

"So how are you calling?"

"I'm at the tunnel."

"Oh, Lordy, Lordy! They could be here at any time!"

George looked quizzically at her.

"Half an hour, maybe," answered the phone. "Gotta go; my train's here. See ya in a few minutes."

She quickly explained the situation to George. Then, glancing down at the rabble, she said, "They're dead meat. What do you think, George?"

He shook his head. "I can't stand them, but I don't want to be responsible for a massacre."

"Good." Wanda leaned over the parapet. "Hey, Goons!"

"What?" one yelled back. Others yelled other things.

"A gang's comin' up the canyon, lookin' for their airplane! Get up here, but leave your weapons behind! Anybody bringin' up a weapon gets thrown off the dam!"

"Right! You just want to save on bread and water!"

George installed the spillway ladder and uncoiled the rope down the chute. There were no takers for the first few minutes. Finally Lew glanced around and loped toward the rope. Hand over hand, he scaled the spillway. Upon reaching the top, he started for the ladder but never made it. Instead, he jerked and toppled over the town side, accompanied by a sharp report from the edge of the bosque.

Before that gunshot had finished echoing, a second shot cracked from the top of the wall near the end of the dam. The blue goon pitched sideways against a cottonwood trunk, his pistol sailing from his hand.

Sunburned and out of breath, Deputy Doug Totten lowered his rifle. "I never shot anybody before. Can't say I like it."

"Last chance!" called George. "We'll cover anybody who wants to come up!"

Nobody dared, or nobody believed. Whichever it was, nobody took the offer.

《　》

The news had not yet reached town, where Rex waited by the bookstore for a tram. *What happens next?* he wondered. The goons were corralled, but for how long? Could they alert the Director somehow, and did he have extras in reserve?

Mike had guided an impromptu Goonville tour the previous afternoon. As they scuffed through the unoccupied buildings, Rex asked if he knew anything of a visitor with a Bible who had paid a call a few weeks back. The young man blanched.

"I wasn't involved!" was all he said.

"Is it worth looking for him?"

"Not anymore."

Goonville might lack people, but there was plenty of contraband. Rumbles torched a warehouse at dawn. Sweet smoke drifted toward Wizmer, empty and unsuspecting.

To the north, smoke. To the south, a new skyline. The left half of the Great Wall was topped by an awning to protect guards from sunstroke, an overgrown polyethylene jug, and the Badmobile. Human silhouettes added a bit of motion to the scene. At the moment, one was lowering the silhouette of a ladder to the spillway. That was curious.

A speck rose in the spillway notch. It morphed into a vertical line, and finally the profile of a very tall man. Suddenly it bent into a parenthesis before pivoting forward to become a falling asterisk of arms and legs, and finally a stationary comma on the slope above the Nimsoo Sea.

Rex could not move, only watch. The asterisk had barely collapsed when a basso rumble echoed from the canyon walls. A baritone shot from the top of the dam precipitated a fresh cascade of echoes. One silhouette ran to the curb above the spillway. Another leaned over the far side, and to the left, a third looked like a hunter in profile.

"You comin', Mister Albert?"

Rex had not even noticed the tram's arrival. "Wha-? Did you see that?!" he exclaimed.

"See what?"

Apparently Charlie hadn't. He was a one task at a time type of guy. It would not be wise to distract him from his driving. "Never mind," replied Rex, hurrying to the back window.

A few others in town also had noticed and were working their way toward the blot on the dam. He must not be imagining things, after all. He called Wanda. She sounded severely frazzled when she finally answered.

"What's going on?" he demanded, quietly enough that Charlie would not hear. "I just saw somebody fall off the dam!"

"Lew. He was changing sides."

"Somebody objected?"

"Yeah; now shut up and listen! A drug gang's coming up the canyon any minute. A real one, and it's gonna get ugly!"

"Great!" he muttered.

"They'll be loaded for bear. We've got popguns."

The tram bumped across the switch on its way to the trestle. A bicycle started up the north trail on the far side, and Rex visually tracked the cyclist. "And a rocket..."

Wanda gasped. "Oh, no, not that thing!"

"What do you know about it?"

"Rumbles told me. Rocketman's crazy, Teerex!"

"Aren't we all? Too bad Old Blue's out today."

"There's Pinky." She sounded resigned.

"Pinky?"

"Tammy's latest toy. A baby switch engine."

"Does it work?"

"She wouldn't have it if it didn't."

"So how do I-"

Wanda interrupted. "Gotta go, Teerex! There's dust down the canyon!" The call clicked off.

The tram rumbled across the bridge. "Charlie!" Rex called, hurrying forward. Stop at the café!"

"Sure, Mister Albert." He decelerated.

"I need somebody who can drive Pinky!"

Charlie stared like Rex had suggested a carjacking. "But that's Tammy's engine!"

"It's an emergency!"

The young man eyed him dubiously. "If you say so, Mister Albert. I'll find somebody."

"Right away! This tram can wait!"

"But the miners…"

"They're safer in the mine. Something bad is happening, and we need Pinky!"

Charlie had always trusted Mister Albert, because Miz Albert was nice. "Yes, sir. I'll find you an engineer right away."

"Thanks! Have him call me." Rex leapt from the tram and started up the north trail. Charlie set the brakes, shut off the master switch, cranked the route sign to "Out of Service", stepped to the ground, closed the door behind him, gave a quick look to see if he had forgotten anything, and galloped into the Terrorist Society. An engineer or two ought to be around for coffee.

The exercise already was doing Rex some good, he thought as he walked briskly up the path. In only a few minutes, he was within opera distance of Rocketman's lair, where Verdi's Anvil Chorus urged him on.

Somebody inside was shouting over the musical anvils. Two somebodies, unless the dragon on the sawhorses had taken to talking back. Rex opened the door, surprising Stan Chess and a darker fellow with a silvery beard. The rocket had been moved and appeared ready to move farther, cradled on the transport.

"Teerex!" Stan called. "Remember Muhammet?"

"Sure I do!" Muhammet had once been a foreign student on an engineering scholarship, courtesy of his government. He had elected to stay in the States after the Shah was deposed.

"We thought tomorrow would be a good day for a launch if somebody could move the propane cars. Goonville is empty, so we can blow it up in good conscience. When the Director comes back, he's homeless!" Rocketman chortled.

"Anything else you need to do first?"

"Nothing. It's all gassed up and ready to go."

Muhammet raised a hand. "The holdup is this cart. If we go too quickly to Wizmer, the batteries will die."

"Not enough oomph," clarified Rocketman.

"What if we bring the launcher south? You said it's on a train car." Rex was getting excited. If he wasn't careful, he might become another Rocketman.

Rocketman the First shook his head. "Too close to the target."

"Can you change the target?"

"Sure, but to where?"

"South of the dam. We're about to be attacked."

Muhammet's silver eyebrows rose. "By the goons?"

"No, by a cartel, and armed to the teeth. They object to our dam wrecking their airplanes."

The rocketeers goggled. Rex's pocket jangled, and he pulled out his phone.

"Hello? … Speaking. … That's right. We need you to take Pinky north right away. There's something at Wizmer we need to borrow. … Of course we didn't ask. … I wouldn't if it wasn't a crisis. … OK, Fredo, we'll meet you at Goonville Gate. Bye!"

He flipped the phone shut. "Stan, I need your Wizmer key."

Rocketman dug the key from his pocket.

"I'll take that," offered Muhammet. "I've used the launcher before. You two follow with the rocket. Now if you will excuse me, Muhammet will bring to you the mountain." He donned his shoes, boarded the bicycle, and pedaled away.

Rex and Stan climbed onto the rocket wagon. A roll-up door opened in the end of the shed, and they were off. The anvils had ceased chorusing, leaving only the hum of electric motors and the crunch of gravel beneath the tires.

"What happened to Arnie and Ben?" Rex asked.

"Arnie's got the gout, and Ben blew his knee out playing racquetball. But if we call 'em, at least they can watch 'er fly."

The rocket's shiny tailfins and black nozzle were only two feet behind their heads. Twenty two thousand miles' worth of fuel followed directly aft. An eddying tailwind wafted a strangely familiar fragrance forward.

"What's this thing run on?" Rex asked.

"Liquid hydrogen and laughing gas."

Of course.

A stubby locomotive, the color of sunburn, chugged through the rail yard. Dust rose from Muhammet's bicycle as he raced the engine to Goonville. The view disappeared when the missile hauler started down the decline to the stream, dodging grabby thickets of catclaw.

They splashed across the stony bottom and whirred up the other side. By the time they reached level ground, an unattended bike leaned against the compound wall. Muhammet stood on Pinky's lower step and gripped a handrail. The engine rolled northward through the gate.

The rocket hauler was losing power. Pinky already was well ahead when Stan parked the oomphless machine alongside the track. "We'll wait for 'em here." He unshackled his dragon's chains and then dug into a side compartment in the carrier. Out came a laptop computer and spool of wire. He connected a cable between the computer and the rocket, booted, and waited.

A distant gunshot echoed. "How long before we're ready?" asked Rex.

"Hour and a half," grunted Rocketman, staring at the monitor.

"You can set up the launcher that fast?"

"It was made for wars. Enemies don't always give you much time." He started typing.

"Hope we have an hour and a half."

Rocketman didn't look up. "No problem for us. Everybody else, yeah. I could push the button right now and this thing would be on its way to the dam. Wrong side, though. Now leave me alone while I plug in the new launch coordinates. Otherwise, no telling where it'll land."

Rex waited uncomfortably. His pocket bleated, and he dragged out his phone.

"Hello?"

"They're here, Teerex." Wanda's voice shook.

"So I heard. What's happening?"

"A goon shot one as soon as he got out of the truck."

"Dumb move. Try not to let 'em know you guys are up top."

She snorted. "Do I look that stupid?"

He glanced toward the dam. "Not from here."

"Thanks. I saw Pinky leave. How long?"

"Stan says an hour and a half."

"That long?"

" 'Fraid so."

She sighed. "Oh, well. Maybe we'll have enough time to evacuate the town."

He nodded. *Silly move,* he thought. *You can't hear a nod.* "Good idea. Don't forget the miners. This thing might knock some rocks loose. Speaking of which, can you see where we are?"

"Goon Plaza?"

"Yep. Soon as you see the launcher go up, you and whoever else is up top need to catch the last train east."

"I don't get to watch, huh?"

"Rocks'll be flying. Remind me to tell you sometime about Head-Smashed-In Buffalo Jump."

There was a pause. "Never mind. I'd rather-" Suddenly a rat-a-tat pattered from the speaker, followed by a longer series. The distant phone clattered and went silent.

"Wanda?"

There was no response, only a rumbling repetition of the cadence from the canyon walls.

《　》

Automatic rifle fire fanned once across the bosque, and once across the top of the dam. The van's windows shattered from front to back. Water spurted from a line of holes in the side of the plastic tank. And, unseen by the gunner, a grey cell phone dropped twenty feet down the upstream side of the Great Wall of Comunicado, bounced twice, and died.

Three bodies lay flat on top of the dam, crowded against the north curb. Six wild eyes flashed from body to body. No blood; everybody was breathing. Doug Totten slid his sunglasses back onto his face so he could more clearly observe Wanda quietly cursing her defunct phone. George pulled its cousin from his pocket and punched in a number.

Beep – beep – beep, etc.

"Hang up your *phone*, Teerex!" he muttered. He slammed it shut, and it immediately jangled. Better put it on vibrate. "Hello!" he whispered huskily.

"What happened to Wanda?" Rex's shout nearly took out George's ear. Maybe he should put Teerex on vibrate, too.

"She's fine, but her phone isn't. Now stop yelling or they'll hear you halfway to Mexico! Don't call unless you have to. We have an evacuation to start and don't need interruptions."

"All right." Rex's pitch and volume dropped by fifty percent. "Before you leave, call and tell me as close as you can where we should aim, okay?"

"Will do. Bye." George fumbled with buttons to mute the ringer. "That's funny; he didn't ask how *I* was doing."

"Fancy that," drawled Doug, crawling on his belly to a drain cutout in the bottom of the parapet. It would be a wet vantage point, with two hundred gallons of water seeking a way out.

Hands on heads, the nine surviving goons shuffled from the bosque toward the trucks. One stumbled. A pistol came up, and then there were eight. The captors noticed that the others had been into the drugs and forced them back at gunpoint to retrieve everything that had not been ingested.

Fifteen minutes had elapsed since Pinky went north.

George made a series of short phone calls.

The bosque was drug-free once again, and the plane wreckage got a last going-over. Unsteady goons climbed at gunpoint up and down the dam, collecting anything they had missed earlier and ferrying it to the other gang lounging around their trucks.

Thirty minutes…

Loaded trolleys and trams filed into the tunnel.

Alpha Goon scoured the dam between the plane and the spillway. Glancing quickly toward the captors several hundred feet away, he stooped as if to pick up spilled cargo. It wasn't cargo, though, but a rope tied to the top of the dam. There was a taker after all, but it was too late. He had only climbed twenty feet when a line of bullets intersected him.

Forty minutes...

"Pinky's coming!" Wanda whispered hoarsely. A feminine iron blob emerged from the upper bend of the canyon, pulling a piece of freight that bore a passing resemblance to the recently departed drill rig.

The goons were reassembled in a line by the trucks. A captor walked behind them with a roll of duct tape, which grew smaller every time he passed a pair of hands or feet. Another man pulled a piece of equipment from the back of a truck.

"Grenade launcher!" whispered Doug.

Fifty minutes...

Pinky stopped in Goon Plaza.

A parade of trams and trolleys emerged from the mountain and scooted around town in search of stragglers.

Fifty five minutes...

Outriggers slid outward from the sides of the mobile launcher. A winch hoisted Rocketman's dragon on board.

An hour...

The rolling parade disappeared, all but one, into the dark.

Doug yelped quietly. "He's got an *axe!*" He slid back from the opening. "Sorry, guys; I can't let 'em do that." He poked his rifle through the hole, aimed, and fired.

Metal clanged onto stone down below. Two blasts of machine gun fire immediately followed. The first whined over the parapet, and the second reduced the Director's supporting cast to zero.

The launcher began to rise.

"Time to go!" called Wanda.

George punched Teerex's name into his phone. "A couple hundred yards south of the bosque, just this side of the biggest boulder. Good luck!" He flipped it shut.

Doubled over, they huffed across the top of the dam and puffed down the lane to the last train east. A two-fingered hand waved them on board.

One hour and ten minutes...

"What're you doing here, Rumbles?" Wanda asked, panting.

"Leaving a gift. Try not to jiggle it." He jerked his head toward a bulging backpack on the bench across the aisle. The new arrivals found seats some distance away.

The trolley began to move, just as the Badmobile exploded into flame. A second blast detonated high on the lane.

"Musta got the grenade launcher working," chattered Doug.

George nodded. "Good! They'll stick close to the bull's-eye. I was afraid they might try to rush the dam."

"There's only five of 'em left," reminded Wanda. "They don't know if we're one or a hundred."

Rumbles gazed toward the receding portal. "They're too smart for their own good. Maybe it'll do them in."

An hour and thirteen minutes...

Rumbles stood and swung the bag onto his shoulder. "Stop at the switch," he ordered. The nervous motorman immediately bumped to a halt, throwing man and bag forward. Three other passengers collectively sucked in their breath while Rumbles grabbed a post and swung like a gate. He straightened, hurried off the car, and laid the bag against the point of the wall where the mine track branched to the left.

"Hope we don't have to use it," he commented while stepping back on board. "It might bring the top down."

An hour and eighteen minutes...

The trolley halted at the Comunicado East platform. Everybody on board hurried through the turnstile and out the tiled exit. Wanda was last. She switched off the lights and locked the door with her master key.

The field house was not made for three hundred people. The hallway and both locker rooms were full without regard for gender or team affiliation.

All eyes in the hall were on Wanda. "Is everybody accounted for?" she asked, scanning the crowd.

"Almost," replied Berno.

Her face snapped toward him. "Who isn't?"

He studied a clipboard. "Teerex, Rocketman, Muhammet, and Fredo should be with the rocket."

"Anybody else?"

He looked at her. "Arnie and Ben begged off on account of gimpiness, but I think they just didn't want to miss the launch."

"Figures. Well, if they die for it, I hope they die happy."

She sniffed the air, "Do locker rooms ever quit smelling?" and called, "Folks, there's more room in the high school. I have a key."

An hour and thirty two minutes...

About half of the mob had filed out the doors in a double line when a jet-like roar over the mountain ended with a thunderclap. The lines stopped while people scanned the brilliant sky above the shadowed cliffs.

"Keep moving!" ordered Deputy Doug.

So they moved. The old school windows rattled less than a minute later. Enough people felt the bump to get conversation rolling. The discussion was interrupted by a monstrous boom that echoed and rebounded between buildings and cliffs.

The shaken crowd hurried to the school, wondering if anything was left on the other side of the ridge.

《　》

It was painless.

The gang was halfway through the first box of grenades when a roar from the north caught their attention. A sharp-eyed fellow spotted a glimmer quickly rising in the sky, and they stopped to watch. They had heard there was a missile range up there somewhere. Men like rockets. Five seconds of roar culminated in a boom, but no explosion. They went back to business as soon as the show was over.

George was good at giving directions. Stan's computer held pristine satellite photographs of the valley, thanks to the same person who had blurred everybody else's pictures. The rocket arrived on target without announcement, five feet north of the boulder and three times more quickly than sound. Though the explosion lasted for only a fraction of a second, a deafening roar continued for more than ten seconds while the straggling sonic boom caught up with its maker. Canyon walls lobbed the noise back and forth repeatedly while airborne debris returned to earth, and then it was quiet.

If a rocket falls in the valley and there is nobody there to hear it, does it make a sound? You, dear reader, have just read the sound. Had you been in the valley, you would not have heard it. Neither would you be reading it.

The boulder had become gravel and dust. The bosque was shattered. Cottonwoods would come back from the broken roots over time to occupy more bottomland than before. The stream, which had formerly run underground south of the dam, oozed from an open wound in the stony canyon floor and began to turn the new, round crater into a new, round pond.

A mile to the north, four men alerted by a tremor watched spellbound as smoke and dust boiled skyward. The awning flew from the Great Wall like a hot dog wrapper from a stadium upper deck. It was still aloft when earth-shaking thunder sent hands to ears. The hands were getting used to it, having done the same a minute earlier when the rocket roared into the sky.

The cacophony ceased four seconds later; residual racket subsided after another ten. If anybody had asked the watchers how long the noise lasted, they would have guessed closer to a minute. The once sharply defined brown plume blurred and grew translucent as the afternoon wind diluted it with air. Just as the gang had done minutes earlier, the missile team returned to their task. The gantry came down, the outriggers were retracted, and Pinky ferried the borrowed launcher back to Wizmer.

Rex and Stan stayed in Goonville. There was only so much room for passengers on the baby locomotive. The rocket man was giddy with excitement, chortling with glee.

"We did it! Did you ever see anything like that, Teerex?"

"Nope. Once is enough."

"What do you mean?" His voice was sharp.

"I wonder how many people it killed."

"They were gonna kill *us!* It's justifiable."

Rex sighed. "I know that. And we're all going to die someday one way or the other, but still…"

"So you're saying I shouldn't have made it?" Stan asked, more quietly than usual.

"I didn't say that. It probably saved more lives than it took. For the time being."

His friend was quiet. "We live in an ugly world, don't we?"

"It's the best we've got for now."

"Meaning?"

"There's a better one coming. I-"

His pocket jangled. He pulled out the phone and read the display before opening it. "Hello, George."

"So you're still with us." The caller sounded relieved.

"And the phones still work."

"Good, twice. What's it like over there?"

Rex scanned the valley. The combination of tremors and sonic booms had taken their toll on Goonville. Misshapen glass panes reflected sunlight at cockeyed angles. To the south, the top of the dam no longer was a simple horizon. Much of the parapet had fallen, and the blackened shell of the van obtruded into a dirty brown sky. "Probably not too many windows left in town. Maybe some dud grenades lying around the dam. My ears are ringing worse'n usual. Otherwise, okay."

"Want a ride?"

"After the others get back from Wizmer. And don't forget Arnie and Ben."

"Will do. We'll send Tammy the Tram. No, make it Doris. She's first in line. But speaking of Tammy, she called."

"Yeah?"

"The Director phoned her from the airport. He's coming home and wants Old Blue in Comunicado tonight to haul out a load of freight. She told him no way on a weekday. He wasn't happy."

Rex shook his head. "Getting pretty sure of himself, isn't he! Think he knows what happened?"

"No. He still thinks he has dope to ship. Tammy said he sounded normal. For the Director, that is. He should be in fine form by the time he gets here in a couple of hours."

"Not for long."

The speaker crackled, like a phone brushed against a moving beard. "Don't count on that," cautioned George. "He'll just threaten to blow the whistle on us. Folks'll cave in."

"I doubt it."

"What do you mean?"

"You'll see. Tell Wanda I'm running the show this afternoon."

"Are you sure?"

"Uh-huh. And we'll need an audience."

"I'll tell her."

Rocketman had been following the conversation with increasing impatience. Finally he could stand it no longer and shouted, "Hey, George, how many people did the rocket kill?"

George paused. "Do you think it got everybody below the dam, Teerex?"

"No question. They were lobbing grenades till the bitter end. Nothing since then."

"Tell him five."

Rex frowned. "Only five?"

"That's right. The rest were already dead."

《 　 》

« 11 »

The Director spent his drive time sharpening his anger to a fine point. So worked up was he by the time he reached the Comunicado turnoff that he nearly missed it, slamming on the brakes at the last second and slaloming from side to side on the gravel road. His suitcase slid back and forth behind the seat.

Shaken, he lowered his speed long enough to decide that the near-death experience was Tammy's fault. If she had not upset him, he would have noticed the intersection in time. That line of thought nearly sent him airborne at the railroad crossing.

He slowed to sixty at Comunicado's 25 MPH sign and slewed to a stop at the ball field gate. It was unlocked. That only angered him more. If his ex-customers ever learned where he lived, the gate had better be locked! He bumped it open with the nose of his truck, but the gate resisted and dragged along the driver's side. The scraping noise set his teeth on edge.

Shadows were growing long when the truck skidded to a stop in front of the field house. Doug Totten's motorcycle rested on its kickstand immediately in front of the building. He must have forgotten to relock the gate after a day of dirt biking. The Director climbed from the cab, pulled out the suitcase, and slammed the door. A long, white scratch from headlight to taillight decided the matter; he would deal with Totten personally.

Various options passed through his mind as he fumbled for the field house key. That bike was Doug's baby. Maybe he should force Doug to tie it to the track in front of Old Blue. No, it might derail the engine. Push it off a cliff. Watch it melt at Environmill. That was as far as the Director got before finding the proper key. He unlocked the door.

The lights were on. That was unusual. Old Doug must be losing it, and that could be dangerous. Something more serious than murder of a motorcycle might be necessary. It also could keep Tammy and a few others in line.

The outside door clicked shut behind him. Suitcase in hand, he stalked down the hallway and inserted his key into the tunnel door even before he had quit moving forward. He twisted it and pushed down the handle.

The key didn't turn. The lever stayed up. The door would not budge. The Director fiddled with key and latch simultaneously, but without effect.

"You're locked out."

He spun around. A pale young man stepped from the alcove by the home locker room door, with the nervous tension of a spooked cat ready to jump in any direction.

"You're out of uniform, Junior," growled the Director, throwing the full force of a baggy-eyed glare at him.

The youngster blinked but did not otherwise move.

"My name is Mike."

It was the Director's turn to blink. Nobody had resisted his orders for a long time, and he had gotten it twice in one afternoon. "Sonny, you picked a bad day to play grownup," he warned as his hand moved toward his pocket.

"His name is Mike." Doug Totten emerged from the visitors' alcove. Unlike Mike, his hands were not empty. "Say his name," he ordered from behind a pistol.

The Director froze. "Mike," he barely grumbled.

"Enunciate."

"MIKE!" He moved his hands away from his body. "Can I get my keys now, long as you won't let me use 'em?"

Doug nodded. The Director pulled the keychain from the door and surreptitiously pressed a fob button against his palm.

"Push it all you want." The young man smirked. "Nobody's gonna answer."

Doug spoke to Mike without taking his eye – or his aim – off his target. "Do you know how to frisk?"

"I've *been* frisked enough, I think I can figure it out."

"Good. Randy, assume the position. Mike, go at it. Be as thorough as you never wanted the cops to be."

The young man had learned well. His subject was quickly relieved of a loaded pistol, a switchblade knife, and a money pouch on the inside of his left thigh. Doug extracted a folded clump of papers and a couple of tiny memory cards from the pouch before returning the cash. "Wouldn't want to rob you. Pull up your pants, and let's go." He returned his pistol to its holster but left the flap unsnapped.

Mike opened the home locker room door. The Director followed, with Doug behind.

Long fluorescent tubes buzzed and flickered below the ceiling, illuminating a room full of people who had not been high school athletes for a long time, if ever. Every bench was filled. A cart of steel folding chairs was mostly empty, its cargo occupying most of the remaining floor space. All seats but two faced two chairs near the door. Only one of the two was taken.

"Have a seat," invited Rex.

《 》

- 192 -

The Director looked around the room. Wanda sat in the front row. Mike and Doug took chairs to her right. Seated by her other side were George and, worse, Berno with his skin still attached. Rumbles leaned against a row of lockers.

"What's this all about?" the Director growled, with as much menace as he could muster.

"You've been evicted," Wanda growled back.

He laughed. "Why? Because some kid-" he glared at Mike, who returned the glare with compound interest, "-turns tail, and the Doc gets away, you think you can run out here and scare me off? I called the rest of my boys. They'll be here any minute."

"Can the bluff!" ordered Rex. "You don't have any boys."

"Right!"

"That's right. A gang worse than yours came up the canyon to see why their airplanes kept disappearing. Your boys were partying hearty around one at the wrong time, and every last one of them got it except for Mike here, because he wised up."

The Director was silent for the moment. "So you lost the canyon. I can help you get it back."

Rex shook his head. "No need. We got 'em all. It's just you and us. Soon as we throw you out of here, just us. Turn around and leave."

"It was just me once before. I can handle that. You know if I go, your secret is blown."

Rex chuckled. "And advertise yourself? I doubt it. We'd go to jail, but you'd die."

The Director's face reddened. "Are you threatening me?"

"I don't have to. Even if the law doesn't pin Billy and Bambee's murders on you, or we don't all charge you with extortion, you're dead as soon as your enemies find you." Rex turned. "He has some, doesn't he, Berno?"

The doctor nodded.

The Director did not move. Rex watched him closely. "You're in over your head, Mel."

"You mean Randy," corrected Wanda.

"He means Mel." The Director looked away.

"What???" The room buzzed.

Rex's blue-green eyes bored into the side of the sagging head. "Randy's dead. He shot himself five years ago at the Coyote Lounge. Didn't he, Mel?"

Once-upon-a-time Randy nodded.

"You mean when Mel-?" Doug stopped.

Rex turned. "-'killed himself'? It was Randy."

"But Bambee saw it happen!" protested Wanda.

"She saw a man shoot the top of his head off. Would you stay around to investigate? I wouldn't. Would you even look back? Not me. There was no autopsy. Why should there be? It was obvious what had happened. There even was a witness. The funeral was closed casket. An undertaker can only do so much."

"That's crazy! Why would Randy do that?"

Rex faced Mel. "Why don't you tell us?"

There was a sigh. "Might as well. He was a hypochondriac. Always dying of something. Finally he decided he had something incurable and miserable, so he'd take the short way out." Mel turned to the crowd, hoping for an understanding face. "And he *was* miserable! Nobody could stand him but his bartender, and that's only because it was my job. His whining could clean out a room full of paying drunks in no time at all."

"He told me he was going to end it all. He just didn't want anybody to know. Insurance reasons, he said, for a kid somewhere. How he ever could have gotten a woman close enough to *have* his kid, I can't imagine, but it must've happened. After five years missing, he'd be legally dead, and the insurance would have to pay up. I tried to talk him out of it like any decent person would, but he'd made up his mind. So I figured maybe we could kill two birds with one stone."

"Bad choice of words, son," groaned Rex.

"Sorry about that. I'd given up on Bambee ever coming around, and finally I decided if I was going to be that miserable, she could have a taste of her own medicine. I'd die, and she'd blame herself for it. Bambee could have had everything I owned, but instead she'd have nothing but misery. I'd get rid of everything but a million or so that I could take with me. And if I *really* played my cards right, I might get the rest of it back. Maybe even Wanda to boot. That part didn't work out too good."

Wanda stared, appalled. Her face blanched, and she hurried toward the visitors' locker room. Mel lifted his hands toward her as if to apologize, but he let them drop after she rushed by. "I didn't realize how much she couldn't stand Randy," he said.

"Maybe it's the Director she couldn't stand!" Rumbles' voice rolled over the crowd.

"Could be," Mel conceded. "Anyway, I said to Randy, 'If you're bound to do such a fool thing, how do you feel about doing a favor for a pal?' "

" 'What's that?' he asked."

" 'Be me. That way you can kill yourself without anybody knowing, and I can kill myself without dying. We both get what we want. We're close enough to the same shape that nobody'll notice if they don't hang around long.' Like you said, Teerex. Randy picked right up on it. Of course, it was just him and me at the bar, and he was on about his tenth shot."

Berno exploded. "Do you *try* to pick the wrong words, or are you just good at it?"

Mel shrugged. "Dunno. Just a natural skill, I guess. Anyway, we set a date. I bought a scooter and hid it in an old trailer near the train tracks, along with some water and food that wouldn't spoil. I made an excuse that Saturday afternoon so I could get out of Comunicado and pick up Randy at his place. He hunkered down in the back seat of the car and snuck into the house across from the lounge. I set out some of my clothes and fixed him up a nice last meal with plenty of drinks, and even got him a box of donuts for breakfast, too. Then I scooted back across the road to get ready for poker night. I didn't tell him that part because he'd want to come over. And I unlatched the bedroom window."

"The next morning, he tromped across the road with a bag full of his old duds and the leftover food so nobody'd know he'd been around, and he hid out behind my place before Bambee got up. She didn't get up any too early. I got out of bed before she did and loaded the shotgun in the bar. Then I parked myself in the office. As soon as she headed into the bathroom, I yelled that I was taking the bills out to the box and went out. I figured she'd be in the john for a while because she'd need a lot of war paint repairs after the night before. So I paid the bills-"

"It was a *Sunday*, for cryin' out loud! They don't pick up mail on Sundays!" interrupted Doug.

Mel released an exasperated sigh. "Think, man! Bambee sure wouldn't pay 'em on Monday! Everything had to be free and clear to keep people from nosing around. Anyhow, *if* you'll let me finish, I went back inside and slammed the door between the house and the bar but stayed in the bar. Then I picked up the gun, tippy-toed out the front door, closed it real quiet, and circled around to where Randy was waiting."

"He looked rougher'n usual. 'Still up to it?' I asked. If he'd said no, I'd just leave."

His audience looked skeptical.

"Honest. Bambee'd be out everything anyway. It was all Wanda's. But Randy nodded, so it was still good."

His audience looked incredulous.

"I helped him through the window and handed him the gun, and he sat down like I told him to. Sideways, so his jowl wouldn't show. 'Good luck!' I whispered."

His audience looked nauseated.

"Then I waited until I heard Bambee in the kitchen, called her through the window, and shut it quick. She'd take a minute or so to get around to seeing what I wanted, which gave me just enough time to hightail it to the trailer. About the time I let myself in, I heard the gun go off."

His audience looked horrified.

"I took the scooter down the track early the next morning after the cops and reporters had all cleared out."

Rumbles clenched and unclenched his fists. "I'm surprised you didn't go to your own funeral!"

"Wish I could've, but I couldn't. People might have noticed, and it woulda been tacky." He attempted a lopsided smile, but nobody returned it. "Look at the good side, guys! Randy got more nice things said about him than he ever would've at his own funeral. A bigger crowd, too."

Tears started down Doug's craggy face. "Mel, every nice thing I ever said about you, I take it all back!"

Mel blinked. Reflected in his old friend's glasses, he seemed to see himself for the first time. "You win," he conceded. "I as good as killed Randy, I guess. But it wasn't murder! He did it, not me. I wasn't even there." He turned so he wouldn't have to look into the lenses. His voice rose. "Bambee as good as killed *me*, and I was just gittin' even. Billy wasn't worth nothin'. He was like shootin' a dog. It's not like I killed 'em slow. None of 'em felt a thing. But *I* felt good! It's like a drug! First the planning, then the shot." A satisfied, glazed mask took over his face.

"What about me?" Berno asked, low and angry. "That wasn't going to be quick."

Mel returned to reality. "I wasn't there. Besides, you earned it. No thanks to you, my customers are gunnin' for me."

"That's the first time I've agreed with them."

The mask returned. "One more. Just one more time! I- I guess if I could kill myself once, I can do it twice. At least I can make it painless. They won't. Or Randy can. With the .22 he used on Bambee and Billy."

"*My* .22?" yelled Rex. "So they can tag me for *three* murders?"

"Calm down. It'll be suicide, same as before. Besides, the numbers are filed off. I'll be using a hot gun. More proof that Randy was worthless." He started for the door.

Wanda, still pale, stood in his way. "Can we trust you to stay dead this time?"

Mel stopped.

"Do you hate me too, Wanda?"

"At the moment, yes."

A tear oozed from the corner of an eye and started down his face. He nodded and cleared his throat. "I can't blame you."

He turned to Doug. "Just for Wanda, could you do one favor for an ex-friend? Follow me. Make sure I stay dead. You can come up with a good story for your old cop buddies about Randy threatening you, or whatever, after you figured out he did in Bambee and Billy."

"That favor I'll do."

"Okay. Let's go."

Wanda stepped aside. Mel left first, followed by Doug with his hand on the grip of his pistol. Most people watched the two men disappear into the hall. A few avoided watching. The door to the football field clattered open and clacked shut. Eventually all eyes but Rex's fixed on Rex. His focused on the doorway.

"Teerex, how did you figure that out?" Jack finally asked.

He didn't turn. "Lots of little things. Berno started it. He mentioned that Randy had gotten plastic surgery. I wondered why anybody would pay good money to look that ugly."

He turned bluish eyes toward Wanda. "You said Ernie the Attorney suggested Mel had cheated to make sure you won Comunicado. Mel was an accomplished cheater, a strategist to the core. He was an expert at telling just enough truth to fool people. 'A good lie, well told and stuck to,' the cheater's motto."

"You also said Randy was lousy at cards. He'd outsmart himself every time. The Director wouldn't play cards. Cheating came naturally to Mel. Anybody who'd ever played cards with Randy would notice the change."

"Then there was the gold. The Director started off on the wrong foot with the whole town. Nobody liked him enough to say anything about gold. It'd be a lot easier for him to 'discover' if he already knew it was around. And when he found it, his reaction was out of character for Randy. A lousy card player with muscle would just say, 'Gimme the gold!' But not the Director."

"Finally, Stan put me on the right track when he said something about assisted suicide. It all clicked later that night after I saw a mountain lion. Cougar, Cat, Catalan, Mel. A different breed of cat."

Wanda studied his face. "I'll never figure you out, Teerex."

"Neither will I," he conceded. "Anyway, Randy wasn't Randy. He looked the part, but he acted more like a Mel gone bad. By becoming Randy, Mel would have an official past if he needed it, but nobody'd want to get close enough to blow his game. So he found some plastic surgeon to do the world's ugliest makeover."

"Keeping the dead Randy alive was about as bad as helping him die. Randy thought he'd be missed, but nobody missed him. His kid'll never see a dime of that insurance money."

Gilbert looked down, slowly shaking his head. "Mel seemed okay when he ran the bar. I never suspected he was that bad."

Rex agreed. "He probably wasn't, at first. But dead men have no friends. Mel was accountable to nobody. He got used to doing whatever he wanted, and he grew worse over time. If he brooded over something, there wasn't anybody to pull him out of it. And he had plenty to brood over. I expect he originally just intended to lay a monster guilt trip on Bambee and move on with a nice nest egg, like he said. Then he found it was harder than he thought to let go of that much money. Maybe his million was running out. It was blackmail time. Randy could do that."

"But his biggest problem was Bambee. She didn't suffer. Instead, she connected with Billy before the real Randy was cold, and she was shacked up within three days. That must have eaten at him more and more."

"It ate at me!" Wanda interrupted. "I shot up a lot of bright red lipsticks!"

"That was all, though. You weren't rotten to the bone."

"Thanks, I think."

"Don't mention it. Eventually Mel decided to shoot up more than lipsticks. While he was at it, he could keep you and me in line by framing the murder on whichever one of us he preferred. Two birds with one stone."

"Did you have to say that?" she groaned.

"He did. That's how he thinks. He didn't stop there, either. Bug my computer to see what I'm thinking. Bug my truck to see where I am. But even that wasn't enough. Booby-trap my truck so it'll crash! One way or the other, I wouldn't be a problem."

"Director Mel had a good thing going. He had power, and he had other people's money at his command. Free dope for selling, and a remodeling business for bad guys. He got to feeling invincible. Nobody could stop him, or their secret town would be out of the bag. It probably only broke a couple hundred laws."

Rex looked around the room. "Then Billy saw one too many locomotives. He tells the railroad some story about seeing a blue train while drunk, and he might as well tell 'em he saw a pink elephant with flanged wheels. Suddenly he's unemployed. He and Bambee check a few things out and decide to try a little blackmail, but they're way out of their league."

"Billy noses around Comunicado. Randy shows up and plays scared. Mel sets 'em straight after he springs the trap. Exit Bambee and Billy."

Rumbles snorted. "That case wouldn't convince any jury."

Rex nodded. "You're right. Circumstantial evidence from bottom to top. It didn't even convince me, so I decided to try a little trick I learned from a reporter." He winked at Jack. "Act like I knew. If I was wrong, Randy'd blow his stack. But if he was already rattled and I hit him with it out of the blue, Mel might cave in. Confessions are admissible evidence."

He raised his index finger. "His customers wanted him dead. That was the first blow." Middle finger up. "His town revolted." Ring finger. "His gang was gone." Pinkie. "His cover was shot." Thumb. "His old friends couldn't stand him." He paused. "And he couldn't stand himself. The last blow." Rex pounded his fist into his other palm.

The questions began.

"What if he hadn't decided to- to do what he's decided to do?"

"Or doesn't do it?"

"We have a room full of witnesses," Wanda reminded them.

"But everybody'd learn about Comunicado if it went to court!"

Rex sighed. "They will anyway. You know that. But I have a few ideas that might make it easier on us."

"Yeah? Like what?"

"Of course, it's up to Wanda. She has the most to lose."

She folded her arms. "Start talkin', Teerex."

He turned to Jack. "First, we need a storyteller."

The discussion was still going two hours later when the field house door clattered open. Everybody froze. Doug Totten slowly walked into the room, looking five years older than when he left.

"Well?" somebody asked.

"He's dead."

"You sure?"

He nodded.

"Did he do it himself, or did you have-"

"He did it."

"How?"

"Just leave it at that, okay?" Doug pulled a folding chair from the cart and carried it to the back corner of the room. He snapped it open and turned it to face the wall. Sitting down, he buried his face in his hands. Everybody watched, but nobody spoke.

A muffled voice emanated from between his fingers. "Keep on talkin'. Never mind me."

《　》

Here is the tale Doug Totten didn't tell...

They walked without speaking onto the foot track. Doug made certain the field house door locked shut behind them.

"Hold on, Mel."

"Yeah?"

"Your key."

Mel's protest stopped when he saw Doug's hand on the butt of the pistol. "Why not? Guess I won't need it anymore." He undid his keychain. "Here."

Doug kept his distance. "Throw it on the roof."

"Yessir." He overhanded it upward. A jangle announced its arrival on target.

Doug was not satisfied. "Show me your hands. Tops and bottoms. Palms open."

"Yessir." No contraband revealed itself.

"Wiggle your fingers."

"What?"

"You heard me." The pistol's safety clicked off. "Spread 'em."

Mel obeyed. Light flashed from a silvery, falling object. A metallic jingle resounded from the hard ground.

"Doug, don't you think we could-?"

"Shut up!"

"But-"

The barrel pointed toward a suddenly silent, wide-eyed Mel.

"Let me tell you what you did," Doug began. "I was a cop for more'n thirty years. A good one. An' then I got caught up in this, this *mess* of yours! I got home the other night and Maria was cryin'. 'What's wrong, honey?' I asked her. I tried to hold her, but she wouldn't have any of it. I asked, 'Can't you tell me what's wrong?' an' she said, 'Somebody once told me all cops can be bought, and I told 'em not *all* cops. But that Director sure found your price!'" His chest heaved. "That's when I decided enough was enough. An' then today I find out the Director was you! Some friend you are! Help one guy who thought you were a friend to kill himself! Give another friend your stuff an' steal it back! Blackmail a whole town! Murder people! Take money to protect murderers even worse'n you! Frame Wanda an' a feller you didn't even know! Lie to your oldest friend an' try to make him just as bad! 'Old buddy, old pal,' you say, 'would you mind killin' me fer old time's sake?' Probably sayin' to yourself, 'If I don't get the drop on you first!'"

His voice cracked. "I'd like to pull this trigger, but I won't unless I have to. No, I'm gonna do what you did. I'm gonna let a man kill himself, and I ain't gonna lift a hand to stop it. But I'm not gonna help him do it, and I'm not gonna tell him everything'll be all right! Maybe I'm not quite as bad as you after all. Just almost." He engaged the safety and lowered the pistol.

Mel watched the weapon return to its holster. His focus remained fixed on its handle even after Doug released it. "What would you do if I *did* get the drop on you?"

"Die. I'd be unbought, and you'd have one more charge to fight. You'd lose, too. Those people in there ain't afraid of you anymore. Wanda can afford plenty of lawyers with what you gave her. That seems fair, maybe the only fair thing in the whole mess."

"What if I run?"

"I'll shoot you, but you won't die. You might be paralyzed, or maybe lose a part or two you'd rather keep, but it'll give you something to think about in jail while you wait for your customers to stop by."

Mel winced. "Well, if that's my choice, let's go. But I need to make one stop in Comunicado first."

"You've already said all the hellos and good-byes you're gonna git!"

"It's a tool shed! Is that all right?"

"Only if nobody's around an' I can see what you're up to."

"Fair enough." Mel climbed into the Director's truck. Doug donned his helmet and boarded his motorcycle. Coming to life, the vehicles moved slowly down the track and through the gate.

Mel drove to the last driveway before the Coyote Lounge, turned left, and crunched to a halt at a tin shed in back. Doug watched, motor idling, while Mel unlocked the shed and pulled out a crowbar. He scratched something into the hood of the truck. Returning to the shed, he extracted a cardboard packing case. He tore the top off with the crowbar and then proceeded to empty the box through the passenger window. Glass bottles crashed inside.

"Hundred eighty proof! Want some?"

Doug shook his head.

Shrugging, Mel reached inside and rescued a bottle. "Guess I'll drink alone, then." He twisted off the cap and took a long swallow before setting the bottle back inside, between the seats. He tossed the lid in after it, followed by the packing case. "Wouldn't want to get busted for littering."

He returned to the shed one last time. Out came a .22 rifle and a box of ammunition. As he loaded the rifle, he carried on a conversation with the just-out-of-reach Doug on the thrumming bike. "Not quite full. Bambee and Billy got a couple." He slid the rifle through the truck window.

"Time to go, unless some old cop wants to run me in for DWI, open containers plural, and a loaded weapon in a moving vehicle. Maybe I'll make excessive noise, too."

"Not this time," Doug replied.

"There won't be a next time." Mel climbed into the cab. He gunned the engine and leaned out the window.

"Changed my mind! See ya!" Gravel flew from all four wheels, and he roared around the building.

Doug quickly shifted and followed at a distance where he could avoid some of the dust. The chase bounced down the empty road at seventy miles an hour, long shadows preceding them in the setting sun. The truck's driver, barely visible through the dusty glare of the back window, could vaguely be seen tipping a bottle to his lips, setting it down, and hoisting it again.

Mel's course became more erratic as the race continued. The brake lights came on just as the truck bounced up the railroad crossing grade, but too late. The suspension bottomed with a bang, and man and machine flew into the air. The truck banked slightly to the right before following an arc to the ground. An explosion announced impact, but there was no smoke, only dust.

Doug skidded his bike to a halt. From his vantage point, only the top of the cab remained visible behind the railroad. He motored slowly across the tracks, one hand on the handlebars, and the other fumbling for his holster.

The truck was upright and off the road. The near front tire was blown, but the engine continued to rumble at idle in a fruitless attempt to drive through a stand of mesquite. Mel leaned over the steering wheel. Pushing away with his hands, he sagged back against the seat and groaned. There was not enough room inside the cab for him to swing a rifle, but Doug was taking no chances. He raised his pistol.

Mel turned his head. "Back's broke," he slurred. "Can't feel my legs. Gonna put me out of my misery?"

"Can't." Doug lowered the weapon.

"I thought not. Back to Plan A. But first, a last cigarette." Gripping the edge of the window with his left hand to keep upright, he fumbled for the electric lighter with his right. "Silly me! I don't smoke," he drawled and dropped the red-hot thing into the cardboard box. A tendril of smoke rose, while Mel dragged the rifle across the cab. "Get lost!" he ordered through the window.

Doug shifted into gear and started down the road toward the Mailpie crossing, keeping an eye to the mirror. A metallic "ping" resounded from the truck behind him. Smoke, then nearly invisible flames, puffed from the open windows.

He continued for a mile before turning around, just in case investigators might be intrigued by an unknown motorcyclist negotiating a U-turn at the scene of a fatality. His heart pounded as he passed the burning truck. Framed by the side window, silhouettes of a body and rifle barrel against a leaping, yellowing background branded his memory. Shattering noises and bursts of blue-and-yellow flame eliminated any urge to stop. The bottles were exploding. So did the windshield, and the mesquite crackled into fiery life.

The deepening sunset over the mountain was brilliant with reds and purples, blues and multiple shades of gold. The colors intensified as the sky grew darker. The motorcycle was half a mile past the crossing when an orange fireball, puny by comparison with the show to the west, reflected in its mirror. That would be the gasoline tank.

A rumble caught up with Doug three seconds later, but he did not hear it over the roar of his engine as he fled.

The *Mailpie Courier Herald* had another busy news week. So busy, in fact, that the Tiny Tots Parade was pushed all the way back to Page 3. That guaranteed plenty of letters to the editor, to complain about the media's obsession with unwholesome topics.

The body of Randy Cogden, a loner, had been found in a burned-out truck near the rail crossing on Comunicado Road. He had driven into a mesquite thicket, ignited combustibles in the cab, and shot himself to death. The motive appeared to be remorse, aggravated by alcohol. "SORRY BAMBEE" had been deeply scratched into the truck's hood. Forensic experts were examining the weapon to determine if it was the same one used in the Flaherty double murder. Cogden had killed himself at virtually the same location. An acquaintance told police that Cogden had been a friend of the late Mel Catalan, who had committed suicide after learning his long-time girlfriend, former dancer Bambee Deere, was romantically involved with family friend Billy Flaherty. She had married Flaherty not long after Catalan's death.

《 》

Maria Totten looked up from her newspaper. "Would you be that acquaintance?

"Could be. The boys at the office knew I'd known Mel. And everything I said was true."

"So's a lot you didn't say."

"Yep."

《 》

Two days later, the state crime lab confirmed that the rifle used in the Cogden suicide also was used in the Flaherty murders.

The Tiny Tots Parade returned to the front page the next day, when an angry parent accused parade judges of taking bribes from other parents. Angry judges accused the parent of offering bribes.

The Prosecutor's Office officially closed the Cogden and Flaherty cases the following Monday, leaving more time to investigate the Tiny Tots brouhaha. Inside the paper, the Letters to the Editor section was expanded to two pages.

《 》

It was a small funeral. A television van was parked down the street, as discreetly as anything with big letters on the side and a motorized radio tower could park. Unless there were vicarious mourners in Television Land, Mel had unfortunately been correct in his assessment of Randy's popularity. Wanda, Rex, and a few others went, not out of respect for the recently departed, but for the long-deceased. The body had been cremated ("Pretty much there already," observed Doug), so pallbearers were unnecessary. The ashes would be scattered in the Malpais.

Most of the mourners, assuming they mourned, were on the downhill side of middle age. There was one exception. A stone-faced teenage boy sat alone in the back corner of the room, as if pushed against the wall by some force of repulsion. "Who do you suppose he is?" Wanda whispered to Rex beside her.

"I have a hunch."

She nodded.

The funeral was short and generic. Nobody knew if Randy had any favorite hymns. Eulogies for a murderer are difficult, and there is little comfort in suicide. After the final "Amen," attendees rose from creaking chairs and shuffled across the carpet to the door, making little sparks when they touched the handle. The prevailing subject of conversation was not the deceased, but how to avoid a reporter patrolling the sidewalk.

The funeral director overheard. He discreetly sidled to an office phone and punched in a number.

"Hello, this is Eddie at the funeral home. ... Well, there's a TV truck outside that I think might be double parked or too close to a fireplug or something. ... You will? Thanks, I owe you one. ... No, not one of those! You aren't ready yet, anyway. Bye!" He quietly set down the phone and slipped back into the lobby.

The chapel was virtually empty. Only the boy remained in his corner, looking straight ahead. Rex nodded at him. The boy's eyes shifted for a moment, and his head barely bobbed.

"I'll be in the lobby," whispered Wanda, easing out the door.

"Would you rather I leave too?" Rex asked the teen.

"Whatever."

"Okay, then, I'll stay." He turned a chair to face the corner, and sat. The boy did not move. "Can I ask you a question?"

"I guess so."

"Was Randy your dad?"

A sudden shudder and reddening face answered the question. "Yeah, I'm the son of that- that-" he erupted with an Oedipal epithet. The dam broke. Tears flowed, and the boy started out of his chair. Rex put a hand on his shoulder.

"Now hold on! I understand how you feel, but-"

"How can you?" the boy sobbed.

"You got me on that one. I know a little bit, though. This is the first funeral I've been to since my wife died. I hate funerals. But there're some things you need to know. I can wait."

The boy sat back down, his shoulders heaving. Rex waited.

"What's your name, son?"

"I'm not your son!"

"What's your name, young man?"

"Randy," he uttered between gritted teeth.

"And you're not proud of that right now."

The boy shook his head. Rex continued. "There are lots of good Randy's. And your dad was better than you think."

"Don't call him my dad! He never was any sort of dad to me!"

"Then why'd you come?"

"My preacher said I needed to forgive him," young Randy grumbled.

"But you don't want to."

His head snapped up, and his eyes blazed. "How can I? He's a murderer! And did you know I sent him a birthday card every year, but he never wrote back for the last five years? Not once! Never called, never nothing!"

Rex's heart lurched. His own eyes got moist. "So he was supposed to earn your forgiveness, is that it?"

There was no answer.

"That's going to be tough at this stage. But I can tell you a couple things you don't know. First of all, your father loved you."

"Right. And that's why he never wrote back."

"That brings me to the other thing. Your dad changed addresses five years ago. He never would have gotten those birthday cards."

The boy glared. "Well, why didn't he tell me he moved if he loved me so much?"

Rex paused. "He couldn't."

Randy studied the older man. "Why not? Was he in prison? Detox? The nuthouse?" Then he asked, a little more hopefully, "Witness protection?"

"Maybe someday I can tell you, but today's not the day. What I will say is that he would get obsessive about things, and then he didn't think straight.

Also, he didn't want anybody to know where he was, and there was a reason. But let's leave that alone. I think your preacher is right."

The boy shifted in his chair. "I'll think about it. But let me tell *you* something! Back when I was a little kid, my dad told me he'd taken out a life insurance policy that I'd get if he died. It was supposed to pay for my college. He was always saying how sick he was. It scared me when he'd say that. I didn't want him to die just so I could go to school. But at least it was something, and I worked hard so I could be better than my dad." His fists clenched. "Do you know how much insurance money you get for suicide? Zero! Now tell me how much he loved me!"

Wanda slipped through the door. "I was eavesdropping. Sorry. What year are you?"

"What business is it of yours?"

"You won't know if you don't tell me."

He answered grudgingly. "I'll be a freshman at State until the money runs out."

"The first part sounds good. How were your grades?"

"Four point one."

"What do you want to study?"

"Physics. And music."

"Oh, really? What type of music?"

"French horn."

Rex and Wanda exchanged glances.

She smiled. "Well, then, Randy, I think you qualify for the first-ever Comunicado Land Company full-ride scholarship for French horn and physics."

He stared, unbelieving. "What do you mean?"

"I mean you're covered, kid. Now do you think you can forgive your father?"

"I'll try! But what do I do to get that scholarship?"

"Nothing. You already have it." Wanda fished a pen and paper from her purse. "Just give me contact information, and I'll get back with you."

"Sure!" Randy started to write. He stopped and looked up. "What time is it?"

"About noon."

He gasped. "Man, I've got to get going! The Las Cruces bus leaves at two!"

Rex opened the front door. "We can take you to the station. I think all three of us can fit in the truck."

"Excuse me!" The sidewalk reporter materialized, with a cameraman in tow. "How do you feel about the murderer committing suicide?"

- 207 -

Rex's mouth tightened, but he did not stop moving. "Death is always tragic. Now if you'll excuse us, we must be going. Anyway, I think your van is about to be towed."

The newsman's head spun toward his vehicle. He expressed a sentiment seldom heard from on-duty broadcast journalists. Rex, Wanda, and Randy hustled by wordlessly. The reporter directed a copious flow of words toward a policeman silently using hand signals to direct a tow truck. The cameraman, trailing his reporter like a mosquito after sustenance, dutifully recorded the scene. The trio from the funeral, forgotten for the moment, piled into Yootibibit with Wanda in the middle.

"Thanks!" said Randy as Rex started the truck.

"No problem. It's too hot to walk."

"I mean for saying what you did. To me, and to that reporter. I was about to say something else to him."

"Like what he was saying to the cop?"

"Something like that."

"I can't blame you." Rex reached for the gear shift but got a leg instead. "Sorry."

"Watch it, Buster!" growled Wanda.

"Okay, you shift."

"That's your job. But I feel like a Wanda sandwich."

"That reminds me. Does anybody want lunch?" Rex asked.

"Thanks anyway," mumbled Randy.

Wanda turned. "You mean yeah, but you're broke, right?"

"Yeah."

"I've got it. We can't have our scholarship student chewing on bus seats."

"Thanks!"

Yootibibit turned into the Headframe Café parking lot. The truck doors opened, and humanity bulged out. "You think we'll still fit after lunch?" Wanda asked.

"Maybe better," replied Rex. "It depends on how the food agrees with you."

"That's comforting."

The café's front window resonated with scratching noises. The proprietor looked up from inside where he was scraping off a credit card decal, and he waved the three in. They filed across a field of sticky curlicues, some of which stuck to their shoes.

"Are you giving up on plastic money, Smitty?" Rex asked.

Smitty continued scraping. "Only that one. They raised their rates, and nobody 'round here uses it anyway."

"Including me. Still take cash?"

"When I can get it."

"We'll swap you some for lunch."

Scrape, scrape. "In a minute. I saw the health inspector down the street. If he sees this junk on the floor today, it'll be in the newspaper tomorrow."

"How about if I finish this while you cook?" offered Randy.

"Sounds fair enough. If he comes in the door, you're the janitor, okay?"

《 》

Rex's phone rang that evening. His own phone, in his own house, in Mailpie. It was in the study; he was in the kitchen. That was how it usually worked. He set down his fish and grease sandwich and retrieved the noisy contraption. "Thither", said Caller ID.

"Hello?"

"Hey. Pop, you're famous!"

"What do you mean?"

"I mean, the other TV station got hold of that news clip when you guys came out of the funeral parlor and the reporter freaked and got himself arrested. I miss all the fun! How'd you get wrapped up in that?"

"Never mind."

"I never do. Who's the kid?"

"The son of the deceased."

Thither's voice dropped. "Oh, man, that would be horrible! You helping him out?"

"We're trying to."

"We?"

"Yeah, me and-" Rex paused.

"Who's the lady?" the Ither interrupted.

"A friend. Maybe I'll introduce you someday."

"That's cool, Pop. Hither and I don't mind. We've talked about it."

"About what?"

"About- about, well, we don't want you to just crawl off in a hole and die! We loved Mom. Always will, but she's gone. We can't move backward, and we won't stay put."

Rex coughed. "Thank you, Son."

"You okay, Pop?"

"Yeah. You've been a huge help."

"It was about my turn. Take it easy, huh?"

Rex returned to the kitchen, where Wanda was demolishing a bag of fried clams. She looked up from the wreckage. "A kid?"

"Yeah, Thither. I mean Arthur."

"I like Thither better. Did he say anything you can tell me?"

"Well, the reporter was arrested."

She hooted. "So there *is* some justice in this world, after all! Anything else?"

He blushed. "I have my children's permission to date."

"You *asked*?"

"No, it was their idea."

Her eyes dropped. She stirred her ketchup with a French fry. "Are you going to?"

"That's up to you."

《　》

《 》

Mailpie's good news advocates finally got their wish a month later, when the *Courier Herald* announced that AOA Enterprises, owner of recycling giant Environmill, had purchased the Mailpie mine property. A portion of the mine would be reopened, not for mining, but for underground disposal of mill wastes. Surplus equipment and demolished metal buildings would be shipped to Environmill for recycling.

That was not all. AOA's parent, the little-known Comunicado Land Company, bought the rail line from Mailpie to El Paso, to transport scrap to Environmill and waste to the mine. It would run under the name of Comunicado Conveyance Company. Within a week, sky-blue locomotives emblazoned with black and gold "CCC" would be running up and down the track.

《 》

"You know they're going to call them Charlie's Choo-Choos, don't you?" Wanda asked.

Rex nodded. "It took me a while to come up with a name that worked."

《 》

The CCC acquired not only the railroad to Mailpie, but the wrecking train stranded there. It would travel around the country, salvaging abandoned rail lines to feed Environmill's furnaces. "There's tons of old railroads out there just itchin' to be tore up," explained spokesperson Charlie Phillips.

The railroad also would extend another direction. The Comunicado Land Company owned some virtually inaccessible property on the far side of the Continental Divide. Engineers had found that the ill-fated Comunicado Tunnel had been close to completion when it was abandoned. A small bore actually was punched later through the last two hundred feet for a failed water scheme, explained historian Doug Totten. Mining engineer Rex Albert told reporters that a few weeks of blasting should suffice.

Then the big one hit.

"GOLD!" The *Mailpie Courier Herald* used its largest font. The Comunicado Land Company discovered gold ore while completing their tunnel. They decided to build a processing plant right at the old Mailpie mine site, in order to simplify mill waste disposal. The facility would produce investment bouillon and coins, among other things, and would be called "Environmint".

As a sign of corporate goodwill, the company entered into a partnership with Comunicado Schools to underwrite college credit programs and refurbish run-down facilities, including the unused football field. A new band room, gymnasium, and locker rooms would be constructed. The old field house would become a brand-new community center, historical museum, and New Mexico's only subway station.

And what of the newly opened land? It would be an experimental community, capitalizing on skills & experiences of older persons, many of whom had been displaced or downsized. The Comunicado Land Company, it turned out, had been quietly identifying and recruiting just such people. The new project would not be merely a senior village, though. Emigrants of various ages had already disappeared into the mountain where, if rumors were true, they boarded a new trolley on a new track and rolled west into their new little world. Rumor also had it that the new residents objected to the name of West Comunicado because they didn't want to "spend all their time in the WC," so it was unofficially called "Geezer Gulch".

The *Courier Herald* dutifully reported the rumors but pointed out that the editors didn't believe them. For all anybody knew, newcomers might actually walk two miles in the dark to a sweatshop in a mobile home camp. There was no way to tell. The company owned the tunnel, a company-owned dam blocked the canyon, a military base blocked northern access, wilderness to the west was full of snakes and wolves, and airplanes were banned.

《　》

Thousands of miles away, red-eyed men crowded around a bed. A middle-aged man with a new face lay sprawled across it, his torso covered by a sheet. A physician stood by his head.

"Aneurysm."

"How can you tell?"

He lifted the sheet, revealing purple flesh. "See? His abdomen is full of blood, but there's none outside. No break in the skin, no blood in the bowel."

"But he can't have an aneurysm! It was repaired when he, he..." The man could not enunciate "was changed".

"All the more likely," explained the doctor. "If his aorta was weak in one area, it could have been in others. A cough or a wrong move could rupture it."

"I don't believe you!" growled a greybeard.

"Then examine him yourself!" shouted the doctor. "Use my scalpel or your own knife; I don't care! I refuse to carve him up any more than has been done already!" He hurried away. The other mourners glowered at the increasingly nervous skeptic.

The commander was buried before sundown, uncarved. The world would not hear of his death any time soon. His lieutenants covertly watched each other even as they threw flowers onto the grave. When eyes made contact, they either locked momentarily or flicked back to the floral heap. No longer bound in purpose to a charismatic leader, there was no unanimity in his followers' vision of future command.

There had been a succession plan, but its author could not enforce it.

《 》

《 》

Rex closed the newspaper he had been reading. A hummingbird buzzed his lawn chair and hurried to the feeder. Most of the Grandithers were down the hill, fishing in the Nimsoo Sea with their parents. The youngest, diapered rump in the air like a dung beetle, stalked a horned toad in the side yard. The reptile skittered away with the mammal in full cackling pursuit.

"How long do you suppose our no-fly zone will hold out?" Rex wondered.

"Long enough," replied Wanda. "Somebody has to bring it to somebody else's attention first. Nobody wants to do the paperwork. I'm not gonna bring it up. Wizmer doesn't care as long as they keep their airspace. There'll be time to so-called build this place from scratch and show it off to reporters before anybody can fly over. Likewise for the satellite censors."

"Maybe we're okay, then."

She slurped the last gurgle of iced tea through a straw and set down the glass. "Worrywarting's my job, not yours. Like that stuff we got from Mel and the airplane gang. Are you sure it can't be traced to here?"

"As sure as I can be of anything. By now, the FBI should have an envelope mailed from someplace else, with a memory card of selected information from Mel about bad guys more interesting than us. And El Paso cops got a tip about a phone somebody ditched in a park."

Can't they trace where the phone was used?"

"Only where there was reception."

"What about Doug's fingerprints on it?"

Rex's grey eyes smiled. "Once a cop, always a cop. His bare paws never touched it."

Smoke rolled upward from the downstream side of the dam. A rumble arrived a couple of seconds later.

Wanda stretched. "That reminds me. We need another load of paint."

《 》

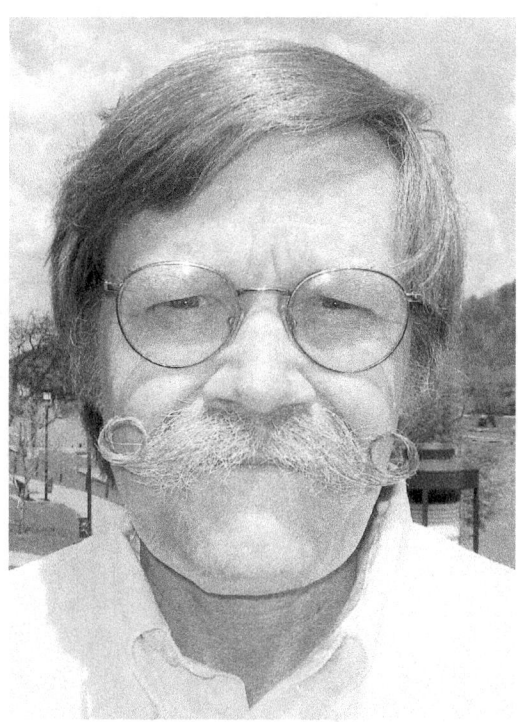

Don Bemis grew up to the sound of trains banging around the clock in the mining city of Carlsbad, New Mexico. Carlsbad is remote, and it is in the desert, but it has a river. The author would like to assure the city fathers that Carlsbad is better than Mailpie.

He played clarinet in the New Mexico State University Band and married Lois, another Aggie clarinetist, before they graduated. Lois is from the mountains of northern New Mexico and never really warmed up to the desert, so they compromised and moved to South Haven, Michigan, in 1979.

Dead Aggies originated as a dream after a two-week, 3,500 mile train journey through the northern United States and Canada. Don and Lois have ridden most of the major North American passenger routes, including some that aren't running any more.

Don and Lois Bemis live not quite a mile from the Lake Michigan shore, ten miles from the nearest passenger station, and less than three hours from the Chicago rail hub. They have five adult children and a growing supply of grandchildren.

www.ingramcontent.com/pod-product-compliance
Lightning Source LLC
Chambersburg PA
CBHW070112260626
47160CB00004B/1439